Praise for the Bestselling
Tea Shop Mysteries
by Laura Childs

❧

Featured Selection of the Mystery Book Club
"Highly recommended" by the Ladies' Tea Guild

❧

"Enjoyable . . . Childs proves herself skilled at local color, serving up cunning portraits of Southern society, and delectable descriptions of dishes."　　*—Publishers Weekly*

"You'll be starved by the end and ready to try out the recipes in the back of the book . . . Enjoy!"　　*—The Charlotte Observer*

"A page-turner."　　*—St. Paul Pioneer Press*

"Tea lovers, mystery lovers, [this] is for you. Just the right blend of cozy fun and clever plotting."
　　—Susan Wittig Albert, national bestselling author of Nightshade

"Delightful!"　　*—Tea: A Magazine*

continued . . .

THE SILVER NEEDLE MURDER

Tea Shop Mystery #9

LAURA CHILDS

BERKLEY PRIME CRIME, NEW YORK

THE BERKLEY PUBLISHING GROUP
Published by the Penguin Group
Penguin Group (USA) Inc.
375 Hudson Street, New York, New York 10014, USA
Penguin Group (Canada), 90 Eglinton Avenue East, Suite 700, Toronto, Ontario M4P 2Y3, Canada
(a division of Pearson Penguin Canada Inc.)
Penguin Books Ltd., 80 Strand, London WC2R 0RL, England
Penguin Group Ireland, 25 St. Stephen's Green, Dublin 2, Ireland (a division of Penguin Books Ltd.)
Penguin Group (Australia), 250 Camberwell Road, Camberwell, Victoria 3124, Australia
(a division of Pearson Australia Group Pty. Ltd.)
Penguin Books India Pvt. Ltd., 11 Community Centre, Panchsheel Park, New Delhi—110 017, India
Penguin Group (NZ), 67 Apollo Drive, Rosedale, North Shore 0632, New Zealand
(a division of Pearson New Zealand Ltd.)
Penguin Books (South Africa) (Pty.) Ltd., 24 Sturdee Avenue, Rosebank, Johannesburg 2196,
South Africa

Penguin Books Ltd., Registered Offices: 80 Strand, London WC2R 0RL, England

This is a work of fiction. Names, characters, places, and incidents either are the product of the author's
imagination or are used fictitiously, and any resemblance to actual persons, living or dead, business
establishments, events, or locales is entirely coincidental. The publisher does not have any control over
and does not assume any responsibility for author or third-party websites or their content.

PUBLISHER'S NOTE: The recipes contained in this book are to be followed exactly as written. The
publisher is not responsible for your specific health or allergy needs that may require medical super-
vision. The publisher is not responsible for any adverse reactions to the recipes contained in this book.

THE SILVER NEEDLE MURDER

A Berkley Prime Crime Book / published by arrangement with Gerry Schmitt & Associates, Inc.

PRINTING HISTORY
Berkley Prime Crime hardcover edition / March 2008
Berkley Prime Crime mass-market edition / March 2009

Copyright © 2008 by Gerry Schmitt & Associates, Inc.
Excerpt from *Eggs in Purgatory* by Laura Childs copyright © 2008 by Gerry Schmitt & Associates, Inc.
Cover illustration by Stephanie Henderson.
Cover design by Lesley Worrell.

ISBN: 978-0-425-22676-6

BERKLEY® PRIME CRIME
Berkley Prime Crime Books are published by The Berkley Publishing Group,
a division of Penguin Group (USA) Inc.,
375 Hudson Street, New York, New York 10014.
BERKLEY® PRIME CRIME and the PRIME CRIME logo are trademarks of Penguin Group (USA) Inc.

PRINTED IN THE UNITED STATES OF AMERICA

10   9   8   7   6   5   4   3   2   1

For Sam. Thanks a million.

ACKNOWLEDGMENTS

Many thanks to Bob, Asia, Moosha, Jennie, and Elmo for all their comments, inspiration, and critiques (as much as dogs can critique). Thanks also to Tom, Sandy, Catherine, and all the good folks at Berkley Publishing, as well as all the booksellers, tea shops, magazines, reviewers, and websites who lend their support.

1

Theodosia Browning pushed open the heavy door and fumbled for a light switch. Dust prickled her nose as she paused in the doorway, then finally found what she was looking for. An electrical hum filled the air as lights flickered hesitantly for a few seconds. Then they arced on, flooding the old kitchen, revealing a half acre of dusty counter space and aging appliances.

Stepping into the dullness of the kitchen, Theodosia looked like a single fresh bloom in a field of brown grasses. English-Irish ancestors had bequeathed her flawless skin, startling blue eyes, and a tangle of auburn hair—the kind of hair the artist Raphael had immortalized in his soft, gilded paintings. Her mother and father, dead many years now, had passed on their calm, resolute, and entrepreneurial spirit. Theodosia's penchant for curiosity seemed to have blossomed on its own.

"How's the place look?" called Drayton. He was still stumping down the stairway, muscling a large wicker basket.

Sixty-plus and dapper, wearing his trademark linen suit and bow tie, Drayton was Theodosia's assistant and catering manager. He'd been with her almost four years now, ever since she'd opened the Indigo Tea Shop in Charleston's historic district.

"Not so bad," responded Theodosia. She knew Drayton would hate it, of course.

"In other words, it's positively antediluvian," said Drayton. Crossing the threshold, he tilted his patrician head back and gave a derisive snort. "Oh my. Martha Stewart meets the Spanish Inquisition."

Theodosia chuckled to herself. Besides being a master tea blender, Drayton was a self-proclaimed arbiter of style and taste. He was also imbued with a keen sense of melodrama.

"We'll do fine," Theodosia told him, balling up a tea towel and wiping clean a wide swathe of stainless-steel counter. The kitchen *was* bad, but she was trying her darnedest to look past that. In fact, most times Theodosia was preternaturally disposed to seeing the positive side of things.

"Thank goodness we're only brewing tea," grumped Drayton. "Imagine if we had to prepare crepes or a raspberry charlotte."

"Then we'd have Haley right down here in the dungeon with us," said Theodosia, pulling a Brown Betty teapot from her basket. Haley was their baker extraordinaire, a gifted young woman who could take eggs, flour, and cream and magically transform them into tantalizing scones, spice breads, and chocolate muffins. Haley Houdini, Drayton sometimes called her.

"Did you know," said Theodosia, looking slightly mischievous as she unwrapped a delicate chintz-patterned teapot, "that there's supposed to be a ghost down here?" Along with a long article in last week's *Post and Courier* about the renovation, there had been a sidebar about the so-called backstage ghost.

This elicited another snort from Drayton. "Having lived some sixty plus years without encountering a true card-carrying member of the spirit world, I find it increasingly difficult to believe in their existence," was his pithy reply.

"Still," said Theodosia, surveying the subbasement kitchen, "I understand there have been some strange goings-on. And Charleston *is* supposed to be the most haunted city in America. More so than Savannah or even New Orleans."

"Perhaps haunted is really just a synonym for history," replied Drayton. He flipped open his wicker basket, pulled out two silver tins of tea, then squinted up at the stone arches that formed the ceiling. "As in the case of this old place. The Belvedere Theatre. Over the past hundred and fifty years it's probably acquired a certain—what would you call it?—karmic buildup of sorts."

Theodosia smiled even as she gave a slight shiver. "It does feel like there might be something." It was cold down here in this strange, dimly lit place and she was dressed in a turquoise sundress and strappy silver sandals. Well, of course, she was. This was August, after all, when Charleston, South Carolina, and the surrounding low country fairly simmered and shimmered with heat. And almost-tropical levels of humidity hung over everything like a soggy towel.

"The Belvedere has a crazy, checkered time line, too," continued Drayton, always eager to talk a little history.

Theodosia unpacked three more teapots, tea strainers, and several tea timers. "I understand this place has been a lot of different things." The Belvedere Theatre sat just a few blocks from her tea shop, but it had been tightly boarded up until this very recent renovation. In fact, being tapped to cater tonight's opening of the Charleston Film Festival was really Theodosia's first peek inside.

"The Belvedere Theatre has basically come full circle," explained Drayton. "It started life as an opera house in the mid–eighteen hundreds, then fortunes shifted and it was used as a warehouse of sorts for years and years. Shortly before World War I, this place was remodeled into the Trident Hotel." Drayton rubbed the bridge of his nose as his eyes traveled across the dilapidated fixtures. "Hence this basement kitchen and the dumbwaiter over there."

Theodosia followed his gaze. "You think it still works?"

"Has to," said Drayton. "How else are we going to get our tea upstairs?"

Theodosia decided this had to be the Belvedere's best incarnation yet, as she stood in the sumptuous lobby, mingling with the opening-night crowd. Women in brightly colored summer dresses, accompanied by men in summer-weight linen jackets, chimed excited greetings, exchanged air kisses, and exclaimed over the gleaming lobby of the Belvedere Theatre. After repeated scrubbings, countless coats of paint, and several million dollars' worth of renovations, the old theater sparkled like a jewel. Black marble floors gleamed, mauve silk wallpaper imparted a soft, romantic feel, and six-tiered crystal chandeliers twinkled overhead.

And how exciting, Theodosia decided, that the theater's very first booking was to play host to the Charleston Film Festival.

Pushing through the crowd, Theodosia could viscerally feel sparks of electricity in the air. The moneyed elite from Charleston's historic district were here, as well as local reviewers and lovers of film. All seemed to be enjoying a heady experience as they rubbed elbows with big-time producers, directors, and screenwriters. In fact, it appeared that most of Charleston's "art crowd" had turned out for tonight's film festival kickoff.

"Theodosia!" called an imperious male voice. "I want you to meet someone!"

Theodosia turned to find Timothy Neville, the octogenarian president of the Heritage Society, pushing his way toward her. Timothy, by virtue of his Huguenot ancestors and Italianate mansion on Archdale Street, enjoyed power-elite status in Charleston. With his bony simian face and small pointed teeth, he was feared, envied, and beloved, precisely in that order.

"Timothy," said Theodosia. "What a marvelous turnout!" Timothy had worked tirelessly with various preservation groups to help raise money to restore the Belvedere Theatre. He had also helped engineer this weeklong film festival, convincing the Heritage Society's board of directors and other civic-minded leaders that holding a film festival would be an exciting cultural event. To say nothing of the fact that cosponsoring the festival would lend a little extra cachet to his beloved Heritage Society.

Turned out in a cream-colored linen suit with a pale peach tie, Timothy looked both dapper and delighted. "This is my granddaughter, Isabelle Neville," Timothy told Theodosia, obviously proud of the young, dark-haired woman whose hand rested lightly on his arm. "Her very first short film is being screened this week."

"Wonderful," exclaimed Theodosia. "What's it called?"

Isabelle turned dark, luminous eyes on Theodosia. "*Reflections in Oil.* It's about some of our local Southern painters."

"Congratulations," said Theodosia. "And good luck, too."

Timothy Neville continued to beam. "Isabelle has a real knack for filmmaking. She shot and edited *Reflections* in her spare time while she was working as a location assistant for Jordan Cole."

"I'm impressed," said Theodosia. Jordan Cole was big-time. A director who'd made his chops with indie films, won major kudos at the Sundance and Tribeca Film Festivals, and gone on to direct major studio motion pictures. "Which film did you work on?"

"His newest one, *Roads End*," said Isabelle. "I came on to the shoot late, but assisted with location scenes in Savannah. And most of the editing was done right here in Charleston at Crash and Burn Studio." She grinned. "It's exciting to have the film premiere here Thursday night."

"Speak of the devil," said Timothy, as a tall man with a square-jawed, sun-bronzed face and blond hair flecked with silver casually cruised by a few feet away. Following in his wake, like a raft of baby ducklings swimming after their momma, were at least a dozen beautiful women in evening gowns.

An entourage, thought Theodosia. *Jordan Cole is traveling with an entourage of women.* And who could blame them? With his craggy good looks and Hollywood connections, Jordan Cole did seem infinitely appealing. She flipped the switch on the tiny digital camera she'd brought along, thought about taking a photo, then didn't.

"Is he a hunk or what?" whispered a voice in Theodosia's ear. A subtle waft of Chanel No. 5 announced the arrival of her friend Delaine Dish. Violet eyes sparkling, Delaine looked utterly adorable this evening in a low-cut pink crocheted dress, her dark hair pulled up in a psyche knot to accent her perfect heart-shaped face.

"I've been trying to wangle an introduction," Delaine explained breathlessly, "but to no avail. I suppose I'll just have to take things into my own hands and go over to Jordan Cole and say how-do." Delaine gave Theodosia a slow wink. It wouldn't be the first time she'd sashayed up to a man and introduced herself. Heck, it wouldn't be the last.

"Have Isabelle introduce you," suggested Theodosia. "She worked with Jordan Cole." She peered at Isabelle, then back toward Delaine. "You two *do* know each other, right?"

Besides owning the Cotton Duck boutique, Delaine was a volunteer and tireless fund-raiser for the Heritage Society. Delaine enjoyed a long-standing relationship with Timothy, but Theodosia wasn't sure whether Delaine and Isabelle were acquainted.

Delaine waved a hand. "Oh sure, we've met lots of times. Hi, honey."

"I think your dress alone will make a grand introduction," said Isabelle with a grin, obviously impressed by Delaine's outgoing nature and cosmopolitan sense of style.

"Oh, you like this?" asked Delaine, feigning innocence as she ran a hand down her hips, smoothing fabric. "The color's called *blush* pink." She giggled. "But I'm thinking it should probably be called *scandal*."

"*How's Drayton coming* with the tea?" Haley asked Theodosia. Posed behind the tea table, wearing a black halter top and long white skirt, Haley fussed with napkins and tiny silver spoons. She'd come along tonight to help pour tea and serve tea sandwiches, once the opening ceremonies were concluded.

"Drayton's downstairs making do with a somewhat primitive institutional kitchen," Theodosia told her.

"Not surprised," said Haley, shaking her head and brushing back her stick-straight blondish-brown hair. "Although everything's pretty fantabulous up here." Here eyes roved the lobby. "This decor is just amazing. No wonder the Heritage Society had to raise millions to restore this place. Oh, and have you laid eyes on any of the famous directors?"

"I just caught a glimpse of Jordan Cole," Theodosia told her.

"Well, I brushed shoulders with C. W. Dredd," said Haley. She pointed across the lobby. "You see him over there?"

Theodosia scanned the crowd, caught sight of yet *another* great-looking film director.

"Yowza," exclaimed Haley. "He is one seriously good-looking guy. Which means this is stacking up to be some week." C. W. Dredd was a Southern boy who'd made good. He'd directed several Hollywood features and also had a new film premiering at this week's festival.

"It's for sure going to be a busy week," said Theodosia, thinking of all the catering jobs she and Drayton had signed on for. She hoped they could pull them off with style and a modicum of grace.

"No problem," said Haley, snapping back into work mode. "In fact, I'm really looking forward to all our little gigs. Nothing like a challenge and a chance to meet new, fun people. So . . . what's our master plan for tonight?"

"Once Drayton finishes brewing the tea, we'll haul it upstairs in the dumbwaiter," explained Theodosia. "Then I'll ferry the dozen or so teapots to you via a rolling cart."

"Great," said Haley. "He's still going with the silver needle?" Silver needle was a white tea from China's Fujian Province. Picked in early spring, its dried leaves resembled white pine needles. Brewing yielded a pale yellow tea with a delicious buttery almond flavor.

"It's still on the docket as far as I know," replied Theodosia, snugging a vase of white roses closer to a crystal candelabra that held tall white tapers.

"Well, good." Haley laughed. "Drayton's never been much of an improv guy so we're probably set."

"You didn't have any trouble getting the tea sandwiches in here?"

"Your sweetie helped me schlep everything in," said Haley. "Now he's gone back for the serving trays." The sweetie Haley was referring to was Parker Scully, Theodosia's sort-of boyfriend and the owner of Solstice Bistro.

"Wonderful," said Theodosia, peering through the crowd, hoping to get a quick word with Parker.

Haley kicked a toe against two red plastic coolers that

took up most of the space beneath the white-linen-draped table. "Lobster salad and chicken salad with chutney, just as you requested."

"Yum," said Theodosia. Haley probably made the finest tea sandwiches south of the Mason-Dixon Line. Some of her other specialties included shrimp salad and dill, cream cheese with pineapple on chocolate bread, and watercress and chèvre on onion tartlets. And, once in a while, when Haley was really off the wall and feeling passionately creative, salmon caviar and crème fraîche on thin-sliced pumpernickel.

"When should I start setting up?" asked Haley. "I don't want to put out the sandwiches too soon and risk having them dry out." Haley was a stickler for order and always liked having things buttoned up nice and neat.

"As soon as Timothy begins his opening remarks you should start setting up," said Theodosia. "He'll segue into introductions of the five major directors who are all in competition for the Golden Palmetto award, then they'll each say a few words. There'll be a five-minute intermission and, after that, screenings of three or four short films. But not everyone will stay to watch the films, so that's when we need to start serving."

"Got it," said Haley. "Where are you off to right now?"

"Backstage," said Theodosia, looping her all-access pass around her neck. She still didn't see Parker and decided she couldn't wait for him any longer. "I want to be ready to scoop up those teapots once Drayton sends them up in the dumbwaiter."

Backstage was dark and about twenty degrees warmer. Theodosia waited patiently next to the dumbwaiter at the rear wall of the theater. A dark blue velvet curtain cordoned off most of the backstage area. Then, in front of that blue curtain was a pair of large white translucent screens, set about three feet apart. Timothy stood at a podium, in front of those screens, addressing a full house. With the grace and poise of an elder statesman, he extolled the virtues of the re-habbed Belvedere Theatre. And reiterated the fact that the citizens of Charleston were thrilled beyond belief to welcome a cadre of illustrious film directors, producers, and screenwriters to their fair city.

As Timothy droned on, the backstage area seemed like a beehive of activity. People whispered, coughed, practiced short speeches, and jostled around in the semidarkness.

"Theodosia?" came a woman's hoarse whisper.

Theodosia peered at a figure that materialized beside her in the gloom. Tall, long dark hair, svelte figure. "Yes?" she said.

"It's Nina," said the voice, more melodious this time. "Nina van Diedrich." Nina was a wealthy, well-connected divorcée who was deeply involved in Charleston's arts organizations. "Isn't this exciting?"

"Wonderful," agreed Theodosia.

"I'm just thrilled at the caliber of talent we've been able to attract," Nina cooed to her. Then she touched Theodosia's arm gently and slipped away. "Ta. See you at the after-party."

Theodosia stood there a few more minutes. Put her ear to the closed door of the dumbwaiter, but didn't hear a thing.

Finally, deciding that Drayton was taking his own sweet time with the tea preparation, Theodosia got a little antsy and began wandering about. Edging into the wings, she found herself in a dimly lit warren of dressing rooms, makeup rooms, and costume shops. The walls here extended perhaps twelve feet high, then ended without a ceiling. Overhead was an intricate hanging maze of ropes, pulleys, and backdrops.

Fascinated, Theodosia eased into one of the dressing rooms where a dozen or so elaborate period costumes hung on a metal rack. They were magnificent pieces, all pure silks and velvets. She supposed volunteers would be wearing these hoop-skirted dresses and elegantly tailored waistcoats in the days to come, when they introduced short films and documentaries of a historic nature.

How like Timothy, she thought, to keep things historically accurate.

Just as Theodosia turned, something bumped hard on the other side of the wall, and she caught sight of something moving in front of her. Startled, she let out a nervous gasp, then realized she'd been tricked by her own reflection in the makeup mirror.

What's got you so jumpy? she thought. Then realized there were voices coming from the cubicle next to her. Low, intense voices.

"I don't know where you get the nerve!" hissed one angry voice.

There was more low murmuring, then a second voice, quivering with rage, responded, "Don't you dare threaten me!"

Curious, Theodosia wondered what was going on in that next room. The argument sounded serious. As though fisticuffs were about to be engaged in.

And then, as if to punctuate the heated exchange, thunderous applause reverberated throughout the theater. And the two people who'd been arguing in the room next to Theodosia fell silent.

Embarrassed that she'd unwittingly eavesdropped on their conversation, Theodosia hesitated for a few moments before making her exit.

But when she walked out of the dressing room a few seconds later, the room next to her was empty. Whoever had been in there feuding was gone.

Wandering back toward the backstage waiting area, Theodosia caught Timothy Neville's words and was cognizant of the fact that he was just about to introduce their first visiting film director. The highly inventive set decorators who'd created the double-screen arrangement now had gigantic klieg lights thrown up against them. So when each director stepped into this brilliant pocket of light before walking out on stage, the audience would see their enormous, larger-than-life shadow projected on the front screen.

"And now," came Timothy's voice as it rose with excitement, "the moment you've all been waiting for. We have a roster of exceptional film directors with us this week, many of whom hail from the South."

Standing backstage, Theodosia saw a shadow loom twenty feet tall on the screen. The first director was now in place and the audience, in response, let out a collective "oooh," obviously excited at what they viewed as a neat bit of showmanship.

Suddenly, there was a scuffle of feet and a second shadow loomed large as well.

What the . . . ? thought Theodosia. She knew this couldn't be part of the script.

"I'd like to introduce," boomed Timothy's voice. "Jordan Cole!"

A loud, sharp bang erupted not twenty feet from Theodosia. Startled, she watched in horror as a dark spatter slashed across the white screen.

The shadow image of Jordan Cole, the director who'd been waiting patiently for his cue, suddenly twisted violently and his hands flew up. The shock from the impact seemed to hold him suspended for several long moments. Then slowly, like a sequence filmed with an undercranked camera, his twenty-foot image imploded on itself and Jordan Cole collapsed like a rag doll.

Screams from the audience almost drowned out a nearby skittering of feet.

What? thought Theodosia, stunned beyond belief. *What just happened here?*

And then someone was moving fast behind her, slipping through the darkness.

"Stop!" she yelled, trying to put some real authority into her voice.

But whoever it was didn't pay a whit of attention to her. There was a loud thunk, then the sound of metal grating against wood. Theodosia's mind suddenly registered the familiar sound: the dumbwaiter!

As the cacophony of screams from the audience out front began to build, Theodosia spun on her heels and raced toward the dumbwaiter. Peering through the backstage darkness, she was just in time to see a shadowy figure jump inside and crouch down. Stunned, Theodosia watched as a single hand snaked out and quickly pulled down the door. She caught just the hint of a gleaming green stone—cuff links perhaps?—then there was a low rumble as the dumbwaiter descended.

People milled everywhere now, pushing and shoving, caught in the throes of panic. Their shouts and cries shrilled in Theodosia's ears.

"Over here!" she screamed. "In the dumbwaiter!"

Nobody paid an ounce of attention.

Got to get the police, she thought. Grabbing a wild-eyed man who tried to rush past her, Theodosia was about to demand the use of his cell phone when a thought struck her like a bolt from the blue. *Drayton!*

"Help me!" she screamed. "I think the shooter is headed downstairs!"

Again nobody listened.

Yanking open the heavy fire door that stood just a few feet from the dumbwaiter, Theodosia uttered a final futile yelp, then threw herself into the back stairwell. Careening downward, trying to descend two steps at a time, Theodosia could almost feel the vibration of the dumbwaiter moving in the wall next to her.

Whoever it was had a serious head start, though. And she knew that when that dumbwaiter hit the basement and the shooter flung up the door, desperate to escape, Drayton would be right in his way!

Poor Drayton, innocently puttering about in the kitchen!

The heel of Theodosia's sandal caught on the lip of a step, causing her to lurch forward and almost pitch headlong down the dank stairs. Grabbing for the handrail, hauling herself upright, Theodosia angrily kicked off the offending sandal, then shucked the other one off, too. Urgency driving her now, she continued her wild descent barefooted.

Then Theodosia hurled herself against the swinging door and flailed her way into the kitchen.

What she saw caused her heart to lurch in her chest and brought a stunned prickle of hot tears to her eyes. Drayton lay crumpled on the tile floor, a terrible tide of red spread out around him.

2

❧

"*I've never been* so terrified in my life," exclaimed Haley as she slid two pans of scones into the huge industrial oven they'd somehow managed to shoehorn into the Indigo Tea Shop's small kitchen. "When I saw all that blood pouring down the side of Drayton's head I thought for sure he was a goner!"

Theodosia nodded sympathetically as she filled tiny cut glass bowls with fresh Devonshire cream. Haley was still young, a college student really, and last night's episode had left her badly shaken. She'd tried to convince Haley to stay home today, to take it easy. But Haley had been adamant. She wanted to be in bright and early this Monday morning, same as always, tending to the morning baked goods and the luncheon entrées, remaining solidly at her post. She was, in short, a tough little kitchen martinet.

Of course, last night Drayton had been even more stubborn and hardheaded. (And thank goodness for that hardheaded part!) After being clobbered on the head by his unknown assailant, Drayton had been whisked to Charleston Memorial Hospital where a frantic Theodosia, Haley, Parker Scully, and Timothy Neville had met him in the ER. Drayton had been remarkably calm, enduring forty-five minutes of medical scrutiny under the watchful eyes of a very competent young resident, an African American woman by the name of Shayla Russell. Dr. Russell had checked Drayton's head wound, performed some perfunctory neurological tests, then made two tiny, precise sutures. She'd set their fears to rest when she explained that head wounds often looked much worse than they really were, something Drayton readily agreed with. To be proactively careful, Dr. Russell had also recommended a head CT, a test that Drayton had completely pooh-poohed. Drayton, of course, had been faultlessly polite but adamant in his refusal. Even though everyone had urged him to have a head scan if only as a precaution.

But then they'd found out about poor Jordan Cole. Brought into the same hospital and pronounced dead on arrival from a shot to the head. That terrible news had put a damper on things, had caused everyone to pretty much run out of steam. They'd stopped pestering Drayton since he really *did* seem okay, and everyone had headed home.

And now Drayton was here at the Indigo Tea Shop this Monday morning, a small bandage on the back of his head. Sitting out front at the little table by the fireplace, talking with Timothy Neville. But from the sound of their raised voices, their mood was none too joyous.

"It's a stupid, ridiculous mistake on their part," snapped Drayton as he dropped a teapot onto the scarred wooden table. "Why on earth would the police want to question Isabelle?"

Tables were set with crisp linens and gleaming silver. Steam gathered in aromatic little puffs above steeping teapots. The aroma of fresh-baked scones and muffins permeated the air. And Timothy Neville had just announced that his granddaughter, Isabelle, was being questioned in last night's murder.

"Just because she *knew* Jordan Cole," Timothy fumed. "Just because she *worked* with him."

"They're questioning everyone," said Theodosia as she joined the two men. She'd overheard Drayton and Timothy express their outrage from her spot in the kitchen. "The police questioned me," she told them. Two police officers had corralled her last night and taken what they'd called a "witness statement." In fact, a whole raft of investigators had been brought in to quiz and grill the people who'd been milling about backstage.

"Only because you were a sort of witness," Timothy told her, still chafing at the indignity of having his beloved granddaughter's character brought into question.

Theodosia poured a steady stream of reddish-black tea into a fine bone china teacup and passed it to Timothy. "Drink this," she told him. "You'll feel better."

Mechanically, Timothy's gnarled hands reached out to accept the cup of tea, then he set it down without taking a sip. "Why do people always say that?" he replied rather crossly. "When absolutely *nothing* could possibly improve my mood this morning."

Theodosia pushed a pouf of auburn hair behind one shoulder. Timothy, she decided, was being even more difficult than his usual taciturn, curmudgeonly self. "This really will help," she assured him. "It's Puerh, a Chinese tea highly effective for calming the nerves. It's also rather strong and functions as a good digestive."

"Calming and strong?" Timothy asked archly. "Isn't that an oxymoron? Like an educated guess or a firm estimate?"

Theodosia was used to Timothy's sharp retorts. "Trust me," she said. "This tea works wonders."

"Last night's tragedy was the worst thing that could have

happened," snarled Timothy. "We've brought in major directors and producers, garnered sponsorship from companies like Crash and Burn Studio and Channel Eight Productions, and caught the attention of hundreds of film fans. And now, what was supposed to be a truly landmark film festival has been marred by murder." He shot a thunderous look at Drayton. "We'll undoubtedly be mired in a police investigation the entire week!"

"The thing is," said Drayton, fussing with his bow tie, "what can *we* do to lessen the negative impact of all this?" As he delivered his words, he stared straight across the table at Theodosia.

"'All this' meaning what exactly?" asked Theodosia.

"We have to ensure that Isabelle is in the clear and carry on with the film festival," fretted Drayton. "That's the priority."

"Whatever we do," said Timothy, "we have to move fast. Nip any problems in the bud, make sure justice is properly served." He finally took a quick sip of tea, then directed his penetrating gaze toward Theodosia as well.

Theodosia set her teacup down in her saucer where it made a tiny clink. "Why are you both staring at me?" she asked.

One of Timothy's heroic eyebrows arched, then quivered. His simian face collapsed into a mass of creases. "I'd say it's rather obvious," he replied, his words clipped and precise.

When Theodosia said nothing, Drayton jumped in to help. "You're friendly with him," he said.

"No way," said Theodosia. She knew exactly who they were referring to. Friendly with *him*. With Detective Burt Tidwell. A strange, beady-eyed bear of a man who headed the Robbery-Homicide Division of the Charleston Police Department. He was also a devious fiend who derived endless pleasure from needling her. "We're not friends," Theodosia told them in a no-nonsense tone.

"I said *friendly*," replied Drayton.

"Big difference," replied Theodosia. "Yes, Detective Tidwell and I have a sort of nodding, tacit relationship, if you could call it that. But I sincerely doubt he's going to pull me inside the fold with his brothers in blue and reveal any investigative insights about Jordan Cole's murder."

"You have to try," insisted Timothy. "We have to know what's going on."

"Especially since we've just kicked off the film festival," agreed Drayton. "And it has six full days left to run."

"Plus Isabelle *is* one of the nominees," added Timothy, as if that little issue wasn't already hanging over their heads. "And who's to say Tidwell won't start badgering some of our important guests and VIPs?"

Theodosia shook her head. "Tidwell's going to carry on his own dogged investigation whether you want him to or not. And having me talk to him isn't going to change things. There's no way Tidwell will take me into his confidence; he's devilish that way. He adores playing cat-and-mouse games, but loathes revealing a single bit of information."

Timothy put a hand on the table and drummed his fingers. "Perhaps there's another way."

"I don't think so," said Theodosia. *Really*, she thought, *there was no way she could get involved.* She already had her hands full this week.

"The thing of it is," said Timothy, "two of our panel judges have already resigned. Traumatized after last night."

"Oh, that's not good," said Drayton, pursing his lips. "Not good at all."

Now Timothy looked distracted as well as nervous. "There are going to be repercussions," he said.

"But the film festival is going to proceed as scheduled, right?" asked Theodosia.

Timothy nodded slowly. "Hopefully, yes. But this festival has been an enormous gamble for the Heritage Society. Not only did we help raise serious funding for the renovation of the Belvedere Theatre, but I'd hate to see my new initiative of partnering with other nonprofits simply disintegrate. It would mean . . . well, the possibility exists that I could be removed from my position." Timothy had been director of the Heritage Society for going on thirty years now and it had flourished under his leadership. In fact, Timothy Neville lived and breathed the Heritage Society. If the organization somehow slipped out of his hands, his spirit would be completely crushed.

Now it was Theodosia's turn to look confused. "So . . . what are you saying?" *A better question might be, what are you asking?* she thought.

Timothy stared over the rim of his teacup at her, his lined countenance and hard eyes giving him the appearance of an old turtle. "I'd like to put you on one of the judging committees."

"Me?" said Theodosia, her voice rising in a squawk. "What are you talking about? I'm not remotely qualified to be a film festival judge!"

"Nonsense," said Timothy, brushing away her protest as though it were an annoying fly buzzing at his head. "You're a former marketing executive who's produced a bevy of TV commercials and short films. That more than qualifies you."

"Maybe so," allowed Theodosia. "But all my production experience is from a few years ago. And all the TV spots and films were financial or retail in nature."

"Of course, you're quite media savvy, too," said Drayton, jumping in, much to Theodosia's consternation. "Which is a huge plus. You've masterminded tons of PR for the Spoleto Festival and done live television. Handled it rather adroitly, I'd say."

"I'm not sure a couple of guest shots on *Windows on Charleston* exactly qualifies me as a media darling," said Theodosia, suddenly feeling both flustered and pressured.

"All I did was talk about how to brew tea." She paused. "And set a nice table."

"Believe it or not," said Timothy, "you're probably more qualified than anyone else we have right now. And besides, serving as a judge would put you squarely on the inside. You could end up being privy to certain information or you might overhear something when you're attending screenings or fancy parties and such."

"That's part of the problem," said Theodosia, trying to make Timothy hear her, make him really understand. "The Indigo Tea Shop has already been hired to cater some of those parties!"

"Oh, Drayton and I can handle all that," said Haley, as she leaned in and set a plate of steaming key lime scones on the table. "I think it sounds exciting to be a judge. Besides, Timothy's right. You might overhear something important. Heaven knows, you're good at ferreting things out."

"The murderer was someone who was *backstage* with you," pressed Timothy. "Which leads me to believe that someone in our film crowd has to know something."

Two fine lines insinuated themselves in the center of Theodosia's normally placid brow. "If I agree to do this," said Theodosia, "are you two sure you can handle things?" Her gaze veered from Haley to Drayton and stayed there. "We've got the Cinema Bistro Café party tomorrow night and the Tea Français on Wednesday."

Drayton waved a hand. "Please. Staging those events will be child's play."

Theodosia wasn't buying it. "You went positively ballistic last week when we hosted afternoon tea for twenty-five women from Goose Creek and you discovered we didn't have a full complement of matching soup spoons."

Drayton gave a casual shrug. "I've mellowed since then."

"Sure you have," said Theodosia. "And when Madewood

Brothers sent Sencha tea instead of Gyokuro, you accused them of being incompetent troglodytes."

"That's because they *are* incompetent," said Drayton. "They bungled the order. Can I help it if I'm fussy about my Japanese tea? No, of course not. But . . . ahem . . . I do see your point."

Theodosia picked up a sliver of lemon and squeezed a few drops into her tea. "You really want me to do this?" she asked Timothy.

His dark, intense eyes drilled into her. "More than anything," he replied. "For heaven's sake, one of the festival's top contenders for the Golden Palmetto Award was *murdered* last night. Probably by someone who rubbed elbows with us. Someone who was skillful enough to insinuate himself backstage with our cadre of southern directors and producers."

"Someone who must have had an all-access pass," murmured Theodosia.

Leaning back in his chair, Timothy put a gnarled hand to the side of his face. "Dear lord, Jordan Cole, one of Hollywood's hottest directors . . . shot in front of five hundred witnesses. And nobody has a single clue that might lead to the murderer's identity."

Except me, thought Theodosia. *I saw that flash of green as the dumbwaiter door slid closed. Had to be cuff links. Or maybe . . . a ring?*

Theodosia pondered Timothy's words, knowing in her heart he was quite correct. Someone had hung around backstage. Someone had gained access. Someone who might still be taking part in the festival.

"Do this," Timothy pleaded. "As a favor to me."

Theodosia sighed. "All right. But, please, assign me to one of the less important judging committees, okay?"

"I'll put you on short films and documentaries," said Timothy, suddenly looking vastly relieved.

Mother of pearl, was Theodosia's first thought. What did she know about short films and documentaries, anyway?

"Cheer up, will you?" said Drayton, seeing the look of panic on Theodosia's face. "It's not like you're judging the Cannes Film Festival or some other big international event. This is just our own local Charleston Film Festival. Our first ever, in fact."

"But hopefully not our last," grunted Timothy.

3

Morning repast at the Indigo Tea Shop usually consisted of scones, muffins, and quick breads served with good morning teas such as Assam, English breakfast, Irish breakfast, or a Ceylon blend. Lunch was generally a cottage tea, a menu that included various combinations of soups, salads, sandwiches, quiches, and desserts. Which, of course, meant a fair amount of prep time.

Haley scurried back into the kitchen where she pulled a second batch of scones from the oven. Drayton slipped a long, black Parisian apron around his neck and busied himself behind the counter, where he had several teapots already steeping.

"You're brewing some Gunpowder tea, too?" asked Theodosia. Drayton had a gift for selecting the pluperfect teas.

His brow furrowed. "Yes, but I don't see my Wedgwood teapot anywhere. Drat, you don't suppose it got left behind last night, do you?"

"It certainly could have," said Theodosia. One of the film festival volunteers had helped her pack everything in a crazy rush.

"That teapot was one of my absolute favorites," said Drayton. "Highly collectible Basalt Capri ware. As you well know, it came from my great-aunt Clauthilde's estate. She was the one who traveled extensively in Europe. Even lived in Lyon a short time."

"I'm sure we can retrieve it," said Theodosia, although she didn't relish venturing back down into the dank basement of the Belvedere Theatre.

Theodosia also had other matters to deal with right now. As the clock edged toward midmorning, her tea shop was rapidly filling to capacity. Customers had caught an intoxicating whiff of Haley's baked goods as well as Drayton's teas, and a hum of anticipation filled the air.

This, of course, was what it was all about. This was what Theodosia had worked for. Never once did she regret leaving the chew-'em-up-spit-'em-out world of marketing to run her beautiful little Indigo Tea Shop. In fact, being a tea entrepreneur was her dream come true. Her floor-to-ceiling cupboards were filled with the world's most exotic teas. From delicately fruited Nilgiris to malty Assams to rich, dark oolongs. Her tea shop itself, a former carriage house, sported pegged wood floors that she'd recently given a red tea wash, battered hickory tables, brick walls, leaded-glass windows, and a tiny fireplace. Of course the place was crammed with items for sale, too. Antique teapots lovingly scouted at local auctions, tea towels, tea cozies, jars of Devonshire cream and DuBose Bees Honey, candles, wicker baskets, and cut glass bowls sat on shelves or were tucked into antique cupboards. The walls were decorated with antique prints and grapevine wreaths she'd made and decorated.

When every table but one was filled, when almost all the

customers had been served scones and tea, Theodosia spun around to find a large hulk of a man standing just inside the front door, staring at her intently. Detective Burt Tidwell.

Rats, she thought. It wasn't exactly what the tea shop needed right now. A big, angry-looking homicide detective hovering like some bizarre, ready-to-pull-its-tether dirigible.

Theodosia did what she always did in times of crisis and duress. She showed Tidwell to a table and brought him a nice pot of tea.

"Mmm, Chinese black tea?" he asked, sniffing expectantly.

Tidwell, she noted, was turning into a fledgling tea connoisseur. "An Empire Keemun," she told him. "The tea that started the Opium Wars."

"See, I am indeed learning," Tidwell responded. "I'm an apt student." He jerked his big head at the chair opposite him. "Sit down, will you?" It wasn't exactly a cordial invitation.

Reluctantly, Theodosia slid into the chair. Then she decided that since she was going to be questioned in her own tea shop, she should get the ball rolling with a few questions of her own.

"Did you find the murder weapon?" she asked Tidwell. Last night there had been a big hue and cry, with at least a dozen uniformed officers running around with crazed expressions, searching high and low for some sort of pistol or gun.

Tidwell took a sip of tea and stared at her pleasantly. "Jordan Cole was killed with a bang stick."

Theodosia stared back at him. "Pardon?" She wasn't sure she'd heard him correctly.

"A bang stick," repeated Tidwell. "Also known as a stun gun for sharks. Divers often carry them as a safety precaution." He looked wildly pleased that he'd caught her so off guard.

"You can't be serious," she said. All along Theodosia had assumed the murder weapon had been some sort of handgun. Something easy to conceal, easy to dispose of. It felt weird to have her paradigm shift so radically.

Tidwell's slightly protruding eyes stared at her without blinking. "I assure you, I am quite serious."

Theodosia was still confused. "But if someone attacked Jordan Cole with a shark stunner, then why wasn't the poor man simply stunned? Why the terrible, fatal explosion?"

"Ah," said Tidwell, delighted she'd asked, tickled he'd been able to ruffle her feathers a bit. "Because we have deduced that this particular bang stick was loaded with a twelve-gauge shotgun shell as well as a CO_2 cartridge. All it took was one good jab and . . . *kaboom*!"

"Is that technical police lingo?" Theodosia asked him. "The *kaboom* part?"

"Forgive me if I indulge in a little colloquial jargon," he replied. "I veer off procedure so infrequently."

Theodosia chose to ignore his remark. "Where would you get something like that?" she asked. "A bang stick?"

"Dive shops, of course," replied Tidwell. "Or one could order via the Internet. Obviously, we're busy compiling customer lists from local dive shops."

"But it's a good-sized weapon, isn't it? How on earth . . . ?"

"Some are three feet long, others run only a foot or so," said Tidwell. "Easily concealed under a jacket." He gazed implacably at Theodosia. "Or skirt."

"I'm pretty sure the person who jumped into the dumbwaiter was a man," she said.

"Witnesses are always pretty sure of their facts until you get them inside a courtroom. Then all bets are off."

"You're in a strange mood," said Theodosia.

"I'm in investigatory *mode*," corrected Tidwell.

"In other words," said Theodosia, "you don't really have a

clue what went down. You're out fishing." She was pleased she finally got in a dig of her own.

Tidwell held up a pudgy hand. "Au contraire," he told her. "I'm following up on several written reports from last night." He peered across at her. "One of them concerns you. What you saw, or *thought* you saw." He pulled a crumpled sheet of paper from his jacket pocket, laid it on the table, and smoothed it.

"So follow up," she told him, anxious to get back to her customers.

"You saw two people arguing," said Tidwell, cupping a plump hand, indicating for her to relate to him exactly what happened.

"No, I *heard* two people arguing," said Theodosia.

"Men?" asked Tidwell.

Theodosia hesitated. "I think so. Maybe."

"Ah," said Tidwell. "Could one of them have been Jordan Cole?"

Theodosia shrugged. "Sure. I guess so." She hesitated. "Although he has . . . had . . . a fairly distinctive voice."

Tidwell nodded. "The east Texas twang."

Theodosia frowned. "I didn't hear anything like that. Then again, they were whispering."

"Could one of them have been the other director, C. W. Dredd? The one who does the political thriller movies?"

"Is he a suspect?" Theodosia asked.

"Everyone is a suspect," responded Tidwell.

"Not terribly productive," muttered Theodosia.

"All right," said Tidwell. "Then please consider this. Could one of the persons you overheard conceivably have been a woman?"

Theodosia shrugged. "Possibly. I guess so."

"Although you didn't actually *see* the two people who were arguing. You only heard them," reiterated Tidwell.

"I only caught faint snatches of conversation," said

Theodosia. As she let her mind wander back, it had seemed like a radio broadcast that wasn't transmitting properly. Bits and snatches of conversation that faded in and out.

"And how soon after you overheard this conversation did the explosion take place?" asked Tidwell.

"Two or three minutes," said Theodosia. "Not long."

Tidwell shook his head and his chin sloshed. "The images of two people made enormous by a rear screen projection. Five hundred witnesses in the audience. Yet no one can identify the killer." He looked supremely irritated.

"That's pretty much what Timothy Neville said," replied Theodosia. "About the identification part." She thought for a few moments. "Tell me, how exactly did the killer get away? I would have thought he was trapped in that basement."

"Tunnel," said Tidwell. "One that leads up and out to a rear parking lot."

"Tunnel," repeated Theodosia. "Yes, I suppose there must be one. For deliveries and such."

"Another question," responded Tidwell. "Did you happen to see Timothy's granddaughter, Isabelle, backstage?"

"Not that I can recall," said Theodosia. She let her mind again rove back to the scramble of police who'd flooded the backstage area last night. "Obviously you located the discarded weapon?" she asked him. "The stun gun?"

Tidwell hesitated a split second. "A small part of it." He glanced down at his paper, then stared at her. "And you say you noticed a hint of green stone. On our fleeing suspect's hand. Cuff links, you think?"

"Or a ring," said Theodosia. "It all happened so fast. And then I was so focused on Drayton. All by himself, downstairs in the kitchen."

Tidwell pulled a pen from his jacket pocket and made a few hasty scratches. "Yes, I have questions for him, too," he said. "I phoned Drayton's home earlier this morning, fully expecting him to be in bed resting and recuperating. Now I find him here instead. Shame, Miss Browning. You don't run a sweatshop, do you?"

"The only sweating we do around here is over a hot stove," replied Theodosia. She glanced across the tea room and saw that Drayton was deep in conversation with Gracie Venable from the Bow Geste hat salon. Gracie was picking up a take-out order of tea and a bag of apple muffins while Drayton chatted with her. "Drayton doesn't like being interrupted when he's with customers," she told Tidwell.

Tidwell settled back in his chair. "Send him over when you can." His head swiveled on his bulbous body as he surveyed the tables around him. "What . . ." he asked slowly, ". . . what is that unusual-looking biscuit the woman in the yellow hat has on her plate?"

"That's one of Haley's cat head biscuits," said Theodosia.

"Strange name," said Tidwell.

"Probably because they're so big and round." She paused. "Would you care to try one?"

"Please," said Tidwell. This time a little sheepishly. "With a generous dollop of Devonshire cream?"

"All right." Theodosia sighed. "Sit tight." She glanced over at Drayton again, saw he was holding up the phone, motioning to her.

Theodosia scurried across the tea room, happy to leave Tidwell behind. She grabbed the phone, whispered, "He wants to talk to you," then put the receiver to her ear. "Hello?"

"Theo?"

"Parker?"

"Everything all right?"

Not really. "As good as can be expected," she told him. "Although Timothy Neville is completely whipped out of shape because the police dared to question his granddaughter, Isabelle. And Tidwell is hunkered at a table even as we speak, glowering at everyone in sight and probably gearing up to beat a confession out of someone with a rubber hose. Thank goodness Drayton is holding his own."

"Drayton's a tough old bird."

"But not exactly a spring chicken," said Theodosia. Her giggle morphed into a choke and tears suddenly welled up in her eyes. She didn't know *what* she'd do if something happened to her beloved Drayton. Probably just throw in the towel. He was as much a part of the tea shop as she was. Haley, too.

"Well, I'm just calling to check on everybody. Make sure you're okay."

Theodosia grabbed a corner of apron and blotted her eyes. "We're okay."

"Tell you what," said Parker. "Why don't I come over tonight and we'll just flake out together. I'll bring the eats, too. Maybe even have Toby whip up something special." Toby was Toby Crisp, Parker's executive chef.

"Can't," said Theodosia. "There's another little problem that's come up. Two film festival judges resigned so I've been shanghaied to take their place."

"Seriously?" said Parker.

"See," said Theodosia. "I thought it was a terrible idea, too."

"No, no, I think it's a fine idea," responded Parker. "You're smart and you know the turf. Film production, that is."

"I sure hope so," said Theodosia.

4

❧

"*Chilled strawberry soup* as a starter," said Haley. "Plus blue crab salad with a mustard vinaigrette and a selection of cucumber-dill and poached-salmon tea sandwiches. It's so warm today I figured our customers would appreciate a cold menu."

"Except for the hot tea," said Drayton, raising one eyebrow.

"Well, that's a given," said Haley. "Since we're a tea shop. But I expect you've prepared a few pitchers of sweet tea, too." Sweet tea was the southern version of iced tea with a little simple syrup thrown in. "You know, my grandmother always used to say, hot day, hot beverage."

"A contrarian philosophy that you've also adopted," said Drayton. "I'd say it becomes you, Haley."

"Thank you, Drayton," she said as she picked up a cleaver and whammed it down on a crab claw, sending shards flying.

"Incoming," said Theodosia, ducking slightly.

Crowded into the doorway of the small kitchen, Theodosia

and Drayton were waiting for the rest of the last-minute menu details from Haley.

"But you *do* have more tasty treats baking in the oven," pointed out Drayton. "So today's luncheon offerings are not entirely cold."

"A batch of cinnamon raisin muffins and a few pans of lemon tea bread," said Haley. She stopped fussing with the crab, put her hands on her hips. "For heaven's sake, I can't *not* bake. Our customers count on us, after all. How many times have you impressed upon me, Drayton, that a proper cup of tea is even better when it's accompanied by a—"

"I know, I know," interrupted Drayton. "Can I help it if I have a sweet tooth? Can I help it if I happen to love a cream scone with my Darjeeling or a madeleine with my English breakfast tea? By the way, you have more biscuits, too?"

"Yes, yes." Haley nodded. Her cheeks were flushed from the heat of the kitchen, her long hair was pulled back into a ponytail, her head was covered with a pink bandana.

"Wonderful," said Theodosia, trying to hurry things along.

"Everything should be out in about five minutes," said Haley. "And if you'll both kindly retreat from my kitchen, I'll have our luncheon entrées good to go in another fifteen minutes."

Drayton threw up his hands in a highly theatrical gesture, then spun on the heels of his well-polished loafers. "I'm out of here," he told the two women.

"You need help?" asked Theodosia. Haley was normally a pretty cool customer, but today she looked slightly frazzled.

"It's just that it's so hot in here and I'm attempting this new vinaigrette recipe. Sure hope it turns out."

"I'm sure it will be stellar," Theodosia assured her. Most new recipes that Haley introduced were greeted with great appreciation from their customers.

Back out in the tea room, Theodosia did a quick perusal of tables. All but three were filled and they still had luncheon customers with reservations who had yet to arrive. So about one walk-in party was all they could accommodate right now. Of course, in an hour or so, when the tables turned over for a second seating, then they could squeeze in a few more parties.

Theodosia picked up her clipboard and consulted the names again. Lillian Hicks and Diane Seifert had called for reservations. But when the front door opened a few moments later and a face peered tentatively across the tops of the tables at her, it wasn't either of those ladies.

"Isabelle," said Theodosia, suddenly putting a name to the face and speeding over to greet Timothy's granddaughter. "Nice to see you again. I didn't know you'd be dropping by for lunch today. Is Timothy . . . ?"

Theodosia suddenly saw a look that was slightly akin to nervousness pass across Isabelle's face.

"No, no, he's not," said Isabelle, recovering quickly. "In fact, my grandfather doesn't even know I'm here." She hesitated. "But I, uh, would like to chat with you if I could."

"Of course," said Theodosia, leading Isabelle over to the small table by the fireplace. "Sit down, relax, get cool. Can I offer you a glass of sweet tea? A small pot of jasmine?"

Isabelle nodded gratefully. "The sweet tea, please."

"Back in a sec," Theodosia told her.

Besides the glass of sweet tea, Theodosia brought Isabelle a crab salad.

"You don't have to," protested Isabelle. "After all, I showed up without a reservation . . ."

But Theodosia waved off Isabelle's protests. "Haley made plenty to go around," she told her.

Then, twenty minutes later, with customers sipping tea and contentedly nibbling Haley's luncheon offerings, Theodosia caught a bit of a break. So she crossed the tea shop and slid into the seat across from Isabelle. "You look worried," she told Timothy's granddaughter. "I'm assuming this visit has something to do with last night?"

"I am," said Isabelle. "And it does." She picked up her linen napkin, dabbed gently at her lips, dropped the napkin back in her lap again. "Miss Browning," began Isabelle.

"Call me Theodosia. Please."

Isabelle smiled. "Theodosia then. I, uh, don't really know anyone in Charleston all that well. You know I grew up here, but moved to Savannah when I was in high school, then went to film school at UCLA."

"Very impressive," said Theodosia.

"Mm," said Isabelle. "The reason I mention all that is because I'm kind of alone here. And I . . . I need someone I can confide in." Isabelle gazed at Theodosia with a bit more intensity.

Theodosia gave a warm smile in return. "And I've been elected?" From the looks of things, it seemed Isabelle might be leading up to a rather serious conversation. "Of course you have Timothy," continued Theodosia. "He's someone you can certainly confide in."

"Not about this," said Isabelle. "You see, I . . ." She stopped, shook her head slowly, tried again. "That is, we . . ."

Theodosia reached across the table and patted Isabelle's hand. "Whatever you're trying to tell me, it can't be *that* difficult. Or even that startling."

"I had a fling with Jordan Cole," Isabelle blurted out.

Theodosia blinked rapidly, taken aback by Isabelle's candor, unsure for a moment what to say. She hadn't been expecting to hear any sort of romantic confession. And, of course, that had to be the precise moment Drayton arrived at their table bearing a steaming pot of tea.

"You absolutely must try this, Isabelle," he urged. "It's one of our summer house blends. Chinese black tea with bits of orange, star anise, and passion fruit. I call it Star-Crossed Love."

"Drayton," said Theodosia. "This really isn't the time . . ."

But Drayton was not to be dissuaded. Placing a dainty china cup on the table, he proceeded to pour Isabelle a serving of tea. "Try it," he urged. "It's one of my secret blends."

"*Why are you* telling me this?" asked Theodosia, once Drayton had moved out of earshot.

"I stopped by Timothy's office this morning after he'd come back from talking with you," said Isabelle. "He told me you were . . . let's see, what were my grandfather's exact words? Oh yes. That you were a savvy amateur sleuth who'd agreed to look into a few things. And that you had a relationship with a certain detective."

"I think that might be stretching things," said Theodosia.

"My grandfather also told me you'd agreed to serve on a judging panel, which would serve as a cover of sorts. Naturally, I assumed that if you're as smart and capable as my grandfather says you are, you'd find out about Jordan Cole and me." Isabelle leaned back in her chair and stared at Theodosia. Not a confrontational stare, but definitely one that said, *Okay, there's a chance I'm going to get pulled into a messy police investigation. Now what?*

"Does Timothy know you were seeing Jordan Cole?" asked Theodosia.

"No," said Isabelle abruptly. "Of course not."

"What about the police? Did you tell them about your relationship with Jordan Cole?"

Now Isabelle looked stunned. "No. Why on earth would I do that?"

Good question, thought Theodosia. Then decided there actually was a very good reason. "How about because you, er, care about Jordan Cole and want to see his killer brought to justice?"

"That sounds weird," said Isabelle. "Like I'm trying to fabricate some sort of alibi."

Theodosia stared across the table at her. "Are you?"

"No!"

"But you really did feel something for him," said Theodosia, in a tone that was much gentler this time.

Isabelle gave a reluctant nod as she worried her lower lip with her front teeth. "I did at the time, certainly. I cared about Jordan very much until I found out there were other women."

"Oh," said Theodosia, suddenly remembering the female entourage from last night. "I see."

Isabelle peered at her, suddenly looking supremely unhappy. "Now it sounds like I might've had a motive, doesn't it?"

Theodosia nodded, almost imperceptibly. "Yes," she whispered, thinking Burt Tidwell might see it that way, too. "I'm afraid it does."

By three thirty that afternoon Theodosia was tired, hot, and dreading the coming evening. True to her nature, she would much rather curl up at home tonight with a good book than go sit in a theater, watch half a dozen short films, and then try to judge them. Of course, it wasn't the watching that had Theodosia worried, it was the *judging* part. That just seemed way too far out of her comfort zone.

"Yoo-hoo, Theodosia!" Delaine's insistent, perpetually cheery voice interrupted Theodosia's reverie of self-pity. She turned to find Delaine Dish pushing her way across the tea room like an entitled duchess, looking resplendent in a sunflower-yellow suit with a matching wide-brimmed straw hat. In her wake, but not to be outdone, was Nina van

Diedrich. Nina wore a slim black sheath dress with a wide crimson belt that reminded Theodosia of a Japanese obi.

Interesting, Theodosia thought to herself. *I always assumed these two were rivals.*

Turns out they were.

Delaine and Nina scrambled for a table, both vying for the best seat. Then, as though a massive switch had been suddenly thrown, both women exploded with high-powered energy. All of it aimed squarely at Theodosia.

"I just *had* to drop by and see how you were doing!" exclaimed Delaine. "After all, you're last night's star witness! You and Drayton . . . oh, how's he doing? Feeling better now?" She cranked her head around, caught sight of Drayton, waggled manicured fingers at him.

"You should have seen *me* last night!" Nina trumpeted. "Being in close proximity to an actual *murder* left me a complete and total wreck! Never in a million years did I suspect I'd have a walk-on role in a real-life murder mystery!"

"But Theodosia was *really* right there," insisted Delaine. She reached over, plucked at Theodosia's sleeve. "Tell us about it! You caught a glimpse of the killer?"

"Really just a glimpse of his hand," said Theodosia.

"And of course we were all questioned by the police," shrilled Nina. "Let me tell you, it's not much fun being interrogated by those people!"

Drayton arrived in the nick of time bearing a pot of tea.

"May I offer you some chamomile tea, ladies?" he inquired mildly. "It has soothing properties, which many people seem to appreciate."

Theodosia flashed him a grateful smile.

But Delaine and Nina were not to be deterred.

"Of course, last night was an utter *disaster* for the film festival," moaned Delaine. "Especially since all us volunteers have worked so hard to make it really special."

"The film festival is proceeding as planned," said Drayton.

"Nothing's changed." He hesitated. "Well, I suppose a few things have been altered."

"Like the molecules of the universe!" exclaimed Nina. "Now everything seems completely different."

"A little less festive," added Delaine. "What with a murder investigation going on."

"I, for one, don't relish returning to the Belvedere Theatre tonight," said Nina. She made a big show of giving a shudder. "Scene of the crime and all that. Of course, I'm the one in charge of tonight's screening." Patting Theodosia's hand as an aside, Nina added, "And I hear *you'll* be joining us. So delightful to have you on our judging panel."

"I don't think we have to worry about being in the Belvedere Theatre," said Theodosia. "The police will probably still be buzzing around." How could they not, she figured.

"But what if the murderer really does return to the scene of the crime?" asked Nina in a hushed tone.

"I'd be more nervous about that so-called backstage ghost," said Delaine, looking jittery. "What if last night's tragedy was some sort of psychic warning?"

"Maybe we should stage a séance," suggested Nina.

"Chills," said Delaine, her eyes widening. "I just got chills."

"*Maybe you should* have dropped Xanax tablets into their tea," Theodosia told Drayton later. "Calm those two nervous Nellies down."

"They do feed off one another, don't they?" responded Drayton. "One always trying to top the other."

Theodosia glanced at her watch. Decided she'd have to shake a leg if she wanted to take Earl Grey for a run, catch a quick shower, then get over to the Belvedere Theatre in time for tonight's screening.

"Hey," said Theodosia, as she pulled off her apron and stuffed it into a wicker bin. "What did Tidwell want earlier?" They'd been so busy all day that Theodosia hadn't had much of a chance to talk to Drayton. About anything besides tea room business, that is.

"Tidwell just wanted to pester me." Drayton sighed. "Wanted to know exactly what I could recall from last night."

"And what do you recall?" asked Theodosia. She, too, had more than a passing curiosity.

Drayton's brow furrowed and one hand crept unconsciously up to the back of his head. "I remember receiving a terrible thwack. And then . . . nothing at all."

5

Click, click, click.

Earl Grey's toenails clicked across the kitchen floor of their upstairs apartment. Theodosia knelt down and put her hands on either side of the dog's head, touched her lips to his velvety forehead. "How are you doing, fella?" she asked.

Earl Grey, her mixed-breed Dalbrador, tea shop dog, therapy dog, jogging companion, and roommate par excellence, gave an answering woof. He was fine. Ready for dinner, if you please, and anticipating a nice evening run.

"But not a long run tonight," Theodosia cautioned him. She stood at the kitchen counter, mixing up his kibbles with a dab of yoghurt and some leftover French-cut green beans. "Remember? We talked about this earlier? I have to go to that screening tonight."

Slightly perturbed now, Earl Grey lifted his head and stared at her. Almost sixty pounds, with wide-set eyes, he was a dog that enjoyed making eye contact with people.

Now his worried stare met Theodosia's questioning gaze. "Rowrrrr?" he asked.

"No, the screening's later," she told him. "So we've still got some time. But first you eat, then we run." She filled a pan of cold water for him. Icy, just the way Earl Grey liked it. "While you eat, I'm going to lay out my clothes for later." She set the two pans on the floor. "What do you think? The black T-shirt dress or the brown sundress?"

Earl Grey hesitated for a moment. "Browrrr."

"Yeah. That's what I thought, too."

"The-a-do-sia!" exclaimed Nina van Diedrich. She threw her arms open wide and rushed to embrace Theodosia as though she were a long lost cousin. As if they hadn't just seen each other a few hours earlier.

"Nina, hi," said Theodosia, slightly put off by the overly effusive greeting. After all, they didn't know each other *that* well. Plus, there was a group of around fifty people gathered in the lobby of the Belvedere Theatre. They'd been talking quietly among themselves; now everyone seemed to be focused on Theodosia and Nina. Not the most comfortable of situations.

"We've been *waiting* for you," said Nina in a loud, take-charge voice. "Didn't want to start the evening without every one of our all-important judges present." Then she clapped her hands together like a strict homeroom teacher and announced, "Everyone, this is Theodosia Browning, one of tonight's judges."

There was a spatter of applause and Theodosia felt herself blushing a deep shade of pink. A shade that probably rivaled that of Delaine's crocheted dress.

"Hello," said Theodosia, nodding, feeling utterly ridiculous at having been singled out. And here she'd thought judging would be a simple and solitary act. Sit in a darkened theater for a couple of hours, watch a few films, jot down your notes, decide which film was the best. Silly her.

Then a young woman with a tousle of reddish-brown curls, a lithe body, and a friendly grin broke away from the group and came hustling up to Theodosia.

"May I escort you in, Miss Browning?" she asked. "I'm one of the volunteers."

"Thank you," murmured Theodosia, as Nina clapped her hands again and made the announcement that everyone should please file into the theater and take their seats.

"You looked like you needed rescuing," whispered the young woman as they walked down the theater aisle together. "Nina van Diedrich can be a real pain sometimes. I probably shouldn't tell you this, but we've all been calling her Nina van Dictator behind her back."

"I appreciate the rescue," Theodosia whispered back. "Thanks."

The young woman stuck a hand out. "Kassie Byrd. Pleased to meet you. I'm a volunteer as well as one of the filmmakers. I did a little piece called *Low-country Ghosts*. Very historical in nature."

Theodosia shook hands with Kassie. "Theodosia Browning. One of the judges. As if Nina hasn't already made that perfectly clear."

Kassie flashed a mischievous smile. "Yeah, she's quite a piece of work, isn't she? On the other hand, maybe *we* shouldn't be talking. People will say the fix is in. Although my film doesn't screen until Thursday night."

"I think that's my night off," said Theodosia.

"Well, good then," said Kassie.

"To be perfectly honest," said Theodosia, as people filed past them and a low hum filled the dimly lit theater, "I have no idea what the judging protocol's supposed to be. I'm not even remotely qualified to be a judge."

"Are you kidding?" laughed Kassie. "You seem like

you're really smart and nice. Which is more than I can say for most of our judges!"

They halted at about the tenth row from the front of the theater. "Here you go," said Nina, handing Theodosia a silver Mylar bag with the words *Charleston Film Festival* silk-screened across it. "Your very own swag bag. Contains your ballot, pen, miniature flashlight, Zagnut bar, bag of kettle corn, official T-shirt, and various other film festival accoutrements. Enjoy."

"Thank you," said Theodosia. "I'll certainly try."

There were four short films being screened tonight, each about twenty minutes in length. And as the evening wore on, Theodosia found every one to be incredibly engrossing.

There was a film on Charleston architecture titled *Gingerbread and Rainbows*. Watching this was great fun because she recognized so many of the palatial homes from the historic district as well as the brightly painted buildings along East Bay Street known as Rainbow Row.

A film titled *Blue Ridge in My Heart* chronicled a troupe of musicians who traveled throughout the South playing traditional Blue Ridge music.

Another film, *Plantation Dreams*, detailed the restoration of an old plantation out on Ashley River Road.

And the final offering, *Oyster Harvest*, was a sort of documentary-style film about a family from Bluffton that had been involved in the oyster industry for the last eighty years.

All four of the films were superb, Theodosia decided, once the curtain fell and the house lights finally came up. Compelling and heart-warming in their own way. Each one deserved an award.

And that, of course, was the problem.

Theodosia had found herself watching these short films

from a typical moviegoer's point of view. Settling back and watching them for sheer enjoyment. But she knew she should probably employ more technical criteria in her judging process.

But what would that criteria be?

Story and theme? Cinematography? Sound or editing?

Theodosia followed the crowd back out into the lobby where refreshments were now being served. She knew she had a difficult task ahead of her. Maybe she should chat with Isabelle about the best way to judge the merits of a short film. Or better yet, one of the other judges. Someone who had experience in this sort of thing.

Nina van Diedrich buttonholed Theodosia the minute her high-heeled sandals hit the marble lobby floor. "Well?" Nina's eyes fluttered and Theodosia noticed that one of her false eyelashes was beginning to peel away from her upper eyelid. "What did you think?"

"All four films were delightful," said Theodosia as they strolled over to a makeshift bar to get a glass of wine. "All seemed like they came straight from the hearts of the various filmmakers. I think ranking and judging them is going to be a difficult task."

Nina shook her head in a cautionary manner and held up a manicured index finger that was painted bloodred to match her dress. "Not really so tough," she told Theodosia. "In my opinion, one film was a complete and utter standout."

Uh-oh. Warning bells echoed in Theodosia's head. Nina sounded suspiciously like a woman with an agenda.

"Nina, they were all great films," said Theodosia, putting more force behind her words this time. As she accepted her glass of white wine from the bartender, Theodosia smiled and eased away from Nina. Turning a little too quickly, she ran smack-dab into a tall man who'd just taken a sip from his wineglass. "Oops, sorry," she said. A couple of drops of white wine had spattered down the front of his shirt.

"No problem," he said, peering at Theodosia, looking almost amused. "At most film festivals, the judges get away with murder anyway." And then, realizing what he'd just said, suddenly looked embarrassed and fumbled to cover his faux pas. "Well, *that* didn't come out quite right," he told her. "Especially after last night." He looked horrified at himself, knowing he'd really bungled his words.

"And you are . . . ?" asked Theodosia. She was amused by his self-effacing manner and a little bit grateful to be talking to someone besides Nina van Diedrich.

"Homer Hunt at your service," said the man. Well over six feet tall, Homer Hunt possessed a large head that bobbed on a skinny stalk of a neck. Homer's complexion was slightly ruddy and his eyes a watery blue. Above his ruddy countenance stretched a wide expanse of forehead.

"You're one of the judges," said Theodosia. She recalled seeing Homer Hunt's name on the ballot she'd scanned earlier. "Very nice to meet you. Are you a filmmaker as well?"

Homer Hunt shook his head. "Oh no. No way. I own Crash and Burn."

"The editing studio," said Theodosia. "Of course." She remembered now that Isabelle had mentioned Crash and Burn. That they were one of the film festival sponsors and the postproduction studio where Jordan Cole's film had been edited. "You edited portions of Jordan Cole's film," she added.

Homer Hunt took a long sip of wine and nodded.

"He must have been amazing to work with," said Theodosia. She meant her statement to be a testament to Jordan Cole's reputation as well as the fact that a director of Jordan's stature had made Crash and Burn his editing house of choice. But Theodosia's words seemed to have the opposite effect on Homer Hunt.

Homer suddenly reared back in surprise. "Not on your life," he snapped. "Jordan Cole was an absolute terror. Nothing we did made him remotely satisfied." He lowered his voice, looking slightly embarrassed again. "Of course, I don't like to speak ill of the dead . . ."

"Or very recently dead," Theodosia interjected mildly.

"The thing is," said Homer Hunt, bending forward, looking gaunt and tense, "Jordan Cole complained the entire time. He claimed that everyone at Crash and Burn was either incompetent or inept and that our equipment was second-rate crap. Can you imagine!" Homer Hunt was beginning to sputter now. "He called our equipment *crap*. And we absolutely pride ourselves on having the latest Avid DS Nitris."

"So working with Jordan Cole wasn't exactly a memorable experience for you," said Theodosia, stunned by the man's vitriolic response.

"Oh, it was memorable," shrilled Homer Hunt. "In fact, I remember hating every minute of it." And then he stomped off.

Theodosia was aware of someone hovering at her elbow. It was Kassie Byrd again.

"Here," said Kassie. "I brought you a few select munchies." She held out a small glass plate that held an assortment of appetizers.

"Aren't you sweet," said Theodosia, readily accepting Kassie's offering.

"Nah, I'm just buttering you up," said Kassie.

Theodosia met Kassie's smile with one of her own. "Are you really?" she asked, injecting a smidgeon of doubt in her voice.

Kassie shook her head. "Nope. I'm not that much of a sycophant. I'm just kind of hoping I can learn something from you. That a few of your entrepreneurial skills will rub off on me."

"What makes you think I'm an entrepreneur?" asked Theodosia, looking slightly bemused.

Kassie ducked her head, the first hint of shyness she'd exhibited. "I saw a piece about you a few months back in the Charleston *Post and Courier.* About how you started the Indigo Tea Shop from a relatively small investment and built it into a successful tea shop, gift shop, and catering service. That's exactly the direction I'd like to go in a few years. Build my own business. You know, start a small film production company." Kassie was rolling now, her enthusiasm almost contagious. "I'm more interested in working with smaller, more creative clients. Like ad agencies."

"They're the ones who usually come up with wacky ideas," agreed Theodosia.

Kassie nodded in agreement. "Oh, and I know you've done a few TV appearances on *Windows on Charleston.* I remember seeing your first pieces. They were really good. I mean, they were fluff stuff, but they were *good* fluff stuff." She glanced nervously at Theodosia, worried now that she'd spoken a little too frankly.

Theodosia grinned at her. "That's okay. I know it was fluff stuff. But it worked. Got my tea shop noticed in the community."

"See," said Kassie, nodding. "That's what I mean, you understand promotion!"

Twenty minutes later, Theodosia was ready to leave. She'd chatted with a few people she knew, managed to avoid Nina, and nibbled what she thought were the best of the hors d'oeuvres—the crab puffs and something called vampire peppers, which were a deep-fried chili pepper that contained a wicked amount of garlic.

Then she remembered Drayton's teapot. The antique Wedgwood teapot that had been passed down from his aunt

Clauthilde. Theodosia didn't relish going back downstairs, but she knew she should check to see if the teapot had been left behind.

No problem, she told herself. The police were probably still poking around down there. There was nothing to worry about.

But when she finally ventured downstairs, there were no police and only a single, dim light illuminating the old kitchen.

Theodosia fumbled for the switches, but flipping them didn't seem to improve the light situation any. Maybe a circuit breaker had been tripped? She thought about turning around, scrambling back upstairs, and forgetting the whole thing. But what if the teapot was there? What if she could just grab it and run?

Grab it and run. That's the ticket.

Feeling her way along the counter, Theodosia squinted into the darkness, wondering where it could be.

But nothing caught her eye.

Possibly, she decided, it had been put away.

So now she had to check under the counters. And there could be anything down there. Mice, spiders . . . creepy things.

Theodosia knelt down and grabbed one of the metal doors. It gave an ominous creak and then slid slowly open. Nothing. But she thought she detected a slight movement, a skittering of tiny feet. Great.

She stood up, shuddered, and that's when her eyes fell upon the wooden door at the far end of the room. Tunnel door?

That door, she decided, was probably the one the killer used to make his escape. After he'd clobbered poor Drayton.

The door drew her like a magnet. She hadn't really noticed it last night. But, of course, they'd been hopping busy then. Searching out spooky tunnels hadn't exactly been top of mind.

Putting a hand on the doorknob, Theodosia gave it a good yank. And wished she hadn't. A damp, musty scent assaulted her nose as she peered in. Nasty. And even though the tunnel sloped decidedly upward, probably came out in the back parking lot, she didn't feel the urge to make that little journey. No thanks.

Slamming the door, she went back to the task at hand. Locating Drayton's teapot and getting the heck out of there. Stepping over to a center island workspace, Theodosia leaned down and opened another cupboard door. And there, to her great surprise, sat Drayton's teapot. Probably someone, maybe even the crime-scene guys, had stuck it down there.

Well, thank goodness. Because it meant she could get out of there right now. But just as Theodosia's fingers wrapped around the handle of the teapot, the single source of light winked out and she was plunged into darkness!

Grabbing the teapot, Theodosia fumbled her way back toward the stairway. Crazy thoughts raced through her head. A blackout had hit the theater. There'd been another murder. And then the most terrifying thought of all.

Someone's down here with me!

That last thought propelled Theodosia up the staircase at lightning speed. She emerged in the back of the theater and rushed down the side aisle, stuffing the teapot into her swag bag as she sped along.

Heart pounding, she emerged at the lobby where, lo and behold, people were still mingling, drinks were still being served, a few waiters still casually served hors d'oeuvres.

Theodosia put a hand to her heart, trying to calm herself, then ducked into the ladies' room. Staring at herself in the mirror, she saw that her cheeks bloomed with color and her hair had taken on a slightly windblown appearance. And even though she felt unnerved, she didn't appear all that agitated or frightened. She looked alive and alert.

Okay then. I guess.

Theodosia patted her hair down, splashed cool water on her face. And decided it was definitely time to call it a night. Enough with the judging and crazy adventures. Time to head home.

But as she pushed her way toward the lobby's main doors, someone reached out from the crowd and put a hand on her elbow.

"You're not leaving, are you?" inquired a resonant male voice.

Theodosia turned her head and suddenly found herself gazing into the limpid brown eyes of C. W. Dredd. And felt herself melt just a little.

Tall, rangy, with a slightly weathered face that made him look like he probably spent lots of time outdoors honing his skiing or surfing skills, C. W. Dredd seemed to convey the same presence and huge personality as the movie stars he captured on celluloid.

This is what it feels like to be starstruck, thought Theodosia. Her knees buckled slightly and she felt the beginnings of an idiot grin creep across her face. Then Theodosia shook her head slightly, as if dismissing that thought. And struggled to pull herself back to the here and now. "I was just on my way out," she murmured to him. *He's just another guy,* she told herself. *So don't act so ditsy.*

"I'd love to buy you a drink," said C. W. Dredd. He moved in closer, invading her space, and Theodosia could smell his aftershave now. Something peppery with a hint of amber.

"Already had a drink," said Theodosia. She wanted to choke, her answer felt so trite and awkward.

But C. W. Dredd just focused his eyes on her and dazzled her with one of his famous smiles. Crinkly eyes, wide grin, white teeth. It was the same smile she'd seen gazing out from glossy magazines. The same confident yet devastating look he flashed at the fawning paparazzi when he strolled the red carpet.

"Are you an actress?" he asked her. He edged even closer and she had the distinct impression that he moved like a panther. Stealthy and confident.

He had a killer pickup line, Theodosia decided, but she wasn't about to bite. "Film judge," she replied. "But just for tonight. Oh, and I guess Wednesday night, too." She stuck out her hand. "Theodosia Browning."

His eyes narrowed slightly. "C. W. Dredd. Say, aren't you the one who saw . . . ?" His voice trailed off.

"Guilty," she said. "Well, not really." His presence flustered her.

"So you're from right here."

Theodosia tried to look friendly instead of someone caught in the high-powered tractor beam of stardom. "Born and bred."

"Love Charleston," said C.W. "I lived just down the pike in Beaufort when I was a kid, but I'm afraid I don't get back to this part of the state as often as I'd like."

"But you do a lot of traveling," said Theodosia. They'd pushed their way outside and were standing on the sidewalk now. It was still warm with a slight breeze, hinting at salt and brine, wafting in from the Atlantic. A silver penny of a moon was just beginning its journey overhead. Theodosia suddenly had the feeling C. W. Dredd was going to take her in his arms and kiss her. She wasn't sure she'd be able to put up much of a protest.

But he just replied, "Lots and lots of traveling. Probably too much. I just wrapped a shoot in Toronto and in a couple months I head for Thailand to direct a World War II piece for Weinstein." He stared at her, obviously interested. "Listen, I'm supposed to attend this dinner thing tomorrow night. Something called a Cinema Bistro Café. Would you like to come along? As my date, I mean? I'd really like to get to know you."

Theodosia backed away from C. W. Dredd even as their

eyes stayed locked on each other. "I'll be there," she told him. "I'll see you there."

C. W. Dredd suddenly looked a little less confident. "How do I know you're not just giving me a line?" he called to her.

Right, she thought as she gazed back at him. *Sure. I'm just shining you on.*

He gave her a crooked smile. "Where will you be?"

"Just look for me at the tea table," said Theodosia as a sudden burst of light assaulted them. She turned her head to find Bill Glass aiming a camera at the two of them.

"Gotcha!" he cried. Bill Glass was a brusque-looking man with slicked-back hair and olive skin. He was also the chief photographer and publisher of *Shooting Star,* a Charleston gossip rag that came out every Saturday.

"Glass!" said Theodosia, unhappy to see him. "What do you want?"

"You two looked so cozy," said Glass in a nasty, nattering tone. "I just had to memorialize it for my magazine."

6

❧

"*Big day today,*" announced Drayton as he folded cream-colored linen napkins into poufy triangles.

"It sure is," agreed Theodosia. Drayton said that every morning. You could set your watch by it. Of course, she agreed with him every morning, too.

"I meant because we've got the Cinema Bistro party tonight. Can you believe we're going to put in a twelve-hour day?"

"It's a good thing Parker and his people are pitching in to help," said Theodosia. Parker Scully was going to prep most of the food at his restaurant, Solstice, then transport it over to the Indigo Tea Shop late afternoon.

"Thank you for fetching my teapot," said Drayton. "I hope you didn't have any trouble finding it."

"Not too much," said Theodosia, suddenly remembering the lights going out and her wild dash up the stairs.

Drayton glanced at her sharply. "How were the screenings last night? Any news to report to Timothy?"

"You mean concerning possible suspects? No, not really."
Theodosia put a few stems of lamb's ears and a spire of Irish
bells into a cut glass vase. Decor for one of her tea tables.
"Well . . . maybe a small nugget of information."

"What?" Drayton asked eagerly. "*What?*"

"While I was doing my bit to mingle last night, I ran
into a fellow by the name of Homer Hunt."

"His company is one of the major sponsors," said Drayton. "Or I should say he is, since he owns the company."

"Yes, and apparently Jordan Cole used his studio to do
quite a lot of editing."

"And?" prompted Drayton.

"And Homer Hunt didn't care for Jordan Cole at all. In
fact, he pretty much accused him of being an obnoxious
prima donna."

"You don't say," said Drayton. "Well, Jordan Cole was a
big-shot film director, so I'm assuming he probably *did*
come across as slightly obnoxious. However, I seriously
doubt the man's bad behavior gave anyone at Crash and
Burn a motive for murder."

"I agree," said Theodosia. "Jordan Cole may have been an
exasperating client, but as far as someone getting vengeful
over it? Just doesn't sound right to me."

They moved about the tea room, arranging tea cups just
so, lighting tea warmers, laying out silverware. Theodosia
loved this time of day. Just before their morning customers
arrived, when everything looked lovely and crisp and perfect.

"Have you thought about the other directors?" asked
Drayton. "The ones who are up for the Golden Palmetto
Award? One of them could have viewed Jordan Cole as a
serious rival."

Theodosia's first thought was of C. W. Dredd. Pressing
close to her last night, smiling his confident, knowing
smile. "A rival for the Golden Palmetto Award?" she said,

keeping her tone light. "I'm not sure it's the most prestigious award a director would want to receive. And consider-
ing this is the first time the award's even been offered, I
don't think directors are exactly drooling over it."

"Good point," said Drayton. He lit the final tea candle,
then tucked his book of matches into an antique sugar chest
that stood nestled against the wall. "So we're not any closer
to digging up dirt on potential suspects." He draped his Parisian waiter's apron around his neck, then tied it carefully
in back. "Too bad. Though it sounds like you did your best.
Kept your ears open just as you promised Timothy."

Theodosia furrowed her brow. "There is one other little
thing."

"Hmm?" said Drayton. Now he was busy adjusting a
pair of old etchings, framed black-and-white prints of rice
plantations, that hung on the brick wall.

"Isabelle told me she had an affair with Jordan Cole."

As Drayton straightened up abruptly, his surprised eyes
sought out Theodosia's. At the same moment a startled
"what!" erupted from the kitchen. Followed by the loud
clatter of a pan hitting the floor.

"Are you serious?" squawked Drayton. "About this al-
leged . . . uh . . . uh . . . affair?"

"You okay in there?" Theodosia called to Haley. Obviously, she'd been listening in on their conversation.

Haley's head popped out from behind the celadon-green
curtain like a manic puppet. "Did you just say what I think
you did?" she asked. Her face was flushed, her eyes bright.

"What do you think I just said?" asked Theodosia.

"That Isabelle, the same sweet little Isabelle who is Timothy Neville's granddaughter, was playing hanky-panky
with Jordan Cole?"

Drayton's mouth twitched nervously as he stared fixedly
at Haley. "You don't have to phrase it quite *that* way," he
told her.

Haley ignored Drayton. "Where did you pick up this juicy little morsel of gossip?" she asked Theodosia.

"Isabelle told me herself when she dropped by yesterday. Of course, she was counting on us to be discreet."

"Hey," said Haley, wiping her hands on her apron and slowly walking toward them, "I'm as discreet as the next person."

Drayton gazed at Haley. "That's based on the theory that *Delaine* isn't the next person in the tea shop."

Haley continued to ignore Drayton. "Get back to the good part," she urged. "So Isabelle was having a torrid affair with Jordan Cole. Wow. He was a real stud muffin and I had her pegged for this sweet, innocent little thing. Guess I have to seriously readjust my perception of that girl."

"According to Isabelle," said Theodosia, "the affair was over. Apparently, Jordan was not . . . how shall I say it . . . not monogamous."

"Oh my," said Drayton, looking almost ashen. "This is definitely not the kind of news Timothy is going to want to hear."

"Fine," said Haley, "then don't tell him."

Drayton scratched his chin, thinking. "Exactly my feeling. In fact, we won't ever mention this again. The information remains confidential . . . buried. Which is probably best for all concerned."

"You don't think we should tell Tidwell?" asked Theodosia.

"Good heavens!" thundered Drayton. "Why on earth would we do that?"

"Because it might somehow be pertinent to the case?" responded Theodosia.

"I can't imagine how it would be," said Drayton, resoluteness in his voice. "Isabelle certainly didn't murder the man. She's a sweet little girl."

Not that innocent, thought Theodosia. *So maybe not that sweet.*

Haley was nodding thoughtfully. "I see your point," she said to Drayton. "This kind of news would just *kill* Timothy."

"And we certainly don't want to do that!" said Drayton.

The Indigo Tea Shop got busy then. And the brouhaha over Isabelle's indiscretion seemed to evaporate like wisps of steam over a teacup.

Haley busied herself in the kitchen, tending to the apple spice cake and cream scones she was baking. As she prepped for lunch, she was already fretting about the Cinema Bistro Café concept they were supposed to pull off tonight.

Drayton hastily brewed tea, filling a waiting cadre of Brown Betty teapots with Ceylon, Dimbula, and jasmine tea. Theodosia greeted and seated guests, then hastily delivered those freshly brewed pots of tea.

When they were finally able to steal a few moments, Theodosia and Drayton each grabbed a cup of Darjeeling and stood at the counter, comparing notes on tonight's upcoming gala.

"You're sure the extra tables and chairs will show up this afternoon?" Theodosia asked him.

Drayton wasn't worried. "I spoke with the manager at Party Central barely twenty minutes ago. He assures me we're on their delivery schedule."

"And you're really okay with having a buffet table?" said Theodosia. It had been Drayton's idea to serve the food buffet-style tonight. A surprising break from tradition on his part since Drayton considered a sit-down meal as the only proper type of meal.

"As you know, I'm not a big proponent of buffets," began Drayton. "But we've got almost a hundred people showing up tonight. And there's simply no way we can crowd everyone into our little tea room."

Theodosia had to agree. Space was indeed limited.

"If we have a scattering of tables inside," continued Drayton, "and set up the rest of the tables out on the sidewalk, there'll be plenty of room for a buffet table as well as social mingling."

"And it's going to be a lovely evening," said Theodosia. As they continued to ease toward September, Charleston's days were a little less humid, the evenings definitely more temperate.

"I think the indoor-outdoor setup will work quite well," said Drayton. "Oh, and I told Party Central to bring us some of those metal stanchions with the velvet ropes."

"So you'll rope off our sidewalk area from the street," said Theodosia. "Excellent."

"That way the seating arrangement will seem cozier and classier," said Drayton. "Plus Party Central is also bringing portable gaslights. That way people won't have to dodder about outside with only tea candles to light the night."

"You've thought of everything," said Theodosia, gratefully. Besides being a master tea blender, Drayton really was an outstanding catering manager.

But Drayton wrinkled his nose slightly and fingered his bow tie. "I wish that were so. I'm positive there'll be something I overlooked. Something that will set off a last-minute panic."

"We'll just do our best," said Theodosia.

As the phone shrilled suddenly, Theodosia reached over and snatched it from its cradle. "Hello?"

"Theodosia," came a nasal, wheedling voice. "It's Constance."

"Yes, Constance." Theodosia took a quick sip of Darjeeling and swallowed it discreetly.

"Constance Brucato. From Channel Eight?" came the voice.

Theodosia sighed. "Yes, yes, I remember." *How could I forget?* "What can I do for you, Constance?"

"It's about the Cinema Bistro party tonight," began Constance.

"Mm-hm," replied Theodosia. She reached over, grabbed her clipboard, and scanned the guest list. Yes, there was Constance's name. Halfway down one of the columns along with several other people from her station. So Constance wasn't just calling to weasel her way in.

"Since Channel Eight is one of the film festival sponsors, we thought we'd do a little taping," said Constance. Now she sounded slightly hesitant.

Theodosia stiffened. "What do you consider a little taping?" she asked. "And who's going to be doing it?"

"I'll be there and my cameraman, Raleigh," said Constance.

Good, Theodosia breathed to herself. Thank goodness they weren't going to send Abby Davis, the somewhat snotty sister of her old boyfriend, Jory Davis.

"Theodosia, will that work?" asked Constance.

"I suppose," replied Theodosia. She knew Constance probably wanted to get some footage she could use on air. But she also didn't relish the idea of a camera crew muscling their way into her tea shop, sticking their camera right in guest's faces.

"We just want to get some people and atmosphere shots," said Constance, obviously trying to reassure her. "We'll edit that together with some more formal interviews of film directors and cinematographers that we've done and run it Saturday morning to generate interest in that evening's presentation of the Golden Palmetto Award. The Belvedere Theatre may be sold out, but there are still tickets left for the simulcast at the Art Center."

Theodosia thought for a moment. "You're not going to put any sort of focus on Jordan Cole's murder, are you?"

"No, no," Constance assured her. "No way. That would be hard news and I'm looking for a soft feature story here.

And to be honest, our station's been downplaying the murder. Since we're one of the sponsors, we're not anxious to have our image tarnished."

Theodosia glanced over at Drayton, watched him measure out scoops of tea leaves. She knew Drayton would hate the idea of Channel Eight showing up tonight. But Drayton hadn't put up forty thousand dollars in sponsorship funds like they had. And Drayton wasn't the one helping to underwrite the event tonight. He was only helping to cater it. "Sure," said Theodosia. "All I ask is that your crew be as subtle as possible, okay?"

"Like a mouse in the corner," Constance assured her. "A handheld camera with a battery pack. No network of cables and cords to trip over, I promise."

"Great," said Theodosia as she hung up. Now all she had to do was break the news to Drayton.

She drummed her fingers on the battered wood counter. "Oh, Drayton," she began.

He whirled toward her, then gazed over her right shoulder as his eyes fixed on someone beyond her. "Hello, Timothy," he said. Drayton's eyes flashed back to Theodosia, silently warning her not to utter a single word about Isabelle.

"Timothy," said Theodosia, turning to greet him. "I didn't hear you come in. Do you have time to stay for lunch?"

Timothy gave a curt nod. "Yes, yes, why not. And I require a word with each of you."

Theodosia escorted Timothy to a table, then had to greet three more groups of arriving guests. That kept her hopping for a while. Until Haley flashed her the high sign that the luncheon platters were ready to be served.

Because today was an extra-busy day for the Indigo Tea Shop, Haley had put together ploughman's platters. This was an assortment of cold sliced ham, turkey, and roast beef with small sides of chutney, Swiss cheese, cranberry white cheddar, strawberries, a sprinkling of toasted pecans, and slices of crusty French bread. A platter for one person consisted of a small bit of each. A platter for four people was considerably more.

Haley's idea was a blessing, Theodosia decided. Because rather than serve their typical three or four courses and deal with all the dirty dishes that ensued, all she had to do was deliver one single platter. Which turned out to be a snap.

And got her back to Timothy's table in record time.

He had just topped a piece of bread with roast beef and was spreading a judicious gob of chutney atop it.

"We have brown mustard, too, if you'd prefer," said Theodosia. "The good, spicy kind."

Timothy shrugged. "This is fine. Sit down, will you? If you can spare a few moments?"

Theodosia dropped into the seat across from him.

"Last night was interesting, yes?" he asked.

"Yes," she said. "In fact, the short films were better than I expected. We're blessed with a lot of talent in and around Charleston."

"And what else have you found out?" asked Timothy. "As far as *pertinent* information goes."

"Oh," she said. "Well, nothing really. Except that Homer Hunt didn't much care for Jordan Cole."

"Mr. Hunt. Another one of our fine judges," said Timothy in a dry tone. "And how did you come by such information?"

"Homer told me."

Timothy looked skeptical. "Told you he didn't like Jordan Cole? Poured his inner secrets out to you?"

"Actually, I kind of poured a drink on him," said Theodosia. "Which was our ice breaker, so to speak. Apparently Jordan Cole did some editing at Homer's studio and is . . . would have been . . . persona non grata."

"Because . . ." said Timothy.

"Because Jordan Cole was rude," said Theodosia.

"Rude," said Timothy, looking unconvinced. "In my book that's not exactly a motive for murder."

"No, I don't think so, either," replied Theodosia as she watched Drayton speed toward them bearing a tray.

"Timothy," exclaimed Drayton. "You must try this black Cameroon tea. I know you'll find it most agreeable. It has an almost chocolaty flavor." Timothy was a known chocoholic with a highly discerning palette that could distinguish one of Fauchon's milk chocolate ganaches from a Callebaut Belgian milk chocolate truffle.

Carefully balancing his tea tray, Drayton placed a second teacup on the table, then poured out a cup of the Cameroon tea. Then he placed another small plate beside it that held two miniature chocolate chip scones.

"The chocolate chip scones are out of the oven?" asked Theodosia. Of course they were.

"Yes," said Drayton, eagerly waiting for Timothy to taste his tea.

Theodosia started to get up.

"Stay a moment," said Timothy. His weary eyes surveyed the two of them. "So you've learned nothing more?" he asked.

A pregnant silence hung in the air.

"That's pretty much it," said Theodosia. She felt awful. Not quite lying to Timothy, but certainly skirting the truth.

Timothy let loose a deep sigh. "Ah well. Perhaps as the week continues you'll pick up some other tidbit of information." He sounded hopeful, but looked distracted.

This time Theodosia made it to her feet.

"Oh, Theo," said Timothy. "Your ballot for last night's judging has to be filled out and returned by Thursday morning."

"Okay," said Theodosia. "No problem." Actually it was a problem, because it meant she was going to have to sit down and sincerely ruminate over the films she'd seen last night. Then select one. "How exactly do I turn in my ballot? Or where?"

Timothy finally picked up the cup of Cameroon tea and took a sip. "Yes," he said, managing a quick smile that looked more like a grimace, "this is quite nice." He turned his gaze on Theodosia again. "Your ballot should be delivered to Crash and Burn studios."

"Sure," said Theodosia. "Great."

7

❧

"I'm about ready to pull out my hair," declared Haley. She was still dashing madly about the kitchen, dumping dirty dishes into plastic bins, pulling pans of scones out of the oven, looking over recipe notes. And shaking her head and frowning.

"Can I help?" asked Theodosia. For someone who was normally very well organized, Haley looked awfully scattered and discombobulated.

"No, but thanks for offering," said Haley. "I've been looking at this recipe Parker gave me and I definitely think it's out of my league. No, I *know* it's out of my league."

"Which recipe?" asked Theodosia, nudging closer.

"This one," said Haley, poking her finger at a five-by-seven-inch card. "The one he said was the *simplest* one. Arugula salad with white truffle oil. Except it's not simple at all . . . it's really quite gourmet."

Theodosia squinted at the recipe. The ingredients and directions didn't seem much different than the recipes Haley pulled off every day. "You can do gourmet," she said, encouragement filling her voice. "In fact, you do it all the time."

"Not really," said Haley.

"I don't think it's the recipe that's got you stumped, I think you're just flooding," said Theodosia. "So much going on today. Why not take a short break and come back to it?"

Haley straightened up and looked around, as if she was coming up for a gulp of air. "All I can say is it's a good thing Parker's doing the really hard stuff tonight. If I had to prepare filet mignon and a potato galette for a hundred people in this tiny kitchen I'd completely freak out."

"You only have to warm them up a little," said Theodosia. "And you'll have help." Parker Scully would be there with his executive chef, Toby Crisp. And Miss Dimple was coming in to help serve.

"But warming up is harder than it sounds," said Haley. "'Cause you always run the risk of drying everything out. Plus I have to worry about the appetizer and cheese plates. And the desserts. Those aren't easy."

"I feel like I should be working in the kitchen with you tonight," said Theodosia, experiencing a sharp pang of guilt. "Instead of attending the party." The plan was for her to be a guest at the Cinema Bistro party; now it looked like she should bag that whole idea.

"No, no," protested Haley. "I'll be okay, really. I just need to take a few deep breaths and get my head on straight. Sit cross-legged on top of my cutting board and do Tantric yoga or something."

"You sure?"

"Yes, of course. I'll be fine. I am fine. And I really want you to play guest and hostess tonight. Really. And continue your sleuthing for Timothy, too." Haley reached up and pulled a plate covered in plastic wrap from one of the metal shelves. "Here, I fixed a small ploughman's platter for you. Figured you'd need your energy." Haley peered sharply at

Theodosia. "You are still doing your sleuthing thing, aren't you?"

"Yes, but I'm not sure it's going all that well," said Theodosia, accepting the plate from Haley. "Or that it was a very good idea to begin with. All I've done is open myself up to a lot more responsibility what with the film judging and all. And here you are, having a kitchen crisis."

"Crisis averted," declared Haley. "I'm fine. In fact, I'd feel a whole lot better if you marched back to your office and enjoyed some much-needed lunch."

"You're sure? You've had lunch yourself?"

"Gobbled tons of cheese and cold cuts. And were they ever good. And . . ." Haley held up a finger. "I intend to attack this arugula salad recipe with renewed energy."

Theodosia took Haley up on her offer. Marched back to her small office, eased herself into her cushy desk chair, and cleared away some of the clutter that littered her desk. Tea catalogs, magazines, a scatter of recipes, her swag bag from last night. Blocking the door to the alley were boxes of teapots yet to be unpacked. In fact, the only organized space seemed to be the wall opposite her desk. She had recently hung an assortment of elegant straw hats there. Trimmed with silk flowers and gauzy ribbons, they were pleasing and restful to the eye—so, yes, now she could dig into lunch.

She munched a piece of Swiss cheese, spread a little chutney on a slice of French bread. And, because Theodosia was a compulsive multitasker, stuck her hand into her Mylar swag bag and pulled out the *Tinseltown Weekly* magazine that was rolled up inside.

Theodosia slipped off her shoes, wiggled her toes deliciously in the plush Chinese carpet that lay underfoot. There, now she felt a lot better.

Tinseltown Weekly was clearly an insider's magazine,

Theodosia decided as she perused it. Devoted to film and film people. The front-page articles were about box-office sales, Hollywood movers and shakers, and upcoming premieres.

Thumbing through a few pages, Theodosia scanned the industry news as well as a list of films that were currently in production. She wondered idly if she'd find C. W. Dredd's name.

And here was something interesting. A gossip column by Peter Pope filled with snippets of Hollywood dirt. Very interesting.

It would seem that Angelina was flirting with a new leading man.

A certain male heartthrob was still blatantly playing the field.

Steven might be spinning off a new production company.

And the first annual Charleston Film Festival was getting under way.

That was certainly nice publicity, Theodosia decided. And what else? Her eyes traveled down the page.

Oh no!

A certain big-time film director was talking trash about a local Charleston editing house!

As she scanned the article, Theodosia wondered if Crash and Burn would be mentioned by name.

Oh yes, they certainly were.

She set the magazine down, let all this soak in. Probably, she decided, this Peter Pope person had interviewed Jordan Cole sometime last week. That's when Cole had delivered his scathing assessment of Crash and Burn Studio. Which meant Peter Pope may have even called Crash and Burn to check his facts. And Homer Hunt would have been tipped off to this rather unflattering mention.

Is that what happened?

Okay, she supposed she could imagine a worst-case scenario and take this one step further.

Such as . . . maybe Jordan Cole's trash-talking had sent Homer Hunt over the edge?

Folding the magazine in half, Theodosia walked out into the tea shop. Drayton was at the front counter, ringing up a take-out order. Theodosia waited until he was finished, then approached him.

"Got something to show you," she said, spreading the magazine article out in front of him.

"Did the film festival get some publicity?" he asked. "Timothy thought it might."

She pointed to the line. "Yes, but there's more to it." She moved her finger down. "Read this part."

Slipping his tortoiseshell reading glasses on, Drayton gazed at the magazine. His half-glasses immediately slid down his nose, giving him the look of a wise old owl. "What?" he asked. "Oh this . . . oh!" he said as he read. "Well, that's rather unflattering I'd say."

"It's more than just unflattering," said Theodosia. "If film people take this seriously, it could mean a major revenue loss for Crash and Burn."

"You make a good point," Drayton mumbled as he continued to peruse the gossip column. "Well, you said Homer Hunt was furious with Jordan Cole. Now we know why."

"Yes," said Theodosia. "But this also gives Homer Hunt a motive!"

"Then we have to show this to Timothy," said Drayton. "Right away."

"You think?" said Theodosia.

Drayton nodded. "He'd want to know."

"I wish I'd noticed it sooner."

"Agreed," said Drayton. "Since he was just here."

"Think we should show this to Tidwell as well?"

Drayton thought for a moment. "Maybe, but let's show Timothy first."

"Okay," said Theodosia. "So . . . you or me? Wait. You've

got the Party Central people arriving any time now and probably have to be here to honcho the delivery. So I better go."

"You don't mind?" asked Drayton.

"It's not something I'm looking forward to," said Theodosia. "Or even have time for. But I'll do it."

Good thing the Heritage Society was relatively nearby. All Theodosia had to do was slip out her back door, zip down a tangle of cobblestone alleys, then take the pathway that led round St. Philip's Episcopal Church. From there it was a matter of making her way down Gateway Walk, a picturesque, rambling pathway that wound through St. Philip's Cemetery and took her through the wrought-iron Governor Aiken gates.

Earl Grey was her accomplice today. Always eager to stretch his legs and accompany his mistress on any errand, Earl Grey strode along slightly ahead of her, tugging at his leash, looking spunky and full of beans.

At about the halfway point, Theodosia could see fresh wooden struts sticking up through the trees that marked the roof of the Featherbed House B and B. The historic old inn had burned down a few months ago and she was delighted that Angie Congdon, the owner, was now in the process of rebuilding.

Continuing on the path past a rose garden, a pattering fountain, and the Charleston Library Society, Theodosia and Earl Grey emerged right at Timothy's back door.

"Afternoon, Camilla," said Theodosia as they entered the gloom of the Heritage Society's great stone building. Actually it was more stately than gloomy, a fine limestone edifice that boasted pecan wood paneling, carved staircases, enormous stone fireplaces, several large galleries, and two levels of underground storage. The Heritage Society, established in the late 1800s and run these last thirty years or so by the iron hand of Timothy Neville, was the official repository of Charleston history. Its three creaking floors contained historic documents, oil paintings, antique furniture, Civil War memorabilia, and much more. There was also a library filled with leather-bound volumes, two large public spaces, and the newly designed outdoor patio.

Camilla Hodges, the Heritage Society's current receptionist, peered through large, green-frame glasses at Theodosia and Earl Grey. She was petite and sixty with a friendly, open face, purple dress, waft of silvered hair, and a little too much perfume. Arpège or something slightly old-fashioned. "I see you brought your friend along," Camilla said, chuckling.

"He's thinking about becoming a volunteer," said Theodosia.

Camilla's chuckle turned to a chortle. Her brown eyes danced, her narrow shoulders shook merrily. "Can he type?" She gazed down at Earl Grey. "Can you type, sweetheart?"

"Nrrrww," was his gruff reply.

"How about fund-raising?" Camilla asked, obviously enjoying this little exchange immensely.

"That he can do," said Theodosia. "In fact, Earl Grey's demonstrations have helped raise almost twenty thousand dollars for Big Paw Service Dogs. And tomorrow night he's going to appear on stage with the Big Paw organization when their documentary is screened."

"Impressive," said Camilla. "Can you say how-do?" she asked Earl Grey. "Maybe give an autograph?"

Earl Grey swept his large paw upward toward Camilla.

"Oh my!" she exclaimed, jumping back suddenly. "You *are* a friendly dog." Earl Grey's oversized paw swiped the corner of the reception desk on its way down, catching a large manila envelope and sending it crashing to the floor. The envelope's contents spilled out everywhere. Money, keys, notebook, cell phone.

"Sorry!" exclaimed Theodosia, bending over immediately to pick things up. As she retrieved the envelope along with a spill of paper money and a set of car keys, she noticed that the envelope carried the return address of the Lady Goodwood Inn. "From the Lady Goodwood," she said, setting everything back on Camilla's desk.

Camilla gave an exasperated eye roll. "I have no idea why they delivered it here." Dropping her voice to a conspiratorial whisper, she said, "It's stuff that belonged to that poor fellow who got killed Sunday night. That director, Jordan Cole."

"You don't say," said Theodosia, trying to keep her tone even. She'd just spotted a key card laying at her feet. She moved forward a half step, put her right foot squarely on top of it. "So the folks from the Lady Goodwood Inn sent his valuables over here?"

"They were returned by the police and then routed over here." Camilla sighed. "Although I don't know what we're supposed to do with them." She grunted as she slipped off her task chair. "I'll go tell Timothy you're here." And then she was off with a faint rustle of nylon.

When Camilla had disappeared from sight, Theodosia leaned forward and picked up the key card.

Hmm.

It was quite obviously the key to Jordan Cole's room at the Lady Goodwood Inn. And probably his other stuff—clothes, personal items, and whatnot—were still there. Probably the room had been paid for until the end of the week. Until the end of the film festival.

Theodosia knew she should just slip the key card back into the manila envelope and be done with it. Of course she should. But then . . . then she couldn't run over to the Lady Goodwood Inn and take a quick peek around.

The police had already been there, she told herself. They already went through Cole's stuff and CSI'd the room or whatever it is they do. So there's probably nothing left to find.

So there's no problem then, right?

Right.

Theodosia slipped the key card into the pocket of her beige crop pants, quickly adjusted her silk T-shirt over it.

Timothy had asked her to do a little snooping.

And this was definitely in the category of snooping.

"Timothy can see you now." Camilla was back and smiling widely.

"Thank you," said Theodosia as she and Earl Grey slipped past the reception desk, slipped past Camilla.

"You know your way, of course," said Camilla, indicating the hallway with her hand and giving Earl Grey a wide berth at the same time.

"Interesting," said Timothy. One gnarled index finger tapped the glossy magazine that Theodosia had presented to him. "Interesting that Jordan Cole . . . how did you phrase it? . . . that he trashed Crash and Burn Studio."

"Drayton and I thought you should know," said Theodosia. "It might be nothing, but . . ." Her words dangled in the air.

"Yes," said Timothy. "It's one thing to insult someone to their face. But when your angry words appear in an industry publication, then it becomes a good deal more serious."

"Serious enough to bring it to Tidwell's attention?" asked Theodosia, even though she knew the answer.

"I think . . . yes," said Timothy. "Not that I want to open up Homer Hunt to any sort of trouble. His righteous indignation is perfectly understandable. But coming on the heels of Cole's murder . . ." He sighed. "Well, this does need to be looked into." He glanced up at Theodosia.

"By professionals," said Theodosia.

Timothy didn't reply. He simply sat behind his enormous

mahogany desk, looking studious and wise and considerably taller in his high-backed leather chair. Theodosia was positive that it was some sort of trick chair. That is was raised higher, set higher, whatever, to give Timothy a larger-than-life presence. Whatever machinations he had wrought, they were extremely effective. Timothy Neville looked like the grand poo-bah chairman of the world with his leather chair, enormous office, bookshelves laden with leather-clad volumes, and tasty art objects. The lighting in the room was low and moody, with just a puddle of bright light focused where the magazine now lay.

"So you'll talk to Tidwell?" asked Theodosia. She watched as Earl Grey padded around the desk and dropped his head in Timothy's lap. Timothy's fingers stroked the dog's head gently. For some reason they had become great buddies.

"I'll speak with Tidwell," said Timothy.

"Soon?"

"Today," said Timothy. "Right now if he can be reached."

"I suppose there's always the chance he could turn up tonight," said Theodosia. "At the Cinema Bistro party." She paused. "You'll be there?"

"Yes, yes," said Timothy, sounding distracted as he studied the gossip column snippet again.

"And you still want me to poke around?" asked Theodosia, willing him to please say no.

"If you could, yes," said Timothy, finally giving her his full attention. "That would be most appreciated." His dark eyes glittered at her and she thought about the key card resting in her pocket. For a split second she wondered if she hadn't somehow been set up. Then she dismissed that fleeting thought from her mind. Timothy Neville wouldn't be that underhanded, would he?

8
❧

"Oh my goodness!" Theodosia exclaimed in a rush as she pushed open the double door. "The tea shop looks absolutely spectacular!"

"Doesn't it just?" asked Drayton, a Cheshire cat smile playing quietly at his lips.

While Theodosia had been at the Heritage Society, the Indigo Tea Shop had been completely transformed into the Cinema Bistro Café. A long table draped with a creamy linen tablecloth held an array of brass food warmers and stacks of white dinner plates. French movie posters graced the walls where grapevine wreaths and old prints had hung earlier. Two large rattan king chairs sat against a backdrop of potted palms, looking very south of France. And the evening's menu was scrawled on a freestanding chalkboard.

There were nine round bistro tables inside the tea shop all draped in creamy linens, too, and topped with pots of yellow and white garden roses. Another dozen tables were on the front sidewalk, cordoned off by velvet ropes. As soon as twilight descended, black wrought-iron lamps would illuminate the scene.

"As you can see," said Drayton, still excited by the magic his team had wrought, "we've graced each table setting with wineglasses as well as vintage crystal glasses. We'll be circulating, of course, with bottles of Côtes du Rhône and Perrier, rather than let our guests schlep drinks from a bar."

"You've done a masterful job," said Theodosia, still marveling at the transformation. "It really does look like a French bistro."

Drayton waved a hand. "Oh, we're not nearly finished. Each table is still going to get a bundle of breadsticks in a country French crock as well as an assortment of olives and cornichons and some red pepper tapenade for dipping."

"Theodosia," called a familiar voice. "What do you think? I hope you're pleasantly surprised."

Miss Dimple, their bookkeeper and sometime helper at the tea shop, popped out from behind the velvet curtains. Well past the age of retirement, Miss Dimple was short, pleasingly plump, and sharp as a tack. She also handled the books for the Chowder Hound and the Antiquarian Booksellers, two other small businesses on Church Street, when she wasn't doting on her two cats, Sampson and Delilah.

"It's *très chic*," said Theodosia, reaching down to put a hand on Miss Dimple's shoulder. "And thank you so much for coming in to help."

Always jolly, Miss Dimple waved a chubby hand. "Honey, you know I love pinch-hitting for you folks. It always seems like more of an adventure than a real job."

"Not to take advantage of you," said Drayton, "but can we count on you for tomorrow afternoon as well?" Tomorrow the Indigo Tea Shop was hosting a Tea Français, an afternoon French tea. Those guests would include many of the documentary and short film writers and producers. Not quite the bigwig sponsors and directors that were expected tonight.

"Oh sure," said Miss Dimple. "As long as I don't have to manage anything tricky . . . like brewing tea."

"No," said Drayton, "I'll handle that."

"No kidding," said Haley, sailing out into the room, bearing two crocks stuffed with plump, crusty breadsticks. "Drayton won't let any of us near his precious teas."

"He's serving something special?" asked Miss Dimple.

"Drayton ordered three different Mariage Frères teas," said Haley. "House blends from their Paris store."

"Ah," said Miss Dimple, nodding appreciatively. "French tea. How lovely."

"Let's hope so," said Drayton.

The afternoon spun into late afternoon as they all engaged in a whirlwind of activity. At five o'clock, Toby Crisp, the executive chef from Solstice, arrived in his catering van with most of the food. At which point things really clicked into hyperdrive. They all helped ferry the food from the catering van into the Indigo Tea Shop's small kitchen, struggling with the still-warm heavy-duty pans. Haley pointed and barked orders like a quartermaster, making sure everything was placed accordingly. Some of the food had to be kept warm, some would be heated up later, and only she and Toby seemed privy to that information.

Finally, an hour before the first guest was to arrive, Haley called the group together.

"We have to go over the menu," said Haley. She was balancing a silver tray filled with cut glass bowls of tapenade and trying to read her checklist at the same time.

"Agreed," said Drayton, taking the tray from her hands. "We need to know which foods will be on the buffet table, which ones we have to serve."

"Not a problem," said Toby Crisp. He was young, smooth-faced, and portly, and looked quietly competent.

He'd honchoed hundreds of catered affairs in his career and didn't seem worried about this one. "The buffet table will include Haley's arugula salad in white truffle oil. Which, by the way, I have sampled and found to be absolutely exquisite."

"Here, here," said Drayton as Haley blushed. Her hard work and determination had paid off.

"And," continued Toby, "we'll be serving our main selections of lavender-roasted chicken breast and parmesan-crusted filet mignon from the buffet table. Along with potato galette and baby green beans with slivered almonds."

"Great menu," enthused Miss Dimple. "So we just stand behind the table and serve guests from the chafing dishes?"

"That's pretty much it in a nutshell," said Toby. "And Drayton will orchestrate beverages. Wine, Perrier, and tea. Isn't that right, Drayton?"

Drayton stepped forward and cleared his throat. "Since our table space is limited tonight, I'm going to make use of our somewhat extensive collection of Chinese teacups. The small blue-and-white ones, sans handles, to be precise. They should fit nicely on the tables along with everything else. Once everyone has their wine or Perrier, we'll make the rounds with pots of either Assam or a Yunnan tea." He gazed around at everyone, looking pleased. "And that should do it."

Haley cleared her throat loudly. "Uh, Drayton, let's please not forget about dessert."

"No, let's not," said Miss Dimple with a laugh. "Since that's always my favorite part of a meal."

"Macarons," said Haley. "Not to be confused with macaroons."

"What's the difference?" asked Miss Dimple.

"My macarons are most like the traditional Italian and French sandwich-style cookies. Very light and crispy, but chewy on the inside. We'll be serving two kinds tonight, almond with chestnut filling and lemon with buttercream filling. Oh, and they'll be accompanied by *citron givré*, which as you all know is really lemon sorbet."

"Yes, of course," said Drayton. "Haley will plate in the kitchen and then we'll bring the sorbet with macarons around to the tables."

"And Haley will be doing an assortment of cheese, too," said Toby. Then chuckled when he saw Haley grinning and shaking her head at him.

"Excuse me," laughed Toby. "I meant to say *assiette de fromage.*"

"Oh!" said Miss Dimple, digging in her apron pocket. "I almost forgot about this." She pulled out a folded piece of paper and handed it to Theodosia. "This note came for you."

"Hand delivered?" asked Theodosia. Her name was written across creamy linen paper in a loopy script.

"Slipped under the front door actually," said Miss Dimple. "Kind of strange if you ask me."

"Okay, thanks," said Theodosia. She wandered over to the counter where she could read the note in private. Unfolding it, she stared at the rather strange words scribbled on the page.

It read: *Please meet me at the Belvedere Theatre at five thirty today.* The note was signed *T*.

Who was T? wondered Theodosia. Timothy? Tidwell? Or was this some sort of trick? And why did they want to meet her at the Belvedere? She shuddered, remembering her experience in the dark last night. Of course, that could have been the janitor shutting off the lights, too. You never know.

She glanced at her watch. It was five twenty. The Belvedere Theatre was just a few blocks away. If she hurried she could just make it.

But should she try to make it? Should she go at all? What if she'd be walking into some sort of setup or trap?

On the other hand, it was possible something positive could come from this, too. A key bit of information. Or even a confession.

Theodosia reread the note, then shoved it into her pocket. "I'm going out for a while," she called to the tea shop in general. "If anybody's interested. Then I'll be upstairs getting ready."

"Hello?" Theodosia's voice rang hollowly in the theater lobby, her footsteps echoing sharply as she took a few tentative steps on the gleaming black marble. Tilting her head back, she saw that only the center chandelier glowed pink and dim. For the second time in as many days, Theodosia wished the Belvedere Theatre wasn't always bathed in such low light. What was the deal, anyway?

"Okay," she said out loud to anyone who might be waiting for her. "I'm here. Now what?"

Her words echoed back at her.

"This better not be a prank."

Still nothing.

Theodosia glanced at her watch. It read five thirty-two. She'd made it pretty much on time. Now she was at a loss as to what to do next.

Creak.

Theodosia's eyes widened and her head snapped around. Yes, she'd definitely heard that. Heard . . . something. And it came from . . . inside the theater?

Okay, she told herself. *I'll play along for a few more minutes. Maybe it is Burt Tidwell, having his silly little fun at my expense.*

She pulled open one of the double doors and walked into the theater. Brass sconces glowed dimly from high up on gold brocade walls. Every plush chair in the large semicircle gallery of seats appeared empty. The large white movie screen hung low over the stage.

"Tidwell?" she called out. Her voice sounded timorous in the large theater. "Timothy?" she called, making herself sound more forceful.

Still nothing.

"Nobody here," she said. She figured it was a prank, *had* to be a prank of some kind. Was C. W. Dredd, the guy she'd met last night, behind this? He'd been fairly forward with her. Was this his idea of a romantic rendezvous? Or was it . . . ?

Theodosia's attention was suddenly riveted by a thin beam of light that pierced the darkness and lit up the screen. She stared up at the balcony where the unseen projectionist must be, but could make out nothing. Then her focus shifted suddenly to the screen as a strange image materialized. It flashed on for just a quick moment. A subliminal visual, really. And Theodosia's impression was that of a strange, demonic bird head. A long wagging tongue had lent an unholy look, a pair of wings arched over bony shoulders.

Theodosia didn't stick around to do an in-depth study of the creature's iconography. She spun on her heels and ran. Ran out of the auditorium, ran out of the theater. Back down Church Street toward safety and home.

"Where were you?" asked Drayton, as Theodosia burst into the tea shop. Then, when he saw she was more than slightly out of breath, he asked, "What's wrong?"

Theodosia dug into her pocket and pulled out the note, then thrust it into Drayton's hands. His eyebrows raised into twin arcs as he hurriedly read the words. "And you went scampering over there?" His voice was heavy with disapproval. "You actually *fell* for this?"

Theodosia shrugged. "I thought . . ."

"You thought wrong," said Drayton with great ferocity. "You could have walked into a very dangerous situation."

Theodosia stared back at him. "You were the one who was so hot for me to investigate."

Drayton's face crumpled instantly. "Dear me, I was, wasn't I?" He grabbed for her hand. "Such a terrible idea on my part. I never thought beyond helping Timothy. I never considered . . . consequences."

"Don't worry about it, Drayton," said Theodosia. "I'm pretty convinced the whole thing was a hoax. A film director trying his best to intrigue or impress."

"You think?" asked Drayton, squeezing her hand again, his eyes imploring forgiveness for his little tirade.

Theodosia nodded.

"So . . . did something materialize?" he asked. "Were you intrigued?"

Theodosia let out a deep sigh. Tell him? Not tell him? "To tell you the truth, Drayton, the whole thing pretty much fell flat."

While Drayton offered to handle all the futsy last-minute details like the lighting of candles and placement of center-pieces, Theodosia ran upstairs to change.

Sprinting past Earl Grey, who was slumped on her expensive damask sofa, enjoying a good doggy snooze, Theodosia peeled off clothes as she raced through her apartment. By the time she reached the bathroom decorated to look like a French boudoir, she was down to nothing. So she jumped into the shower.

When she emerged five minutes later, looking pink and damp like a freshly steamed rock shrimp, she'd almost forgotten the note and her ill-advised trip to the theater. She wrapped up in a fluffy white robe she'd liberated a long time ago from the Four Seasons Hotel in New York, then slid onto the padded wrought-iron chair that sat in front of her vanity.

Tonight was a party and she was going to have a good time, she decided. Parker would be there tonight and she was planning to wear a new dress. First, of course, she had to make herself pretty.

Makeup was fairly easy for Theodosia. The high humidity in Charleston kept her complexion fresh and dewy soft. So all she really needed were a few tiny dabs of makeup base blended with her favorite moisturizer. Got to add a little mascara, of course, because there wasn't a woman alive who couldn't use a little judiciously applied mascara to thicken her lashes. Eyebrow gel gave added definition to her already naturally arched brows. And a touch of Chanel's Summer Plum Glossimer slicked on her full lips. *There.*

Her hair was another matter.

Thick, full, bordering on amazingly abundant, Theodosia's hair was coveted by everyone except her. She was the one, after all, who had to tame it.

Tonight, however, she decided to throw caution to the wind. She'd just pull it all into a low, loose ponytail and allow any tendrils that curled around her face to have their way. No glossing creams, no gels. Just au naturel.

Now to get dressed. A cowl-neck halter dress of pale green chiffon, hand-painted with a few orchid blossoms. On her feet, gilt-heeled green sandals to match.

Theodosia added a bangle bracelet and her diamond stud earrings, then walked out into her living room, tottering a bit on her very high heels.

"What do you think?" she asked Earl Grey. "Do I look like a sophisticate or a character from *Gone with the Wind*?"

The big dog slowly craned his neck around and appraised her with sleepy eyes.

"Grrarawir," said Earl Grey.

"Yeah, that's what I thought, too."

A low whistle greeted Theodosia's arrival downstairs.

"Parker?" she said.

Parker Scully peered out from behind an enormous floral centerpiece, all wide smile and cobalt-blue eyes. "Boy, are you ever dolled up!" His voice was filled with admiration, and a grin lit his boyish face.

Theodosia favored Parker with a warm smile. "You think so?"

He ran a hand through his tousled blond hair as he studied her carefully, obviously liking what he saw. "Yeah, your outfit's really great. Especially that pale color and those floral thingy designs—hey, are those hand-painted?"

"They are," she told him, enjoying his perusal of her wardrobe.

"And I love the high heels. Very sophisticated. Kind of wicked looking, too."

Theodosia raised the heel of her right foot and crooked her foot sideways for better viewing. "Very Delaine," she told him. "They're Prada slides she insisted I buy. On sale, of course."

"Well they certainly look top dollar," said Parker. "Doesn't she look great?" he asked as Drayton went scurrying by.

"Lovely," said Drayton, barely glancing over.

"You didn't even look!" cried Haley, who was right behind him.

"That's because I've got you beating at me with a stick," complained Drayton.

"Because we still have a million things to do!" shrilled Haley.

But Parker was still taking his time, admiring Theodosia.

"You should wear dresses more often," he told her. "I mean, you always look great, but tonight your outfit is exceptional."

"You look real pretty, honey," said Miss Dimple, who had toddled out from the back room.

Drayton finally managed a dutiful glance at Theodosia. "She is awfully gussied up, isn't she?" he said.

"That's because Theodosia's supposed to be a *guest* tonight," Haley told him. Not a worker bee like us. Theo gets to hobnob with all the fun, hip film people."

"My dear Haley," said Drayton, "most film people are neither fun nor hip. They toil in an industry that seeks only to create a fleeting cinematic image that bears no resemblance to reality."

"Thanks a lot, Drayton," said Haley in a wry tone. "You really have a knack for taking the mystery out of things."

"And the fun," added Miss Dimple.

9

❧

Candles flickered and a buzz of conversation filled the air as guests seemed to arrive in droves. Some 100 people had been on the official guest list for the Cinema Bistro Café, but now it appeared that almost 150 had shown up to crowd into Theodosia's little establishment.

Luckily, no one seemed to mind. Groups formed and re-formed, the talk all seeming to follow a few general themes. Were the police any closer to catching Jordan Cole's killer? Which director was going to take home the Golden Palmetto Award Saturday night? Were there any more of those delicious basil shrimp appetizers?

"Theodosia," said Constance Brucato. "I'm just going to have Raleigh move slowly through the tea shop with a handheld camera, okay?"

Theodosia stared at Constance, who looked very glammed up in a bright red cocktail dress. "You're going to just film or do actual interviews?"

"Interviews, yes," said Constance. "A few. And only if

people really want to participate. We're not going to be pushy."

"Please don't be," said Theodosia, who knew firsthand just how pushy Constance could really be.

"Oh," said Constance, grabbing hold of Theodosia's arm and steering her over to a tall man with a shock of white hair. "I want you to meet Linus Gillette. Mr. Gillette is the general manager at Channel Eight."

"The boss man," said Linus Gillette, showing a toothy smile in his suntanned face and extending a hand to Theodosia. "And we're about to change our name to Trident Media. Our new name's a nod to the three counties that comprise the Charleston metro area, plus we're going to be acquiring a few local stations."

"Theodosia is the owner of the Indigo Tea Shop," Constance explained to Linus Gillette. "And she taped a couple of segments for *Windows on Charleston*."

"Of course she did," said Linus. "And we just might ask her back again some time." His eyes crinkled warmly, but his manner was slightly pompous.

"Time permitting," Theodosia told him. In her mind their previous arrangement had been quid pro quo. Channel Eight had needed content for their TV program, so she'd done a knowledgeable presentation on tea. It had been a strictly business relationship, no one had done anyone any favors.

Luckily, Theodosia was saved from a fairly boring one-sided conversation with Linus Gillette by Kassie Byrd, the volunteer and filmmaker she'd met the other night.

"Excuse me," said Kassie, looking adorable in a chocolate-brown skirt and tank top and a stunning coral necklace. "Could I get a photo of you with some of the other judges?"

"Absolutely," said Theodosia, slipping away with Kassie. And when they were out of earshot, she added, "You rescued me again. Thank you."

"I thought your eyes looked a little glazed over." Kassie laughed. "And since Nina van Diedrich tapped her magic wand on my head and pronounced me event photographer, I thought I'd put my questionable talent to good use."

"It's most appreciated," said Theodosia, as they pushed their way through the crowd. "Where do you want me to stand?"

"Over there with the others," said Cassie. She'd already rounded up six other film judges and the group was milling about in front of the wall of movie posters. "Theodosia, you stand in front of Homer, okay?"

Theodosia slid in front of Homer Hunt, who gave her a smile and a whispered, "Nice to see you."

She gave him a tight nod, wondering if this innocuous-looking man was capable of extreme violence.

"Say tea," urged Kassie. And then she was snapping away and they were all smiling, trying to appear normal and natural while being blinded by the brilliant flash. "Perfect," chirped Kassie. "One more and then . . . okay, we're done. Thanks, guys."

Theodosia was still seeing white flashes dance before her eyes as she fanned herself. "Warm night," she said to Kassie. With the press of people everywhere, the temperature in the tea shop was starting to climb.

"Before I moved back here to Bowman, I lived in Santa Fe for a while, so I'm used to a little heat," Kassie told her. Then Kassie suddenly dropped her voice and murmured, "Boy, would I ever love to be a production assistant for that guy!"

Glancing across the room, Theodosia saw that "that guy" was C. W. Dredd, the film director who'd waylaid and flirted with her last evening.

"He's an absolute doll," said Kassie appreciatively. "And he's . . . oh, good heavens, he's headed right for us!"

Catching sight of Theodosia, C. W. Dredd gave a slow

wink, then sauntered toward her. The crowd, as if sensing his star power, seemed to part like the Red Sea.

"Hiya," he said, staring right at Theodosia. "How's the star witness tonight?"

"Excuse me," said Kassie, slipping away, looking more than a little envious.

"Did you send me a note earlier?" asked Theodosia.

He smiled at her. "A note?"

"You didn't ask me to come to the Belvedere Theatre?"

Dredd shook his head, still looking slightly amused. "No. Should I have?"

"You're sure?" asked Theodosia.

"Hey, why would I send you some crazy note when I knew you were going to be here tonight?" His voice was the consistency of melted butter. Confident melted butter.

"I pretty much have to be here," Theodosia told him. "Since I live here."

That brought him up short. "Huh?"

"This is my place, Mr. Dredd," said Theodosia.

C. W. Dredd let a slight frown mar his perfect brow, then he seemed to shake it off. "Call me C.W., okay?"

"Okay." *Whatever.*

"So," he said, letting one hand wander up to Theodosia's shoulder, where it rested possessively. "This is your tea shop." He glanced around, taking in the pegged floors, wooden beams, and colorful tins of tea stacked floor to ceiling. And seemed to like what he saw. Then his eyes fixed on the small wooden sign that hung over the counter. "The Indigo Tea Shop. Cool name. And this place is quite charming. It kind of looks like it could be a movie set. Like a very clever art director envisioned it and brought it to life."

"Thank you," said Theodosia. "I think."

"So . . . if this place is yours, you pretty much have to stick around tonight. You can't run off on me." C.W. dialed up his smile several degrees.

He had her there. "No, I suppose not," said Theodosia.

"So, you, uh, live upstairs?"

Theodosia nodded.

"How about a tour?"

Parker Scully was suddenly at Theodosia's elbow. "Theo?" Parker said anxiously, "there's a problem in the kitchen."

"Problem in the kitchen," Theodosia told C. W. Dredd. "Gotta run."

"Hey, I'm saving a place for you at my table. Hurry back."

"Maybe," Theodosia said over her shoulder. Then she ducked through the velvet curtain after Parker. "What's wrong?" she asked him.

Parker turned to face her, supreme unhappiness written across his handsome face. "The problem is . . . that guy was hitting on you."

"That's not a problem," Theodosia told him. "It's a fact of life. A guy like that, he probably hits on every available female on the planet."

"Is that what you are?" asked Parker. "An available female?" He sounded angry, but looked worried.

"I'm not really sure," said Theodosia. This was a conversation she'd known they were going to have eventually. But this felt like a strange time to get into it.

Parker put his arms around Theodosia and pulled her close. "I think you're really quite *unavailable*. In fact, I think you're going to be very, very busy in the coming weeks and months. So busy you'll probably never find time to say hi to that guy again." His lips closed on hers.

"Well, this is a fine situation," said Drayton as he sped out from the kitchen. "We're running around like maniacs and you two are out here canoodling."

"Who's canoodling?" called Haley from the kitchen. She sounded harried but interested.

"Theodosia and Parker," replied Drayton.

"Well, I'm glad *somebody's* having fun," said Haley. "Because I'm about to go insane."

"Toby had to run back to Solstice for more chicken and steak fillets," Drayton explained to Theodosia. "We've had so many extra people show up we're running low on food." He suddenly looked very serious. "I believe we have a few party crashers."

"Or guests who brought guests," said Theodosia. She was still nestled comfortably in Parker's arms.

"Anyway," continued Drayton. "Timothy Neville and Isabelle are sitting at the head table without any food."

"Did they want chicken or beef?" called Haley.

Drayton glanced at Parker, who seemed to be on top of things, despite his angst over C. W. Dredd moving in on his girl.

"Chicken," said Parker.

"I have two lavender-roasted chicken breasts left in here, but that's it until Toby gets back," called Haley.

"Plate them up and I'll deliver them," said Theodosia.

"Oh, now you're working?" asked Drayton, raising a single eyebrow.

"When did she ever really stop?" called Haley. "C'mon in here, Theo, I'll have 'em ready in a sec."

"Are we okay now?" Theodosia whispered to Parker, gently extricating herself from his embrace.

"Absolutely," he replied. "As long as you tell that other guy to get lost."

Which might be a problem, Theodosia decided. Because she had a feeling that when a woman told C. W. Dredd to get lost, he just got more interested.

"*Timothy*," *said Theodosia,* swooping down on Timothy Neville's table. "I have your lavender chicken. Yours, too, Isabelle."

"Thank you," said Timothy, eagerly accepting the plate. "And by the way, this is a lovely party."

"Drayton was the mastermind," said Theodosia. "And you have Parker and Haley to thank for the food . . ."

"We'll be sure to thank them," said Isabelle, "Everything's been perfectly lovely."

Theodosia waved a hand at Miss Dimple, who came scurrying over with a bottle of wine. "If you could take care of Timothy and Isabelle here . . ."

"That's right," directed Timothy. "You go mingle."

And mingle she did. Theodosia was introduced to several other film festival judges, two more directors, and a cinematographer named Ernest DeWitt, who wore a loop around his neck and introduced himself loudly to everyone.

Constance Brucato and her cameraman, Raleigh, also moved relentlessly about the room. The second time Raleigh grabbed at one of the cheese plates that was lined up on the counter, Drayton snapped, "Could you please not help yourself to those?"

Raleigh glanced at Theodosia, a helpless look on his face. Obviously, he hadn't eaten yet and hoped she might intercede on his behalf.

"What if you finish your interviews as fast as possible and then I fix you a special plate," Theodosia suggested.

Raleigh gave a grateful nod. "Sure thing," he replied as Drayton continued to grumble under his breath.

Delaine Dish, fashionably late and dressed in a sleeveless, scooped-neck black dress, finally arrived in a flurry of shrill hellos, ecstatic hugs, and carefully delivered air kisses.

"I was wondering if you were going to make it," said Theodosia, as Delaine came scurrying over to her.

"Busy, busy, busy," cooed Delaine. She adjusted the diamond pendant that hung from her neck and gazed about the room, looking slightly predatory. "But I certainly wouldn't miss this. Mmm," she said as though savoring a piece of chocolate. "Lots of pretty people." By *people* Delaine meant *men*.

Theodosia glanced down at the see-through plastic bag Delaine had slung across one of her arms. She could see that it swathed a gorgeous blue knit dress. "I see you brought a change of clothes, just in case. Want to stash it in my office?" They were standing just a few feet from there.

Delaine focused on Theodosia and grinned from ear to ear. "Silly Theo. This dress is for *you*. I know how much you admired mine the other night, so I brought you one just like it." She paused, breathless. "Of course, since pink is *my* signature color, your dress is blue. Periwinkle blue to be exact. Perhaps, with a few minor adjustments to your wardrobe, blue could become *your* signature color."

"Thank you," said Theodosia, gently taking the dress into her arms. *Signature color? Probably not.*

Nina van Diedrich chose that exact moment to join them. "What have you got there?" she cooed enthusiastically. "A new dress?"

"I brought it for Theodosia," said Delaine. "Because she simply went gaga over my pink one."

Nina snatched the blue dress from Theodosia's hands. "May I?" she asked, then quickly slipped off the plastic without waiting for an answer. "Adorable," Nina declared, holding the dress up. "And it goes beautifully with my darker coloring, too, don't you think?"

Theodosia was forced to admit it didn't look half bad.

"But I have a drop-dead *purple* georgette silk dress at my shop," Delaine told Nina. "Which would be even *more* perfect for you, Nina dear."

"I don't know," said Nina, who seemed totally smitten by the blue knit dress. "I'm awfully enamored of this one."

"Tell you what," said Theodosia. "If you think the blue suits you best, then you should have it."

"Really?" squealed Nina.

Delaine looked like she was ready to rumble. "But I brought that dress specifically for *Theodosia*," Delaine told Nina. Her violet eyes glittered, her nails suddenly looked razor sharp. "I ordered it especially for her. She's going to wear it tomorrow night when she accompanies Earl Grey on stage."

"I am?" said Theodosia. This was the first she'd heard of Delaine's wardrobe edict.

"Of course," said Delaine. "Doesn't Earl Grey have a blue collar and wear a blue service dog cape?" She grabbed for the dress and began to pull it away from Nina.

"Well . . . yes," mumbled Theodosia. It had never occurred to her that she had to coordinate her outfit with her dog's.

"Then it's settled," said Delaine, still trying to wrest the dress back from Nina. "This is Theodosia's dress."

"You can't just order another one?" asked Theodosia. Nina looked like she never wanted to give the dress up.

"Not on such short notice," said Delaine, through clenched teeth. This time she managed to pry the dress from Nina's clutches. "Perhaps you'd better put this dress in your office, Theo." As she handed Theodosia the dress, Delaine's voice was dangerously shrill. "For safekeeping."

"I'll take it back for her," said Nina. "No problem."

"Actually, it would be a problem," muttered Delaine as Nina finally dashed off.

"Face it," said Theodosia, trying to jolly Delaine out of her mood. "She admires your taste and style."

"I suppose you're right," said Delaine. "And speaking of style . . ." Her eyes were suddenly focused on C. W. Dredd, who seemed to have a perpetual group of admirers clustered about him.

At that exact moment, C. W. Dredd looked up and

locked eyes with Theodosia. Then a crooked smile flashed across his handsome face.

Delaine took in their little exchange. "I was going to flirt with C.W. myself tonight, honey. But it looks like *you* made a mighty big impression on him.

"Not my intention," whispered Theodosia. "Especially when Parker is hovering in the kitchen and there are sharp knives all around."

Delaine gave a little shiver. "There's nothing like having two men fight over you. So romantic and thrilling. Reminds me of earlier times when men actually fought *duels* over women." She got a dreamy, faraway look in her eyes. "Gee, those were good times."

"Not for the men, they weren't," replied Theodosia.

10

❦

Maneuvering her Jeep down the bumpy cobblestone alley, Theodosia pulled up to the back door of Floradora Flowers. Jumping out, she flipped open the rear hatch of her vehicle, then rang the back bell. As she waited, she marveled at the tangle of wild roses and lush magnolia bushes that Hattie Boatwright, the owner of Floradora, had been able to coax from the almost hardpan soil. Theodosia wondered if Hattie used muracid, coffee grounds, or some kind of witchcraft. Theodosia noted that all she had growing at the back door of the Indigo Tea Shop was one miserable, scraggly magnolia plant that hadn't done a thing in three years except look sickly. Although, when she thought about it, Earl Grey might have something to do with that.

Theodosia heard one lock being undone as well as a second one. Then Hattie Boatwright, her Church Street neighbor and fellow small business proprietor, pushed open the door and beckoned her inside.

"You're early," said Hattie. She was a small woman in her

late fifties, dressed in khakis, with a mop of dark, curly hair and a perpetually cheerful nature.

"Sorry," said Theodosia. "Just trying to get a jump on the day." It was Wednesday morning, just a few minutes shy of eight thirty.

"That's okay, honey," said Hattie. "I always come in early on Wednesdays and Fridays. That's when my new shipments arrive."

Following Hattie through the workroom, Theodosia marveled at her inventory of flowers. Hattie had coolers filled with tulips, roses, daffodils, and genestra, as well as tall metal containers brimming with coneflowers, hollyhocks, and fairy roses. Just like her tea shop with its aroma of bergamot, jasmine, and rose hips, there was definitely an aromatherapy effect at work here. The sweet scent of the flowers made Theodosia want to curl up under a bower of ferns and take a nap.

"So how did the rose bouquets work out for your little soiree last night?" asked Hattie.

"They looked adorable on the tables," said Theodosia. "In fact, they were so enticing that more than a few of our guests took them home."

Hattie gave a slight grimace. "That's the problem with small bouquets. Which is why I prefer gigantic arrangements skillfully weighted down with rocks. Much more difficult for people to spirit away."

"Drayton wanted different flowers for today anyway," said Theodosia.

"What's the occasion?" asked Hattie. As their florist of choice, Hattie had provided elegant rose-and-baby's-breath bouquets for Victorian teas, lilies and asters for Easter teas, even orchids for bridal teas.

"Today's our Tea Français," said Theodosia.

"Ah," said Hattie, sliding open the door of one of her coolers. "No wonder Drayton wanted French lavender along with Peruvian lilies, El Toro roses, and hypericum berries. I had to order the lavender special from a dealer in Provence."

"That's our Drayton," said Theodosia. "Never one to make things easy."

Hattie pulled out a cardboard tray full of flowers and peered at her. "I heard your film festival ran into some trouble. It's a sad thing, that director getting killed on stage. Are the police any closer to finding who did it?"

"I don't think so," said Theodosia, acutely aware that the key card to Jordan Cole's room was resting inside her handbag.

"Too bad," said Hattie. "Well, hopefully nothing else will pop up to jinx you." Hattie balanced the tray full of flowers as she thrust a stack of French market baskets into Theodosia's hands. "You carry the baskets out and I'll bring the flowers. But I think we'll have to make two trips."

Theodosia dropped the flowers and baskets at the Indigo Tea Shop and bid a hasty greeting to Drayton and Haley. They both looked a trifle tired this morning, but so did she. After staying up late last night, Theodosia figured her eyes could benefit from a pair of damp tea bags. Tea bags applied to the eye area were always a soothing and surefire trick to reduce puffiness.

Maybe she could squeeze in a quick siesta after lunch, Theodosia decided. But for right now, as she cruised down Meeting Street, then turned into the parking lot of the Lady Goodwood Inn, she had to remain sharp and focused.

Stepping inside the Lady Goodwood Inn, a historic whitewashed building fronted with a row of tall, graceful columns, Theodosia glanced about nervously. She for sure didn't want to run into Frederick Welborne, the inn's general manager. He was an affable man who'd been at the Lady Goodwood for at least two or maybe even three decades. But her mission today of making a foray into a murdered man's room didn't exactly come under the heading of social call. So she'd rather not answer any questions. Or have any witnesses.

Tiptoeing down the long carpeted hallway, Theodosia glanced in at the Magnolia Room, a large, elegant room painted in broad pink-and-cream stripes. She'd helped cater more than a few wedding receptions in that lovely room. Then she was dashing past the French tapestry that hung in the foyer and heading for the elevator.

Theodosia had just pushed the call button and was waiting impatiently, when one of the office doors in the wood-paneled wall burst open. And the last person in the world she expected to see came bustling out.

"Delaine!" exclaimed Theodosia, before she could catch herself.

Delaine stopped up short and put a hand to her chest. "Theo!" she cried with a tiny little squeak, as though it had been light years since they'd seen each other instead of just last night.

"Delaine," said Theodosia again, but with slightly less enthusiasm. "What are you doing here?"

Delaine casually brushed a microscopic piece of lint from her pale blue silk blouse. "I just picked up a batch of gift certificates for the Heritage Society's silent auction," said Delaine. She tilted the white leather folder that was clutched in her hands. A few more seconds ticked by and then Delaine narrowed her eyes. "A better question might be what are *you* doing here?" Delaine cocked her head like a curious magpie awaiting an answer.

"Uh . . ." began Theodosia.

"Well?" said Delaine, edging closer.

"I was . . ." Generally fast on her feet and quick with a reply, Theodosia fumbled for an answer.

That was enough for Delaine. Now she definitely knew

something was up. "Okay, Theo, you'd better tell me what's going on." Delaine put a hand on one jutting hip, assuming an aggressive pose.

Reluctantly, Theodosia opened her handbag and pulled out the key card.

"What's that supposed to be?" asked Delaine. Now her nose twitched in disinterest.

"Key card," said Theodosia.

"I can see that," said Delaine, letting a slightly bored tone edge into her voice.

"You've got to keep this quiet, okay?" said Theodosia.

Delaine looked insulted. "Of course, I'll keep it quiet. You know me, I'm the height of discretion. If you say mum's the word, then mum's the word."

Right, thought Theodosia.

"Now tell me what's going on," continued Delaine. "What's the big secret with your silly little key card?"

"I'm pretty sure it's the one that unlocks Jordan Cole's hotel room."

Delaine's eyebrows lifted into sharp arcs, her glossy lips pursed. "Are you kidding me?" she exclaimed. But the look on Theodosia's face told Delaine she was quite serious.

Now they both gazed at the gold key card that glinted almost hypnotically in the light from the glass and brass sconces that hung on the wall.

"Where did you get it?" demanded Delaine. "Better yet, *how* did you get it?"

Theodosia waggled an index finger. "Found it at the Heritage Society yesterday afternoon. Apparently the police sent Jordan Cole's personal effects back to the Lady Goodwood, and they sent it over to the Heritage Society. Long story short, the envelope spilled onto the floor and I picked up the key card when no one was looking."

"Awfully reckless of you," breathed Delaine. Obviously, Theodosia had captured her interest.

"I suppose."

One of Delaine's fingernails tapped at the hard plastic key card. "I want in on this, you know."

"You can't be serious."

"Yes, I think I am," said Delaine.

"There's no reason both of us should get in trouble," said Theodosia.

Delaine fixed her with a wicked grin. "Who says we're going to get in trouble?"

They rode the creaking elevator to the third floor, then tip-toed down the length of plush Oriental carpet. At the end of the hallway, they faced a set of double doors that bore a polished brass plaque. The plaque read Santee Suite.

"This is it," said Theodosia. Now that she was here, she was flirting with second thoughts.

"Try the key card," urged Delaine, pointing toward the slot in the door.

Theodosia touched the card to the slot, hesitated a moment, then slid it in. There was a soft click and then the door unlocked.

They found themselves gazing about a sitting room that was resplendent with plum-colored carpeting, two Queen Anne wing chairs, and lovely antiques.

"What a beautiful suite," said Delaine, pushing her way in. "And look at all the antiques. Magnificent."

Theodosia knew the smart thing to do was to get in and get out as fast as possible. If they didn't dawdle, didn't spend too much time here, they wouldn't run the risk of having housekeeping or hotel management walk in on them.

But Delaine was completely entranced with the decor. "Look at this art glass parlor vase lamp, Theo. I do believe the brass metalwork is by Plume and Atwood! And this drum table is simply amazing."

"Delaine," said Theodosia. "This isn't *Antiques Roadshow*. By my estimation, we've got about two minutes tops to do a quick snoop." Her head swiveled left then right, took in the open briefcase still sitting on the coffee table, the pack of cigarettes next to it.

"Fine," snapped Delaine. "So what are we looking for anyway?"

Theodosia crossed the carpet, heading for the bedroom. "I really don't know," she said over her shoulder.

Inside the bedroom, time had stood still. Jordan Cole's sport coat was tossed across the bed, his suitcase sat open on a luggage rack. A glance into the bathroom revealed toiletries and a shaving kit sitting on the blue tile counter. Theodosia peered at it. Hermès aftershave. Nice.

A thin white film that Theodosia figured had to be fingerprint dust covered everything. Yes, the police had been through here with a fine-tooth comb, probably. So what was left to find? Maybe nothing.

Delaine came up behind Theodosia. "This is quite a lovely bedroom, too," she declared. "Nice and cozy. Although I can't say I care much for those chintz curtains."

"Clock's ticking," murmured Theodosia. "Check the nightstand, will you?"

But Delaine seemed to have lost her edge. "This is just making me feel sad," she said. "Looking around a dead man's room. Don't you think the police have already pawed through everything?"

"Probably," said Theodosia. She walked over to the closet, pulled open the white slatted doors. A few shirts and pairs of slacks hung in there looking desultory and unworn, along with another sport coat, an elegant British tweed. Two pairs of shoes sat on the floor of the closet.

"Anything?" called Delaine.

"Nope," said Theodosia. She hadn't really expected to find anything, yet she still felt a tinge of disappointment.

Somehow, the key card dropping at her feet had seemed a fortuitous sign.

Drawers slid open, then were closed again as Delaine checked the dresser. Still Theodosia stared into the closet. She reached out a hand, felt the tweed sport coat. Why, she wondered, would Cole bring a tweed sport coat to Charleston in summer? Then answered her own question. Probably because he'd flown in from cooler climes. Like London. Her hand sought out the fabric again. It was soft and light, unlike any tweed she had felt before. Had to be . . . a bespoke piece?

Theodosia checked the label on the inside of the jacket. Nothing.

No label at all?

Curious now, she pulled the jacket open a little more. Finally located a small label that was almost hidden near the seam of the lining. It said *Chittleborough & Morgan, Savile Row.*

"Find anything interesting?" asked Delaine. "Uh-oh!"

Theodosia glanced over at Delaine. Her eyes had gone wide and she was suddenly skittering toward the closet. Delaine mouthed "maid" to Theodosia and gestured frantically toward the door. Then Delaine was pushing her way in, shoving Theodosia and squashing her into the closet, pulling the doors closed behind them.

Silently, they stood hunched together in that narrow, dark space. Delaine put a finger to her lips. Theodosia rolled her eyes. Like she was going to blurt something out now?

Theodosia wondered exactly what the maid was doing. Then decided she was probably changing towels, dusting a bit, doing her normal housekeeping chores. As she'd deduced earlier, the room was probably paid for until the end of this week.

Scrunching sideways, trying to find a more comfortable position, Theodosia's hand brushed up against the jacket that was hanging there. No wonder it was such an elegant jacket, she decided. It was a Savile Row jacket. A one-of-a-kind, hand-tailored piece. Her fingertips edged inside to the silk lining, savoring the feel. And hit . . . a slight bump.

A bump? In a Savile Row jacket?

But, yes, there was definitely some sort of bump or glitch. Something that maybe shouldn't be there.

There was the faint sound of a door closing and then Delaine said, "I think she's gone."

"Delaine," said Theodosia, still standing in darkness.

"Um-hm?" Delaine opened the closet door and peered out.

"Do you know anything about Savile Row tailoring?"

Delaine turned back and gave a tiny frown. "A little."

"Do they ever put . . . um . . . hidden pockets in jackets?"

"You mean a cosh pocket?" asked Delaine.

Theodosia's fingers continued to probe around. "That's a real thing? What did you call it . . . a cosh pocket?"

"Cosh pockets are designed for gentlemen who wish to discreetly conceal money, a small weapon, whatever," said Delaine. "The tradition dates back to the eighteen hundreds."

"Interesting," said Theodosia, her fingers again running over the slightly concealed bump in the fabric.

"So is that what you found?" Delaine sounded only slightly interested.

"Yeah, maybe." Theodosia's fingers finally worked their way into a hidden seam. "Got something here."

"What is it?" asked Delaine.

"Hang on a minute," said Theodosia.

"What?" asked Delaine. *"What?"*

Theodosia grasped a small metal object between her fingers and slid it out from between the seam that wasn't really a seam. Cradling it in the palm of her hand, she showed it to Delaine.

"A camera?" said Delaine, peering at it. "And so tiny. Must be digital."

"It is," said Theodosia. It was a tiny Leica M3. The two women continued to stare at it.

"I wonder," said Delaine slowly. "Could there be any photos stored on it?"

Theodosia's heartbeat quickened. "I think we should definitely take a look." They moved closer to the window, where the light was considerably better.

"Hurry up then," urged Delaine. "Turn it on."

Theodosia pushed a few buttons and a tiny screen lit up. "According to the digital counter there are, let's see, twenty-two images stored here."

"Can we scroll through them?" asked Delaine. "Do you know how to do that?"

Theodosia nodded. "I think so." Her fingers probed at the buttons and, a few moments later, they were flipping through a mini slide show.

"Looks like he took mostly shots of his movie crew and cast members," said Theodosia. "There seem to be location shots, too."

"Where are the most recent photos?" asked Delaine.

"I'm getting to those," said Theodosia. "I think." She continued to press the tiny button with her index finger, finally coming to the last shot.

It was a dark, moody shot of a dark-haired woman. But it was difficult to make out the woman's face.

"Can you tell who this is?" asked Theodosia, squinting. "She kind of looks familiar, but . . ."

Delaine shook her head no. Then she pulled a pair of glasses from her handbag. A pair of sleek caramel-colored frames that sported glittery double Cs on the bows.

"I didn't know you wore reading glasses," said Theodosia. This was the first time she'd seen Delaine in any kind of eyewear besides dark sunglasses.

"I don't," snapped Delaine, quickly pulling them off.

"Whatever," said Theodosia, knowing Delaine was exceedingly vain when it came to her appearance. "The thing of it is, can you tell who the woman is?"

Delaine slid her glasses back on and squinted at the tiny image. She said nothing for a few moments. Then her eyes widened in surprise. "The drapes," she said. "They're the same chintz drapes that are hanging in this room."

Theodosia lifted her eyes and stared at the burgundy-and-blue chintz drapes that hung behind the king-sized bed. She was beginning to get a nervous, fluttery feeling in the pit of her stomach.

"And the woman?" she asked cautiously, even though she was pretty sure who it was. "Who do you think it is?"

"Oh my goodness!" Delaine crowed excitedly. "I do believe it's Nina van Diedrich!"

11

❧

"I can't believe it," muttered Drayton. "I can't believe Nina van Diedrich was having an affair with Jordan Cole."

Delaine tapped her little finger against her teacup. "That man must've had scores of women swooning over him."

"Take a number and get in line," added Theodosia. "Like at a deli counter."

The two women were back at the Indigo Tea Shop, sitting in the corner with a stunned Drayton. They were sipping cups of Assam, a hearty, bracing tea with a slightly malt-like flavor.

"You're talking about a dead man," hissed Drayton. "A man who had romantic liaisons with Nina van Diedrich *and* Isabelle Neville."

"What!" Delaine emitted an ear-piercing yelp.

Drayton gazed across the table at Theodosia. "You didn't tell her?"

"I was about to," said Theodosia.

"Are you serious?" screeched Delaine, clearly stunned.

"Cole was romantically involved with Isabelle, too? Timothy's young granddaughter?"

Theodosia nodded. "I guess she's not so young after all."

"Whoo!" said Delaine. She took another sip of tea, pulled herself together, then gazed at Theodosia with slightly slanted eyes. "And just when were you fixing to tell me about little miss Isabelle?"

"Look," said Theodosia. "Does it really matter?"

"Of course it doesn't," said Drayton, cutting in. "The issue now is, what exactly should we do with this newfound information concerning Nina?"

"I think we have to inform Tidwell," said Theodosia.

"What about Timothy?" asked Drayton.

"We'll tell him, too," said Theodosia. "But later."

"And tell him about Isabelle, too?" asked Drayton.

"Let's cross that bridge when we come to it," said Theodosia. "The thing is, we have a strange, rather uncomfortable situation at hand."

"Deliciously strange," agreed Delaine.

"And if you want to project a worst-case scenario," continued Theodosia, "you could argue that either Isabelle or Nina found out about the other, had a possible confrontation with Cole . . ."

"And things turned violent," finished Drayton.

"Good gracious," murmured Delaine.

"So the way I see it," continued Theodosia, "this case is definitely out of our hands."

"No," said Drayton, shaking his head solemnly. "I think it's still very much in our hands."

"What do you mean?" asked Delaine. She was snapping her head back and forth, following the conversation like she was watching a tennis match.

"A digital photo isn't proof of anything," said Drayton. "Nor is a romantic entanglement, no matter how well documented."

"You mean Tidwell isn't going to move on this," said Theodosia. Now that she stopped to think about it, she knew Drayton was probably right. It wasn't illegal to be romantically involved with someone. And to charge someone with murder required substantial proof.

"Tidwell will certainly want to question Nina and Isabelle," said Drayton. "But I don't think it will go much further than that."

"I guess I see what you mean," said Delaine, looking slightly confused now.

Theodosia gazed at her teacup, an Ainsley floral print done in colors of yellow and light pink. It caught the light and reflected it back at her in a colorful swirl. "So what exactly are you saying, Drayton?"

"That we share this recent photo with Tidwell and continue to poke around," replied Drayton.

Delaine nodded slowly, as if she was reluctantly seconding Drayton's vote.

"Maybe we've gone as far as we can," ventured Theodosia. "Maybe we're not going to turn up anything else."

"My dear Theo," said Drayton, a knowing smile spreading across his lined face. "If your wily sleuthing this morning is any indication, I would say you're just warming up!"

Haley brought them a plate of scones while Drayton went off to call Tidwell.

"Everything okay?" she asked, setting the still-warm scones on the table, then placing a small cut-glass bowl filled with Devonshire cream next to them.

"Just dandy," said Delaine, reaching for a scone. "Tell me, dear, do you know how many fat grams are in one of these?"

"Hardly any," said Haley, deadpan.

"Actually, Haley," said Theodosia. "Things aren't okay.

We just came across some rather startling information."
And she quickly related to Haley how they'd found the little camera and the picture it contained.

Haley gave a low whistle. "Sounds like somebody's gonna get hauled down to police headquarters and put in one of those tiny, airless rooms with the one-way glass."

"Wouldn't it be great if this murder investigation could be wrapped up nice and neat before our big award show Saturday night?" asked Delaine.

Haley gazed at Delaine as though she were a deluded child. "That's not how things generally work," she told her. "Usually murder investigations are messy things that drag on and on."

"You're awfully young to have such a cynical view of life," snapped Delaine.

"I'm not cynical," responded Haley. "I'm just a realist."

Twenty minutes later Burt Tidwell came charging into the tea shop. He loomed in the doorway, his face a darkened thundercloud. Then he caught sight of Theodosia and Delaine. Threading his way through the tables, moving quite precisely for such a large man, he eased his bulk down in a wooden captain's chair across from them.

"I was told you wanted to see me," Tidwell announced in his gruff tone. "Something about a liaison the late Jordan Cole was having, although Drayton, being Drayton, was rather circumspect on the phone."

"Yes," said Theodosia. "We came across some information that could be key to your investigation." She had a feeling this was going to be a somewhat troublesome exchange.

"Well, you're too late," said Tidwell, suddenly looking smug. "I just had a talk with the girl this morning."

"You . . . what?" began Theodosia. *What's he talking about?* she wondered.

"Isabelle Neville told me all about her previous relationship with Jordan Cole," said Tidwell. "Although to hear her confess it, I must say it sounded more like a schoolgirl crush."

"And you were questioning Isabelle . . . why?" asked Theodosia.

"It came to our attention that Isabelle was fired from Cole's film crew."

"Are you serious?" said Theodosia. This came as a major shocker. "I was under the impression the two of them had a successful working relationship. That she was a location assistant and had even been present for some of the final editing."

"Not at all," said Tidwell. "In fact, according to some of the crew members we talked to, the girl caused quite a commotion."

"That is so weird," muttered Theodosia. Had Isabelle been lying all along?

"Do you still consider Isabelle a suspect?" asked Delaine. She hadn't said anything until now.

Tidwell seemed to weigh his words carefully. "Probably . . . not. But we still need to investigate a few details." He leaned back in his chair and the aged wood emitted a groaning protest. "Now, what is so all-fired important that you had to call me out and interrupt my busy day?" His dark eyes darted from Theodosia to Delaine.

"Uh . . ." began Delaine, then chickened out.

"We've been doing a little investigating of our own," began Theodosia.

"When have you not." Tidwell sighed. He rolled his eyes to signal his disapproval.

"At the Lady Goodwood Inn," continued Theodosia.

Tidwell suddenly stiffened in his chair. "Don't tell me."

"Actually, *in* the Lady Goodwood Inn," said Delaine.

Tidwell held up a hand. "Please. Please don't tell me you

ladies actually gained access to Cole's room." His beady eyes
drilled into them.

"Suite," said Delaine.

Tidwell glared at her. "What?" came a rumble deep
within his throat.

"It was technically a hotel suite and not a room," said
Delaine. "Actually, the Santee Suite. Rather tastefully fur-
nished, too. Nice carpet, good quality antiques . . ."

Tidwell cut her off. "You snuck inside Jordan Cole's hotel
room!" His voice had taken on a thunderous quality.

"In a manner of speaking," said Theodosia.

"Either you did or didn't enter the premises," said Tidwell.

"When you put it like that," said Delaine, trying her
best tiptoe diplomacy, "I'd have to say we sort of did. Just to
look around, of course, not to steal anything." She paused,
then let a touch of excitement enter her voice. "And we
found something, too."

Tidwell's eyebrows lifted a millimeter.

"Something the police overlooked," added Theodosia.
There. She knew that would annoy as well as intrigue him.

"Ladies," said Tidwell, looking very put upon, "you are
dithering. If you have something to say, then kindly say it."

Theodosia placed the small silver camera on the table in
front of her.

"A digital camera," said Tidwell, his voice condescend-
ing now. "And what lovely images does that contain? Vaca-
tion photos?"

"Show him, Theodosia," said Delaine.

"Yes, show me," said Tidwell with a sigh.

Turning on the camera, Theodosia clicked through the
photos until she came to the last one. She set the camera
back down, placed an index finger firmly on top of it, then
slowly slid the camera across the table toward Tidwell.

One of Tidwell's pudgy fingers reached out to hook the

camera and tow it the rest of the way. He lowered his giant head and stared at the tiny colored image. Then, like a helium balloon slowly deflating, Tidwell let out a long, low whistle of air.

"Nina," he finally muttered. "Well, I'll be."

12

❧

Just when the tea shop was filled with luncheon customers, just when Drayton had handed Theodosia a pair of teapots brimming with Ceylon tea and brisk Nilgiri tea, Constance Brucato called.

"What is it, Constance?" asked Theodosia. She was standing at the front counter, doing a balancing act with the steaming teapots, holding the receiver in the crook of her neck.

"I need your help, Theo."

"Now what's wrong?" Theodosia glanced at the front door, saw three women standing there, waiting to be seated. "Drayton," she hissed.

"The interviews from last night are all good," said Constance in her slow, thoughtful tone. "But the edit looks too lighthearted. I think we need a different perspective."

"What perspective is that?" asked Theodosia.

"I was actually thinking of *your* perspective," said Constance. "You're one of the film festival judges, so I was wondering if we could get a few comments from you that might helpfully add a more cohesive note."

Theodosia was both flattered and perplexed. She wasn't quite sure what she could add. "I suppose . . ."

"Great!" chirped Constance. "Could you be at the studio tomorrow morning, say around nine?"

"And this will take how long?" asked Theodosia.

"Not more than an hour," assured Constance. "Certainly no longer than ninety minutes . . . two hours at the most."

"See you then." Theodosia sighed.

"We're jammed," said Drayton, once Theodosia was off the phone. "We had four extra parties show up . . . walk-ins."

"Where did you put them? In my office?" All the tables were filled, but the tea room didn't look overly crowded.

"Outside," said Drayton. "So you're going to have to put on your track shoes and play waitress this noon, okay?"

"No problem," said Theodosia. As a sole proprietor she knew it was her duty to wait tables, wash dishes, do whatever it took to keep the place humming. She'd been in far too many fancy restaurants where managers and maitre d's fiddled haughtily with their reservation book while patrons stood waiting and waiters and busboys struggled to stay afloat. There would be none of that nonsense at the Indigo Tea Shop.

"And these," said Drayton, thrusting a handful of menus at her, "are the menus Haley printed for today. But realize they're fairly limited. Just soup, salad, sandwiches, and scones."

Haley's "fairly limited" menu turned out to be shrimp bisque, crab salad tea sandwiches on nut bread, chicken salad on croissants, fruit salad, and lavender scones. Not so limited at all.

Customers seemed delighted by the offerings, especially

the ones who were seated outside. A temperate breeze wafted down Church Street and the sun sparkled overhead, gilding the surrounding brick buildings and making everything sparkle. Summer but without the sizzle.

Jenny Foster, one of Theodosia's regular customers and the proprietor of the Giddy Gnome Garden Shop over on Market Street, grabbed her by the arm as she dashed past.

"Drayton mentioned this was a Ceylon tea," said Jenny. "Is it similar to the Kenilworth Estate he brewed last week?" Jenny had been in with some friends for a tea party.

"Actually," said Theodosia, "the Kenilworth you enjoyed is a black tea from the Dimbula region of Ceylon. The one Drayton's serving today is Nuwara Eliya orange pekoe. Golden, bright, delicately perfumed. Smell that aroma? It's almost like savoring the bouquet of a fine wine."

"You're right," said Jenny. "It's a very subtle aroma." She grinned. "Almost perfumey."

"The important thing is," said Theodosia, "do you like it?"

"I love it," said Jenny. "And my friends and I love coming here."

"Thank you," said Theodosia. "That's high praise and I appreciate it."

Now, Theodosia decided, if they could all just push through until about two o'clock, then take an hour to set up for the Tea Français, they should be fine. Well, hopefully fine.

Luckily, Haley was on top of things in the kitchen. And then Miss Dimple showed up early to help. Hustling about efficiently, clearing luncheon plates, delivering dessert plates of cookie and bars, pouring refills of tea.

When two o'clock rolled around, Theodosia hung her CLOSED FOR PRIVATE PARTY sign on the front door and pushed up her sleeves. Time to prepare for the Tea Français, their nod to the Cannes Film Festival.

"This is going to be a snap," announced Drayton. He snapped his fingers sharply as if to prove his point.

"Whoa, big guy," said Haley. "We've got tons to do."

"You're not going to beat me with a stick again, are you?" asked Drayton, playfully.

"Did you get those French toile pillows to rest against the chair backs?" asked Haley.

Drayton nodded. "Marianne Petigru dropped them off just before lunch. They're all jumbled in Theo's office. In fact, there are so many poufy pillows back there it looks like a royal pasha could settle in quite comfortably."

"Excellent," said Haley. "And we've got the little French flags?"

"Check," said Drayton. He cocked his head and narrowed his eyes. "Say, just who's supposed to be catering manager here anyway?"

Haley gazed at him impassively. "That would be you, Drayton."

"So why are *you* suddenly jumping in to oversee every last, lingering detail?"

"Because I'm the resident nitpicker." Haley laughed, then turned and dashed back into her kitchen.

"I'll say," muttered Drayton as he headed for his counter to check his tea for what had to be the fourth or fifth time.

"Drayton seems all atwitter," Miss Dimple remarked to Theodosia.

Theodosia waved a hand. "Don't mind him, he's always like that. In fact, I think it pleases him."

"Do you think I cannot hear you talking about me?" called Drayton. "I'm just across the tea room, not some gaping, phantasmal abyss."

"Gaping, phantasmal abyss?" said Miss Dimple, lifting her brows and looking to Theodosia for an explanation.

"Oh," said Theodosia, very nonchalantly. "Drayton finally crumbled under societal pressure and got cable TV.

And if you ask me, he's completely hooked on the SciFi Channel."

"Am not," said Drayton in a small voice.

"*How many guests* today?" asked Miss Dimple.

"Should be around forty-five," said Theodosia. She and Miss Dimple had been working steadily for the last half hour. Setting tables, laying out silverware, adding finishing touches.

The plates, saucers, and teacups were the Genoa pattern produced by J & G Meakin in England, an elegant cream, black, and gold scrollwork pattern.

Stemmed water glasses were cobalt and gold Val Saint Lambert cameo glasses from the early 1900s.

Tiny pressed glass compotes held thin-sliced lemon.

Silver cachepots brimmed with sprigs of fresh lavender and the flowers that Theodosia had picked up earlier.

Finally, silver was laid out, candles were lit, and soft music came across the stereo system—A piece from the *Come Away with Me* album by Norah Jones.

Miss Dimple put a hand to her ample bosom. "It looks like an Old World painting," she declared. "Like a still life you'd see in a museum."

Theodosia had to agree. With the afternoon sun filtering through the antique lead-pane windows, the tea shop seemed to have taken on a wondrous glow.

Even Drayton stopped his fussing to come take a look. "Lovely," he declared. "Perfect."

Now Haley joined them. "Now we're cooking," was her succinct comment.

"No, my dear, *you're* the one who's doing the cooking," shot back Drayton.

"What is on the menu?" inquired Miss Dimple.

"Three fairly simple courses," said Haley. "We'll begin

with lavender scones accompanied by Devonshire cream and the Earl Grey jelly Drayton ordered from Mariage Frères in Paris. Second course will be quiche Lorraine with a citrus and spinach salad. Third course will be three different savories."

"Here comes the good part." Miss Dimple chuckled.

"Asparagus and prosciutto tea sandwiches," said Haley. "Cranberry-cheddar cheese with smoked turkey tea sandwiches. And apple and goat cheese bruschetta."

"You've outdone yourself again, Haley," said Theodosia. "We really should offer this menu to our regular customers, too."

"Agreed," said Haley. "But don't you want to hear about the desserts, too?"

"Please," begged Miss Dimple.

"Calla lily cookies," said Haley. "Which are really sugar cookies that I shaped into a sort of leafy form and filled with a date and chocolate mixture."

"Excellent," declared Drayton.

Pleased, Haley adjusted the tall chef's hat Parker Scully had presented her with. "And we've also got sponge cake with strawberries as well as strawberry cobbler."

"You must have gotten an exceedingly good deal on strawberries," said Drayton with a laugh.

"I did," agreed Haley.

"Now tell us about your teas, Drayton," urged Miss Dimple. "You've been so mysterious about them."

Drayton pulled himself into a ramrod posture and gazed at them from beneath hooded eyes. "As you are aware, Mariage Frères is the oldest tea importer in France. They are also recognized for their prodigious skill in mélange—or blending. Thus I have ordered three teas for our sublime sipping enjoyment today."

"Why do I feel like I'm watching an episode of *Masterpiece Theatre*?" Haley quipped to Theodosia.

Theodosia gave a knowing, conspiratorial smile.

"The first is Marco Polo tea," said Drayton, undaunted by Haley's flip comment. "A black tea flavored with Chinese fruits and flowers. Second is Fondateur, a smoky blend of Chinese tea with fruity top notes. And finally Mirabelle, a black tea that's been delicately scented with the French Mirabelle plum. All very French, all quite delicious for our Tea Français."

"Oh, and one more thing," said Theodosia. "As the pièce de résistance, Haley has tried her hand at the art of decorating sugar cubes." She turned and smiled brightly at Haley. "You want to show them what I think is rather amazing for your very first attempt?"

Haley gently lifted the lid off a small tin box and they all crowded around, curious.

"Well, I'll be," exclaimed Drayton.

There were pristine white sugar cubes decorated with gold fleur-de-lis, yellow sun emblems in honor of Louis XIV, and blue, white, and red French flags.

"And, look," said Drayton. "She's even done Napoleon's favorite bee motif! I'd have to say well done, Haley!"

13

❧

A low hum filled the tea room, punctuated by tiny clinks as bone china teacups gently met saucers. The aroma of fresh-brewed tea infused with plums, citrus, and rose petals hung redolent in the air. Add in the fresh-baked scones and the aromatherapy factor at the Indigo Tea Shop was beyond heavenly.

"A lovely tea party," declared Miss Dimple. She had a large silver tray propped against one hip and was waiting patiently as Haley loaded her up with plates of scones.

"It's nice that the directors, producers, and cinematographers of the documentaries and short films have a special event, too," said Theodosia. "I sometimes think they're the unsung heroes of the film industry."

"What are you talking about?" asked Drayton as he rushed into the kitchen.

"The short film people," said Haley, then stopped to consider how she'd phrased her words. "Well, I didn't mean to say they're short *people*."

"We know what you mean, dear," said Miss Dimple.

"Hah!" exclaimed Drayton. "That fat-cat director who was flirting so outrageously with Theodosia last night has just turned up like the proverbial bad penny."

"What!" said Theodosia. "You mean C. W. Dredd? He's here?"

Drayton nodded. "Unless he has an identical twin brother. Give me two more bowls of Devonshire cream, will you, Haley?"

Haley quickly dispensed creamy dabs into small glass bowls shaped like glass slippers.

Theodosia was suddenly in a tizzy. She scurried over to the green velvet curtain and peeked through. Yes, there he was. C. W. Dredd. Larger than life and oh so attractive. Laughing his hearty laugh, sauntering from table to table. Escorting a tall, dapper-looking man that Theodosia had never seen before.

"But he's not supposed to be here!" Theodosia hissed to Drayton and Haley when she was back in the kitchen.

"Well, duh," said Haley. "Guess he didn't get the memo."

"It's not a problem," Drayton assured her. "We've got more than enough food."

"That's not the issue," said Theodosia.

"He does lend a sort of . . . golden-boy image to the event," said Miss Dimple in a wistful tone. Even she had fallen under the spell of the megawatt director.

"I'm going to go out and talk to him," said Theodosia. "Ask him to please not upstage this event."

"I don't think he'd do that," said Miss Dimple.

"Sure he would," said Haley.

"Theodosia!" exclaimed C. W. Dredd when he caught sight of her. "There's someone I want you to meet." His grin was warm and his eyes roved over her appreciatively.

"What a surprise," said Theodosia, showing considerably less enthusiasm. "I wasn't aware you'd be attending our little tea. In fact, I didn't notice your name on the guest list."

C.W. shrugged good-naturedly. "You never know where I'll pop up. But, hey, I want you to meet Johnny Fleming." He turned to the man who stood next to him. "This is the tea lady I was telling you about. Theodosia. Isn't she something?"

"Nice to meet you, nice to meet you," said Johnny Fleming. He was a square-jawed, intense-looking man who gripped her hand hard as he glanced surreptitiously about the tea room, aware of the stir he and C.W. were causing.

"Johnny's a producer," explained C.W.

"Yes, I'm aware of that," said Theodosia. Johnny Fleming was another big name in Hollywood. A producer whose stock in trade was action pictures. Not her kind of film, but they pulled in megabucks at the box office.

"Johnny's just asked me to direct his new picture," said C.W. "We start filming in two weeks."

"Short notice," said Theodosia. "I thought you were headed off to Thailand."

"Yeah, well." C.W shrugged. "We made a few calls and squeezed this in, too."

"Truth of the matter is," said Johnny, smiling at Theodosia like a friendly barracuda, "I originally had Jordan Cole signed on. But . . . hey, those are the breaks, huh?"

"Is that what you call it in your industry?" asked Theodosia. "A break?"

"I got actors under contract and a crew ready to roll," said Johnny. "I'm just lucky I was able to grab this guy. Hey, pictures are a tough business, doll. What with movie completion bonds, distribution deals . . ."

"All business is tough," said Theodosia. "But that doesn't mean it has to be mercenary."

"Oooh," said Johnny Fleming, clapping a hand to his

chest as if he'd been stabbed. "A feisty one." He nudged C. W. Dredd appreciatively.

"She's a pistol," agreed C.W.

"Gentlemen," said Drayton, arriving just in the nick of time. "Allow me to escort you to a table."

Which gave Theodosia the opportunity to flee into the kitchen.

"That C. W. Dredd is absolutely maddening," she complained to Haley.

"Yeah, but he's also a total hunk," said Haley.

"Everything he says sounds scripted," said Theodosia. "As though he's playing a part."

"That's because he is," responded Haley. "He's playing at being a big-shot film director."

Uninvited guests or not, the Tea Français appeared to be a rousing success. Delaine, seated at one of the large round tables, couldn't say enough good things about Theodosia and Drayton and the Indigo Tea Shop. She happily regaled her tablemates with tea trivia she'd picked up on her many visits.

"Did you know," said Delaine, "that Queen Anne really popularized tea in the early seventeen hundreds when she started drinking tea for breakfast instead of ale?"

Everyone giggled over that one. "And you know what else?" said Delaine. "Drayton has one of the rarest teas of the world in his collection. A tea that costs over six hundred dollars a pound." That elicited oohs and aahs.

"What tea is that?" asked one of the women.

"Kilburn Imperial white," responded Drayton. "From Sri Lanka's Handunugoda Estate. Fantastically delicious and oh so delicate."

And then one thing led to another until Drayton was asked to recite one of his favorite tea poems.

"Oh no, I really couldn't," he protested rather weakly.

Which of course brought encouraging cheers. So Drayton pulled himself to his full stature and, in his best oratorical style, let his voice ring through the tea shop:

> *"Now Tea's a tricky, skilled affair,*
> *Demanding discipline and care.*
> *The little Cuppa tree is grown*
> *Up in the hills, a rainy zone.*
> *The tea trees on the misty mount*
> *Are far too numerous to count;*
> *But each is tended, come what may,*
> *By someone every seventh day."*

A round of applause followed Drayton's recitation. And in that moment, Theodosia noticed Bill Glass standing just inside the front door.

She hustled over to him, annoyed. "What are you doing here?"

"Whoa," he said, holding up a hand in an attempt to deflect her indignation. "If you must know, Linus Gillette asked me to drop by. Wanted me to get a few still shots we could both use. You remember Linus, don't you? One of the festival *sponsors*?"

"You'd better be quick about it, Glass," warned Theodosia.

But Bill Glass's sharp eyes were already scouring the room. "Holy cow," he said under his breath when he noticed C. W. Dredd and Johnny Fleming. "I thought this was supposed to be the B squad today. But you've got some real celebrities here."

"Afraid so." Theodosia sighed. This was exactly what she didn't want. Having two Hollywood pros upstage the independent directors and producers.

As Bill Glass fiddled with the two cameras he had slung

around his neck, an insinuating grin crept onto his dark face. "Every time I run into you, that guy, Dredd, is nearby. Seems like you two are awfully cozy."

"Dream on," said Theodosia.

Once the cookies, sponge cake, and strawberry cobbler had been consumed, once third and fourth refills of tea had been poured, Theodosia's guests began to wander about her shop.

Last week Haley had put together a number of different themed gift baskets. And those were proving to be extremely popular. One was a spa basket that featured a selection of Theodosia's T-Bath products, a sea sponge, and a tin of relaxing chamomile tea. Another was a mystery basket that included a mystery book, a blue teacup covered with yellow stars, and a tin of Lapsang souchong, the smoky, mysterious blend from the Wu Yi Mountains in southern China.

The antique secretary, highboy, and shelves of the Indigo Tea Shop also held a newly replenished assortment of teapots, marmalade, tea towels, herbal soaps, scone mixes, and dried flower arrangements.

Theodosia was busy stocking tins of their own house blend of Earl Green Tea when Kassie Byrd, the volunteer who'd been shanghaied to take photos last night, approached her.

"A wonderful tea," gushed Kassie. She'd already picked out a tea towel and a jar of honey. "I love how the ritual of tea helps you slow down and relax."

"It does, doesn't it," said Theodosia. "And it's amazing how many people mention that."

"Probably because people are always on the go twenty-four/seven," said Kassie. "And when they finally get a chance to unwind it just feels so good." She held up a teacup without handles that featured a matching lid and saucer. "What can you tell me about this?"

"That's a traditional *guywan*," said Theodosia. "A Chinese tea bowl. Lots of people favor them because of the lid—keeps your tea nice and hot. I import those directly from Canton, although now the city is technically known as Guangzhou."

"Gotta have it," said Kassie. "And could your chandelier be any cuter?"

Theodosia lifted her eyes to the chandelier that hung overhead. Instead of eight small shades over the bulbs, it featured eight colorful and slightly tipsy teacups. She had simply drilled out the centers of the teacups and saucers, glued them in place to serve as shades, then whitewashed the lamp's hardware. Now it glowed enticingly in the far end of her shop.

"It looks like something out of Alice in Wonderland," said Kassie. Then added slightly wistfully, "I don't suppose that's for sale, is it?"

"No," said Theodosia. "But I do have some dried grapevine wreaths that are decorated with teacups. Also very cute."

"I think I might like one," said Kassie.

"Sure thing," said Theodosia, her eyes scouring the walls but not finding one. "But I'm going to have to run back to my office. I'm positive I've got some stashed there."

Just as Theodosia was about to duck through the velvet curtains, she ran smack-dab into Isabelle Neville.

"Hi, Theo," said Isabelle. "Lovely tea." Her manner was cool and formal, almost as though she were testing Theodosia.

Theodosia jumped right into the fray. "Isabelle," she said, "I wish you would have been straight with me."

"What?" Now surprise showed on Isabelle's face.

"I wish you would have told me about getting fired from Jordan Cole's film crew."

Isabelle's eyes blazed with indignation. "Where on earth did you hear that?"

"Actually, Detective Burt Tidwell mentioned it just this

morning." Theodosia kept her voice low, but the intensity in her tone indicated she meant business.

"Well, he was quite mistaken," said Isabelle. She had a tin of jasmine tea in her hands. Now she reached over and put it back on the counter.

"I don't think so," said Theodosia. "I know Detective Tidwell quite well and he is many things—boorish, brash, and blunt to name a few. But he is rarely mistaken."

"Don't try to involve me in this investigation," said Isabelle. And now she was no longer the doe-eyed, soft-spoken granddaughter of Timothy Neville. Her eyes snapped, her features hardened, her voice was like flint striking granite.

Theodosia studied Isabelle's demeanor. And decided something just didn't ring true. This morning Tidwell had pretty much told them that Isabelle was no longer a suspect. But Isabelle's defensive posturing didn't seem to jibe with this. Could Isabelle actually be hiding something? Maybe. It was possible, Theodosia decided. Experience had taught her that pretty much anything was possible.

Delaine was suddenly hovering at their elbows. "Well, hello, you two. Oh, don't you just look too serious for words."

"Nice to see you, Delaine. Great tea, Theodosia," said Isabelle. And then she slid away from them.

"Yes, it was a very delightful tea," cooed Delaine to Isabelle's back. Then she shrugged and focused her full attention on Theodosia. "In fact, I was able to get acquainted with Mr. C. W. Dredd. Lucky me, his table was situated right next to ours. He certainly is an entertaining fellow. And all those stories he tells—about real Hollywood stars! Kind of dazzles a girl."

"He's Mr. Showbiz himself," said Theodosia, her mind elsewhere.

"And so fun to flirt with." Delaine paused. "You don't *mind*, do you, Theo? This could be a somewhat delicate matter and I certainly don't want to tread on any toes. But I *do* know you're extremely sweet on Parker Scully."

"Be my guest," said Theodosia.

"You don't mind?" asked Delaine, sounding thrilled.

"Not in the least," said Theodosia.

"Wonderful!" exclaimed Delaine. She gazed out across the tea shop, letting her eyes settle on C. W. Dredd. A satisfied smile played at her lips. "Oh, and dear . . ." Delaine touched a hand to Theodosia's arm even as her eyes followed Dredd's every move. "You *are* going to wear the blue dress tonight, right?"

14

Theodosia stared at her reflection in the antique mirror. The aged, wavering glass gave her face a soft-focus appearance, almost like a dream sequence in a film. Then she decided the last few days *had* been almost dreamlike. Starting with the violent murder of Jordan Cole, the killer's frantic escape, her two strange encounters at the Belvedere . . . three if she counted meeting C. W. Dredd. And everything culminating in her suspicions about Nina, Isabelle, and Homer Hunt. And, yes, even C. W. Dredd himself.

Then she felt a tug on her arm and Theodosia was brought back to the here and now. She was standing in the crowded hallway at the Heritage Society wearing the blue knit dress Delaine had given her. Earl Grey, duded up in his blue service dog cape, stood at attention beside her. All around them guests greeted one another, sipped flutes of champagne, and buzzed excitedly about the documentary screenings that were about to begin.

"Theodosia." Timothy was suddenly at her side, looking

thin and elegant in a severely tailored tuxedo with a bright blue cummerbund.

"Timothy," said Theodosia. "An excellent turnout." Timothy was always going on about "numbers" and "impressions." A far cry from the old days before money was tight and all he cared about was a show or exhibition that appealed to a limited audience.

But Timothy didn't want to chitchat about marketing success tonight. He leaned in so close Theodosia could smell his aftershave lotion. "Have you gleaned anything more from Tidwell?" he asked.

"Not really," she told him. Theodosia wondered if it was common knowledge yet that Tidwell was questioning Nina about the photo image that had turned up on Jordan Cole's camera. Then she figured that if Timothy knew, he would have mentioned it straight off.

Normally composed to the point of being a martinet, Timothy was fidgeting tonight. "I'm upset that Burt Tidwell keeps coming back to Isabelle. And all because she worked on Jordan Cole's final film. It's preposterous, really."

"Yes," responded Theodosia. "It is rather disconcerting." She looked around for Isabelle, finally located her across a sea of folding chairs, chatting with a group of people. Isabelle glanced over once, saw Theodosia talking with her grandfather, then seemed to renew her efforts at being sociable. Isabelle appeared to be giving both of them a wide berth tonight. Theodosia wasn't sure if Timothy had learned about Isabelle's previous relationship with Jordan Cole or if he was still in the dark. Whatever the case, she didn't want to be the one to bring it up.

Parker Scully was suddenly at her elbow. "They're going to start the screenings any minute now, so we should probably get the star over to his group." He gazed down at Earl Grey with affection. "Want me to take care of that?"

Theodosia nodded as she handed Parker the leash. Earl

Grey was going to appear onstage when they introduced the Big Paw documentary. He was one of the first dogs to complete therapy dog training with them and it was a real honor for him to be present tonight.

"Okay then," said Parker as the two of them trotted off together. "Time for your close-up."

"You'll continue to keep your eyes and ears open?" asked Timothy, still hovering. "As we discussed?"

"Of course," said Theodosia, feeling awful. It seemed that every new revelation was something that had to be kept quiet or couldn't be discussed freely with Timothy. Theodosia hoped with all her heart that Burt Tidwell and his crackerjack team of detectives would wrap this investigation up fast. Because it was killing her.

And then Parker Scully was back to escort Theodosia to her seat.

"How's he doing?" she asked as the lights began to dim and a spotlight lit the front of the auditorium. She was worried that the crowd might make Earl Grey nervous and had taken the precaution of feeding him only half a cup of kibbles tonight.

"He's a champ," Parker assured her. "He'll do fine."

This evening, Linus Gillette was doing the honors at the podium. He thanked everyone for supporting the first-ever Charleston Film Festival, put in a somewhat heavy-handed plug for the newly named Trident Media, and then gave a short but heartfelt introduction of the documentaries. There would be three films, he told them. All quite wonderful, all deserving of an award.

And then Melinda Ash, current executive director of Big Paw, emerged, leading Camille, a hearing dog, and Earl Grey, their star therapy dog. The trio was followed by Cleo McLean, a longtime volunteer, who led Elmo, another hearing dog, and Honey Bee, a seizure-alert dog.

A spatter of applause began in front, then built to a

deafening roar. The dogs pricked up their ears and looked around expectantly, as if to say, *All this for us? Gee, thanks.*

"Thank you," said Melinda, taking her place at the podium and addressing the audience. "When we undertook the task of bringing service dogs to Charleston some four years ago, we never dreamed we'd enjoy such success. Or that we'd receive so many requests." She gave a sad smile as she gazed out over the crowd. "Please, enjoy this film about our amazing dogs and the many tasks they perform for our clients. And realize how many people with disabilities are on waiting lists to receive dogs like these."

"Woof," said Earl Grey, adding impetus to Melinda's words.

Theodosia's heart was near bursting with love for her dog. He looked so serious standing there on stage. As though he knew he was truly an ambassador for his fellow canines. Haley and Drayton, who were sitting in the row behind her, clapped and stomped as the dogs once again received an enthusiastic hand.

And then the documentaries began.

First, of course, was *Cold Nose, Warm Heart: The Service Dogs of Big Paw*. Theodosia was thrilled to see the footage of Earl Grey at the O'Doud Senior Home. One of the residents, who was blind and wheelchair-bound, didn't have a lot of options for activity. But when he tossed a rubber ball for Earl Grey, the dog would bump and bounce his way down the hallway, skittering on the linoleum and painting an audio picture for the man. Then Earl Grey would bring the ball back and snuggle affectionately in his lap.

The Last Confederate Funeral was the second film. It chronicled that somber yet amazing weekend in April of 2004 when the crew of the Hunley, the submarine that disappeared during the Civil War, were finally given a proper funeral and burial. Reenactors from all over the eastern seaboard took part and a crowd of 50,000 people lined the

streets of Charleston to watch horse-drawn limbers carry the
bodies to Magnolia Cemetery.

The final film was a wonderful documentary titled *The
Pelicans of Cat Island.* Located near Beaufort, the Cat Island
footage gave a marvelous, never-before-seen glimpse of the
rare white pelicans that resided there.

At the cocktail party following the screenings, Theodosia ran
into Kassie Byrd.

"More tough voting choices?" Kassie asked her.

"Once again, the films were all great," said Theodosia.
"But I did disqualify myself from voting on the Big Paw
documentary."

"I love that about you," said Kassie. Then added, "I wish
you were judging tomorrow night."

"That's when your film's being screened?"

Kassie nodded. "*Low-country Ghosts.* Got my fingers
crossed."

And then they were both engulfed by friends and film fans.
Delaine was clutching the arm of C. W. Dredd, introducing
him around, looking as though she never wanted to let go.

"Hi, Theo," purred Delaine. "I decided it would be great
fun to introduce C.W. to some of my friends."

"And you *do* seem to know everyone," said C.W. His eyes
twinkled as he gazed at Theodosia. "Hello there, tea lady.
Nice to see you again."

"Hello," said Theodosia, giving him only a cursory glance.
Instead, she turned her full focus on Delaine. "You and I need
to talk."

Delaine frowned slightly. "Right now? Surely it can wait
until later."

Theodosia put a firm hand on Delaine's elbow and pulled
Delaine toward her. "I promise I'll give her back," she told
C. W. Dredd.

"Hey, no problem," said C.W., looking slightly relieved. "Take your time."

"Well, that wasn't very nice," said Delaine, beginning to pout. "C.W. and I were just getting to know each other. And I think we're quite simpatico, if you know what I mean."

"This will only take a second," said Theodosia.

"What's so important?" asked Delaine, tapping the toe of her stiletto.

"Nina's here tonight. I think we should talk to her."

Delaine pretended to look confused. "About what?"

"Don't play dumb with me, Delaine," said Theodosia. "You know exactly what I'm talking about. This is the perfect time to confront Nina about her relationship with Jordan Cole."

Delaine's lip curled. "I thought Detective Tidwell was going to do that. He represents the law, after all."

"For all I know he *has* talked to her," said Theodosia. "But I have a feeling Nina van Diedrich is more likely to pour her heart out to us than to Burt Tidwell. He has a rather nasty habit of bullying people."

Delaine's eyes suddenly widened and her face contorted. "Oh! Speak of the devil," she said under her breath. "Better shush." Nina van Diedrich was slaloming toward them through the crowd.

"What are you ladies shushing about?" asked Nina. An inquisitive gleam lit her eyes.

But Delaine was adept at handling sticky social situations. "We're talking about who best deserves the award in the short film category," she said, offering up a smooth, face-saving white lie.

"I think they should all win," added Theodosia. "A three-way tie."

Nina rolled her eyes. "That just isn't possible. The whole concept behind a film festival is to give out *one* award in each category."

"Well, we know *that*," said Delaine.

Nina's eyes suddenly honed in on Theodosia's blue dress. "I see you're wearing my favorite dress."

"You really covet it, don't you," said Delaine, suddenly sounding more than a little catty.

"You're still going to get one for me?" Nina asked Delaine. "I'm crazy about this black cocktail dress I'm wearing, but it doesn't hold a candle to Theo's blue dress."

Delaine offered a simpering smile. "I'll *try* to get another, but I'm afraid I can't make any promises."

"Maybe if I arranged a little something for us," said Nina, a sly smile crossing her face, "it might put you in a more generous frame of mind. Willing to return a favor of sorts."

"What on earth are you talking about?" asked Delaine.

"What if I told you I could arrange a séance?" Nina murmured.

Delaine's eyes suddenly went round. "Seriously? You mean at the Belvedere Theatre?" She could barely control her excitement.

Now Nina was the one who looked like the pussycat who'd swallowed a whopping big canary. "I can take care of everything," said Nina. "What say we all get together tomorrow at five o'clock? I know for a fact the theater will be empty then."

"Interesting idea," said Theodosia. But what was Nina really up to?

"I'll handle all the details," promised Nina. "I even know a woman, a genuine psychic, by the name of Zelda Keen. She can act as medium for us."

"It *does* sound awfully exciting," said Delaine, casting a hopeful, inquiring glance at Theodosia.

Theodosia had a decision to make. She could step on Burt Tidwell's toes and confront Nina right now, ask her point-blank about her relationship with Jordan Cole. Or she could let this little séance scenario play out. Maybe, possibly, Nina had some sort of confession to make. And Theodosia simply needed the right venue from which to pry it out of her. As well as a modicum of encouragement.

"Okay, Nina," said Theodosia. "Count me in."

"Me for sure," squealed Delaine.

"You know, ladies," said Nina. "I do have an ulterior motive for staging this séance."

"Oh really?" said Delaine.

Now what? wondered Theodosia.

Nina reached into her jeweled clutch purse and pulled out a folded piece of paper. "I received this yesterday." She held it out stiffly and Theodosia was the one who accepted it.

"What is it?" asked Delaine as the paper was unfurled.

"Not sure," said Theodosia, scanning the note. "All it says is *Be prepared for an encore.*" She rubbed a corner of the paper between her thumb and forefinger. The paper was very similar to the strange note she'd received yesterday. Maybe, Theodosia decided, she should nose around some of the local stationery stores.

"*Encore,*" puzzled Delaine. "What's that supposed to mean?"

"No idea," said Nina. "But I plan on asking Zelda Keen what she thinks. See if she picks up any weird vibes."

"An encore is a repeat performance," said Theodosia. "If you ask me, this note sounds like some kind of warning."

"Oooh," gasped Delaine, clearly intrigued. "Creepy."

15

❧

"*You're sure I* can't give you a ride home?" asked Parker Scully. He was standing with Theodosia and Earl Grey outside the Heritage Society on the recently installed patio. Palm trees swayed in the slight evening breeze, a small waterfall pattered delicately down a tumble of stones and swirled in a miniature pond where tiny golden fish darted. Other guests had spilled outside, too, and were milling about. Some sat at wrought-iron tables, others were shadowy figures wandering through foliage that seemed to have spurted and grown at an accelerated pace.

"Thanks, but no thanks," said Theodosia as she tried to gently reel in Earl Grey. He'd been wagging his tail, sniffing at everyone who drifted past them, obviously still charged up from his stage appearance. "The walk will do us both good. Give Mr. Earl Grey a chance to stretch his legs and relax before bed. And help me clear my head."

"Your head needs clearing?" asked Parker. "You've got problems spinning around inside that clever brain of yours?"

He reached a hand up, rubbed gently at the base of Theodosia's neck.

"Not big problems, just . . . dumb stuff," she told him, relaxing at the touch of his fingers. Parker was hitting the pressure points and little knots of tension were dissolving like magic.

Parker smiled a lazy smile. "My little Sherlock Holmes," he murmured. "Hot on the trail of the bad guys."

"Not really."

Parker cocked his head sideways and his blue eyes were suddenly piercing. "You're telling me you're *not* doing your own brand of sleuthing?"

"Not exactly," said Theodosia.

"Yeah, right," said Parker. "Hey." And now he stopped rubbing and put both arms around her. "I worry about you. You're one of those people who go charging in, full speed ahead."

"Drayton's been talking again," said Theodosia. She was pretty sure Drayton had spilled at least some of the beans to Parker.

"Drayton is a very wise man," responded Parker. "Who worries about you. Almost as much as I do."

"Please don't *worry* about me," said Theodosia. That was the last thing she wanted. To cause someone distress.

"The thing is, you get involved in these bizarre investigations," said Parker.

"Only peripherally," said Theodosia.

"You put yourself in harm's way."

"I'm in no danger, truly," responded Theodosia. *Oh yeah? What about that note that lured me to the theater? That could have turned out badly.* "Look," said Theodosia. "I'll be fine, really."

"Are you talking about tonight or in general?" asked Parker.

"Both," said Theodosia.

That seemed to satisfy Parker for the moment, for he pulled her even closer and kissed her. A nice, intense, full-on smacker that went on and on until she was practically breathless.

"What say we . . ." began Parker. But Earl Grey had suddenly wrapped his leash around their collective knees and was pulling so tight he was about to cut off circulation.

"Hey, ease off, boy," said Parker, grabbing Earl Grey's collar and guiding him in a circle around them. "You got us all tangled up." He cocked an eye at Theodosia. "Did you teach him that? To be a chaperone?"

"No, just a therapy dog." Theodosia laughed.

"Well, I could use a little more of our brand of therapy," murmured Parker. And he kissed her again.

A few minutes later, Theodosia was on her way home. Still feeling warm and tingly from Parker's embrace, but also letting thoughts of Nina's note and the upcoming séance percolate in her brain.

Tugging at his leash, almost strutting as he walked ahead of her, Earl Grey snapped at fluttering white moths that had emerged from Jessamine bushes to revel in the velvet darkness.

And Gateway Walk *was* dark tonight. For some reason, Theodosia had assumed that scores of tonight's film attendees would be walking home this same way. That there would be a veritable parade of people along the four-block route. But no soft snatches of conversation floated back at her, no patter of footsteps echoed behind her.

"Weird," she murmured, stepping up her pace a bit.

It wasn't until she'd crossed King Street and passed through the wrought-iron Governor Aiken gates that she heard the first hint of someone behind her.

Not really a footstep, more like a scrape. Like a shoe catching on the uneven surface of one of the paver stones.

Theodosia paused at the rose garden and, like a cartoon bubble forming above her head, her silent words were, *Who's there?*

But now the night was silent, save for the whirring chirp of a few cicadas.

Nothing, she told herself. *Just hearing things.* Then she suddenly recalled the words inscribed on a nearby plaque.

> *Through hand-wrought gates, alluring paths*
> *Lead on to pleasant places,*
> *Where ghosts of long forgotten things*
> *Have left elusive traces.*

Ghosts, she thought to herself. And wondered why the ghost thing kept coming up.

And then . . . *snap!*

Theodosia's heart lurched in her chest. Her hand jerked sharply, telegraphing to Earl Grey that something was possibly amiss. He paused in mid stride, looked up at her, concern flickering in his limpid brown eyes.

Was someone following her? she wondered. Or was she just jumping at shadows?

Yes. Probably. Jumping at shadows. Stop being so silly.

"C'mon, boy," she murmured reassuringly to him as they walked on. After all, her dog was with her. Granted, Earl Grey was a therapy dog, not an industrial-strength *guard* dog, but a large dog offered a significant presence, didn't it?

Nearing the Gibbes Museum of Art now, Theodosia noted that a few lights burned in upstairs windows. Probably, she decided, there was some sort of meeting going on. An acquisitions committee. Pondering over the purchase of some marvelous oil painting or charcoal drawing. Or volunteers planning a fund-raiser. Whoever was behind her was proba-bly late for one of those meetings.

And when she finally emerged at Meeting Street, golden drips and drops of light from the wrought-iron streetlamps pooled at her feet in a most reassuring manner. Stretching to her left and right, stately Charleston mansions that had stood for a century also lent a feeling of solidity and safety.

Theodosia and Earl Grey crossed the street and took the path that passed along the right side of the Circular Con-gregational Church. They were headed into the part of Gateway Walk that was the darkest now. Of course, it was also the most beautiful. Gigantic boxwoods, yews, and azal-eas formed a leafy bower around them. Pittosporum stretched overhead. Arbors and trellises heavy with foliage were tucked enchantingly along the walkway.

Ssst!

The sound came out of nowhere. Unexpected. Chilling. A hiss that was both eerie and yet somehow personal in na-ture.

This time Theodosia definitely knew she was being tar-geted.

She stood stock-still. "What?" she called out. Earl Grey snapped his head around, looking alert and very on guard.

A low chuckle floated back at her. Closer now, but off to her left. Theodosia tried to concentrate, to ascertain if the sound had been made by a man or woman, but it was too hard to tell.

"Not funny," said Theodosia. And then she continued walking. Not running, but definitely moving with purpose.

Chink!

A small rock landed on the sidewalk ahead of her, then skipped off to the side.

What the . . . ?

Some idiot was pitching rocks at her!

There was the soft rustle of leaves and then a larger rock

hit just ahead of her. Almost the size of a tennis ball, it smacked hard on the pavement, then spun wildly away.

"Stop it!" she called.

More laughter floated toward her. Mirthful, but with a nasty, harsh undertone. As though whoever was doing this was having a good deal of fun at her expense.

"Owrrr!" Earl Grey yelped sharply, then spun in anger and surprise. Another rock had sailed out of the darkness and clipped him in the hindquarters.

That was enough for Theodosia. She wasn't a coward. In fact, her first instinct was to stand her ground and have it out. But with no weapon at her disposal and feeling vulnerable in the darkness, this was no time to be reckless.

Theodosia and Earl Grey took off running.

Now she could definitely hear footfalls behind her.

Conditioned from countless morning and evening jogs through White Point Gardens along the Battery, Theodosia and Earl Grey fairly raced down the narrow path. Crape myrtle slapped at her shoulders, wisteria grabbed at her ankles. She knew if they could make it to St. Philip's Cemetery, there would be any number of gravestones, monuments, and statues to duck behind for cover.

They dove behind a white marble sarcophagus topped by a statue of a kneeling angel just as a hail of rocks came down upon their heads. Luckily, there was a shelflike projection at the base of the angel that they could snug themselves under.

Angry to the point of boiling, Theodosia motioned silently to Earl Grey, telling him to lie still. Then she quickly gathered up as many of the rocks as she could.

"Joshua fought the battle of Jericho," she muttered to herself as she half stood and peered out into the darkness. "And the walls came tumbling down." Theodosia let fly the rocks, one after the other. Sending them soaring into the nearby bushes.

On the fifth rock, she was rewarded with an angry gasp. She'd finally found her target. Good. She wound up like a major league pitcher and slung the last three rocks in the same general direction. Then Theodosia grabbed Earl Grey's leash and they took off.

This time they were flying down Gateway Walk, pounding the pavement hard, revved up into overdrive.

They burst out onto Church Street and never let up their pace for the next two blocks. Until they reached the back door of the Indigo Tea Shop.

Upstairs, safe and secure, Theodosia put Earl Grey to bed with a kiss and a few gentle pats. Then she wandered into her bedroom and gazed at herself in the mirror.

Her hair swirled about her head like Medusa. There was a small scratch above her left eye. Her blue dress carried a wide smear of dirt and the hem drooped.

"What a night," she muttered. "From exhilarating to utterly crappy in the space of about ten minutes."

Pulling the dress and everything else off, feeling world-weary yet relieved, Theodosia climbed into the shower and stood under the hot, soothing jets.

Who, she wondered, had been so intent on spooking her tonight? And with all that rock tossing, had they intended serious harm?

Ideas circled inside Theodosia's head like chase lights on a theater marquee.

Finally, makeup removed, hair combed out, fresh cotton nightgown swaddling her, she tiptoed over to her bedroom window and looked out. Tops of trees swayed gently in the night air. Moonlight dappled the peaked and gabled roofs. A few lights twinkled from second-story bedrooms. Charleston's historic district presented a picture-perfect image of peace and tranquility.

She wondered if danger was still lurking out there.

Theodosia gave a deep sigh as weariness overtook her.

Better, she decided, that she not tell Parker about the rock throwing. He'd just worry all the more.

She crawled into bed and pulled the comforter up to her chin. But it was a long time before she was able to fall asleep. And when she did, she dreamt of a strange bird with a wagging tongue.

16

❦

"You made it," purred Constance as she bustled across the lobby of Channel Eight, soon to be known as Trident Media, to greet Theodosia. "And you look just great, too. Perfect for an on-camera interview."

Dressed in a wrap dress with a blue-and-white design slightly reminiscent of Japanese kimono fabric, and feeling recharged this morning, Theodosia was hoping to tape her commentary as quickly as possible and hurry back to the tea shop.

"We'll just pop into Studio B," said Constance. Without waiting for a reply, she headed down a long hallway hung with large, bright corporate-looking oil paintings and some so-so fiber artwork. Theodosia followed closely on Constance's heels. Praying Abby Davis didn't come flying out like a harpy to accost her.

They pushed through a heavy door that gave a pneumatic hiss and entered a large TV studio. Though dimly lit and devoid of people, the studio was cluttered with cameras, cables, lights, and all manner of equipment. Over in one corner loomed the large, boomerang-shaped news desk. It was dark now, but come six o'clock it would be lit like a three-ring circus and filled with carefully made-up talking heads. In another corner was a full kitchen with acres of counter space. Theodosia had worked in that studio kitchen last year when she'd taped her tea segments.

"What I thought we'd do," said Constance, all bustle and business, "is have you sit on this stool . . . here." She indicated a tall wooden stool set against a backdrop of white seamless paper. "And I'll toss a few leading questions to you."

"Okay," said Theodosia. Easing herself onto the stool, she was suddenly reminded of the murder that took place behind the white scrim at the Belvedere Theatre. And the thought chilled her so much goose bumps rose on her arms.

Whoa, girl, take it easy, she admonished herself. *Just 'cause you're fixated on that murder, and some moron put a scare in you last night, doesn't mean you have to go all jittery.*

"Relaxed?" asked Constance.

"Sure," lied Theodosia.

"Just answer any way you feel like," instructed Constance. "As you probably know, my questions won't be heard in the final edit, just your comments. And we'll probably use whatever you say as voice-over for footage we've already shot."

"Got it," said Theodosia. "You pretty much want a PR narration, right?"

"Right," said Constance. She picked up a set of headphones and adjusted them on her head. "Tully!" she suddenly shrieked.

The lights in the control room snapped on suddenly and a young man came flying out the door.

"Yes, Constance," he answered.

"Whenever you're ready," she said coldly. She turned to Theodosia. "New intern."

"Where's Raleigh?" asked Theodosia. He was the long-suffering cameraman who had been at the tea shop the other night. The one who had worked with Constance for any number of years.

"Control room." Constance nodded toward a long window that oozed blue light. "Managing the board."

Tully attached a tiny microphone to Theodosia's collar. As if by magic, the overhead klieg lights snapped on and Theodosia was bathed in bright light.

"Not too bright," she told Tully. Theodosia knew from previous TV experience that bright overhead lighting often made for dark circles under the eyes.

"Not to worry," said Tully. "I'll give you plenty of fill." He pulled two tripod lights close to her, turned them on, fiddled with each for a few moments. Then he was behind one of the large cameras, edging it toward her on silent pneumatic wheels. "You look great," said Tully. "Now say something."

Theodosia looked directly into the camera, smiled, and said, "Something."

Tully pulled on his headset and began talking directly with the control room. "Okay? Not too hot? Yeah. Here, too." He leaned around toward Constance. "We'll roll tape on your say-so."

"Go," said Constance.

"Go," said Tully.

Then Constance was firing questions at Theodosia from her prepared list. How did the notion for a Charleston Film Festival come about? Do you think the fact that they were able to attract big-name directors helped with attendance? As a festival judge, what are the criteria you use for judging a film's merit?

Theodosia answers were breezy, truthful, and right to the point. She knew Constance would probably use just snips and snatches of her words anyway. Most TV editing was all about sound bites. Not much story, really. Just a hot music track with some hard edges you could cut to and a few snatches of voice-over. Besides, how long would the promo piece run, anyway? Thirty seconds? Probably.

"That's a wrap," yelled Constance. And the hot lights were blessedly dimmed.

"Well done," came a deep voice from the corner.

Theodosia blinked, but could see nothing but bright spots dancing in front of her eyes.

Then Linus Gillette emerged from the shadows and walked across the studio toward her. "We sure appreciate your doing this."

"No problem," said Theodosia.

"You're a natural," said Linus.

Theodosia shrugged. "Not really, but it's kind of you to say so."

"Did we ever talk about giving you a permanent segment on *Windows on Charleston?*"

Right, thought Theodosia. *Especially when Abby Davis, the host of* Windows, *hates my guts.*

"No, we didn't," put in Constance, eager to score points with her boss. "But we should."

"I'm afraid that wouldn't be possible," said Theodosia. "Since most of my mornings are taken up at the tea shop."

Linus spread his arms in a munificent gesture and let forth a rolling laugh. "But this is *television.*"

"And the Indigo Tea Shop is a thriving, hands-on business," said Theodosia. "Really," she demurred. "It's what I do."

"Suit yourself," snapped Constance.

Linus Gillette watched as Tully unclipped Theodosia's microphone. "And how is our new intern doing?"

"Coming along," said Constance in a grudging tone.

"He did a great job," volunteered Theodosia. She figured somebody had to give the kid a word of encouragement.

Tully gave her a quick wink. "Thanks," he muttered under his breath.

"We'll have this edited together when?" Linus asked Constance.

"Probably by early afternoon," Constance assured him.

"You know," said Linus, leaning toward Theodosia in a conspiratorial manner, "this matter with Jordan Cole has been very upsetting."

Constance nodded in agreement. "Very upsetting." Although she didn't look all that upset.

"As a sponsor we're concerned with . . . what would you call it?" said Linus. "With possible blowback. From the terrible circumstances this past Sunday. The accident."

"You mean the murder," said Theodosia.

Linus looked suddenly unhappy. "The last thing I want is for Trident Media to get hung out to dry on this."

"Why would that happen?" asked Theodosia.

"Oh," said Linus, stroking his chin thoughtfully, "if this story somehow spun out of control. But, of course, that's not going to happen. And I've had assurances from the Charleston police that they're working round the clock on this."

Tully pulled the two tripod lights away from where Theodosia was still seated. "Did you know that Jordan Cole used to be an intern here?" he asked.

Linus and Constance instantly turned their heads in tandem and frowned at him.

"First I've heard," said Theodosia. She gazed at Linus.

"Years ago," said Linus, waving a hand. "And he wasn't even a very proficient intern. In fact, I think we probably fired him. Always trying to run things *his* way."

"Imagine that," said Theodosia. "His directorial skills emerged early on."

Linus shook his head. "I'm just glad that whole mess last Sunday hasn't cast a pall over the rest of the film festival. And our rehabbed Belvedere Theatre."

"It is a beautiful theater," agreed Theodosia.

"It should be," said Linus, proudly. "I was on the restoration board."

"Pardon?" said Theodosia.

"For the Belvedere Theatre," said Linus. "I was the one who was most instrumental in bringing in architects and restoration specialists."

"I understand a huge amount of work was done," said Theodosia.

Linus grimaced. "You don't know the half of it. They had to remove sheet-metal cladding that had been installed in a bad nineteen fifties modernization effort. That was a monster. Then there was the restoration of all the interior cornices and parapet balustrades. And, of course, all new seating had to be created."

"Well, it looks amazing now," said Theodosia.

"You know the light fixtures that extend around the proscenium?" he asked.

Theodosia nodded, although her mind had long since jumped into hyperdrive.

"All those had to be recast," said Linus. "A costly and time-consuming process."

"Sounds like you know that old theater rather well," said Theodosia.

"Like the back of my hand," crowed Linus. "I've crawled through the rafters, scoured the subbasement, and hung over the edge of the balcony."

But did you ever take a ride in the dumbwaiter? wondered Theodosia, as she suddenly saw Linus Gillette in a whole new light. *Or write a threatening note?*

17

❦

So, of course, Theodosia was the last one to drop off her ballot. Carla Wilf, the receptionist at Crash and Burn Studio, told her so.

"Sorry about that," said Theodosia. "Hope it's no trouble for you."

Carla shrugged from behind the antique library table that served as the front desk. "Not really." She was a forty-something woman in tight jeans, a Tweety Bird T-shirt, and the occasional blond dreadlock clipped into her rather wild, shoulder-length blond hair. A flower child stuck in a sort of time warp, but probably the perfect receptionist for the sort of artsy business Crash and Burn had turned out to be.

"This is a great-looking studio," commented Theodosia. Crash and Burn was located on the first floor of a rehabbed warehouse in the French Quarter, that area in Charleston around Philadelphia Alley, State Street, and Queen Street that had blossomed into a mixture of offices, studios, trendy bars, and gift shops. The floors were genuine cypress and the

walls were a sort of Tuscan yellow brick. Two red-leather director's chairs and a pair of club chairs in a black-and-white
Holstein cow pattern served as lobby seating. A squiggle of
pink neon formed a free-form sculpture.

On the walls were dozens of framed photos that depicted
Crash and Burn's various editing suites. Other photos featured well-known directors who'd worked there, as well as
actors who'd done voice work there—what the industry
called Foley work, redubbing sound and sound effects into
motion picture footage.

"So, you're enjoying our wall of shame?" asked Carla.

"It's a lot of fun," Theodosia told her as she studied the
various photos. "I actually recognize some of the people."

"Oh sure," said Carla. "We get lots of actors through
here. Although most of them are C-list as opposed to A-list,
if you really want to know the truth. Say, do you want to say
hi to Homer?

"Why not," said Theodosia. "If he isn't too busy."

"I'll buzz him." A half dozen silver bracelets jangled on
Carla's wrist as she punched buttons.

"You guys even do underwater filming," said Theodosia,
pointing at a color photo that showed a salmon-colored reef
with a cloud of blue and yellow striped fish hovering nearby.
"Wait a minute, Crash and Burn doesn't do actual filming,
you only do editing."

Carla waved a hand. "Yeah, but the underwater stuff is
Homer's big thing. He's a real dive freak. Always taking
trips down to Belize or Barbados."

"Homer's a diver," said Theodosia, suddenly thinking
about the bang stick that had killed Jordan Cole.

"Best sport in the world," said Homer Hunt as he crossed
the lobby toward her. "Hello, nice to see you again."

Theodosia spun around to face him and shake his out-
stretched hand. "I've done a little snorkeling, but diving
always seemed a little risky," she told him.

"Nonsense," said Homer. "It's perfectly safe if you take the right precautions."

"The shark thing is what makes me nervous," said Theodosia.

"Sharks can be a factor," admitted Homer. He tapped the photo she'd been studying. "This dive, off the coast of Tobago, we encountered a whole pod of Caribbean reef sharks. Luckily they had other things on their primitive little brains that day."

"But what if you really had to defend yourself?" asked Theodosia. "Would you use one of those stun sticks?"

Homer shook his head. "I'm an avid spear fisher. So a JBL Woody, a type of sling spear, is my weapon of choice." He grinned and the lower half of his face seemed to float widely atop his stalklike neck. "Nothing like nailing a grouper or sea bass."

"Sounds exciting," said Theodosia, although she really didn't think it did. She wasn't anti-fishing or even anti–spear fishing. She ate fish, *loved* fish, in fact. She just didn't feel the need to dive into the briny depths, confront her future entrée, and lance it in person.

"Say now," said Homer, eyeing her. "You're not going by the Belvedere Theatre today, are you?"

"I wasn't planning to," said Theodosia. "But I could make a stop if there's something you need. It's on my way."

"You're a dear," said Homer. "I have a box of award statues that need to be delivered."

"Sure," said Theodosia, without much enthusiasm. "No problem."

The trophies were tall and flangelike. Artsy bordering on ugly, they rattled like crazy in the back of her Jeep. Theodosia breathed a sigh of relief when she pulled up in front of the Belvedere Theatre. Now her only problem was finding somebody to help schlep them in. But there should be somebody at the theater, shouldn't there? It was getting close to lunchtime and more film screenings were scheduled for tonight.

Theodosia stood in the empty lobby and gazed around. Her first thought was, *Oh no, not this again*, until she heard voices coming from the back of the theater. She pushed open one of the side doors, sped through the auditorium itself, and emerged in back.

Nina was standing there, giving final instructions to a handful of volunteers. She almost did a double take when she saw Theodosia. "Theodosia? What are *you* doing here?"

Theodosia pointed with her thumb toward the theater lobby. "I've got the award statues. Homer asked me to deliver them."

"Bless you," said Nina, putting a hand to her chest. "At least someone is pitching in to help." She faced her volunteers once again. "So everyone needs to be back here by six o'clock, is that understood?" Heads nodded as Nina broke away from the group. "You need help carrying them in?" asked Nina.

"Yeah, there are two boxes. More bulky than heavy."

As they made their way through the auditorium, Nina put a hand on Theodosia's arm. "It's all set."

"What's all set?" asked Theodosia.

Nina gave a little shiver. "Our séance. Remember?"

"Oh that," said Theodosia. For some reason, she'd forgotten all about it. After last night's mad chase and this morning's rather strange revelations, Nina's séance had completely slipped her mind.

"Five o'clock," Nina told Theodosia. "And then it's off on a journey to the spirit world with Madame Zelda Keen."

"I hope Madame Zelda is prepared to cut a few corners," said Theodosia. "Isn't there another screening of short films tonight? And then the after-party at Solstice?"

"I don't think it's smart to rush these things," cautioned

Nina. "When you pierce the membrane of the spirit world, you have to tread very carefully."

Theodosia stared at Nina. She seemed to be taking this séance very seriously. Of course, just last night she had tried to use this same séance as a bargaining chip to get a blue dress from Delaine.

The blue dress! Wait a minute. Could someone have thought . . . ?

Theodosia stood stock-still as a bizarre thought washed over her. Had she been stalked last night because she'd been wearing that blue dress? Had someone seen Nina flitting around with the blue dress the night before and surmised that it belonged to her?

In other words, thought Theodosia, *did someone follow me last night and toss rocks at me because they thought I was Nina?*

The possibility did exist.

So maybe Nina had nothing to do with Jordan Cole's murder? Or else . . .

Maybe Nina did have a hand in it. And now someone was after her!

A block from the Indigo Tea Shop, Theodosia stopped at Cutter's Stationery and Card Shop. Mrs. Lettie Kern, a woman who'd worked there since time immemorial, greeted her when she walked in.

"Hello, dear," said Lettie. Lettie called everyone dear. Or lamb, if she really liked you.

Theodosia touched an index finger to her collarbone. "It's Theodosia, Mrs. Kern. From the tea shop down the block?"

Recognition dawned on Lettie's lined face and her bright blue eyes danced merrily. "Of course," she said. "All that lovely tea." Lettie's head bobbed and her white pouf of hair moved like fine cotton candy. "And that fellow, Drayton. With the fine manners."

"He's a charmer," replied Theodosia. "But I was wondering if you might help me with something." Theodosia dug in her handbag and pulled out the note she'd received two days ago. "Can you tell me, was this particular notepaper purchased from this store?"

Lettie reached for bejeweled spectacles that dangled around her neck from a bejeweled chain. "Let me take a look, lamb."

Theodosia handed her the paper.

Lettie rubbed the paper between her thumb and index finger, gave it her studious consideration. "Avignon," she finally pronounced.

"Come again?"

"This looks like notepaper by Avignon. From their Heritage collection."

"Lettie," said Theodosia, "do you recall anyone buying a box of this notepaper recently?"

Lettie wrinkled her nose, thinking. "I believe someone might have purchased a box earlier this week."

Good, thought Theodosia, *now we're getting somewhere.*

"Was it a man or woman?"

"Maybe . . . a woman?" said Lettie, though it sounded like she was guessing.

"A young woman?"

"Definitely young," said Lettie, not sounding all that sure.

"Twenties?" asked Theodosia.

Lettie's face telegraphed her confusion. "Perhaps."

"Or maybe a little older?" prompted Theodosia. "Forties?" The possibility existed that Nina might have sent Theodosia a note, then sent another note to herself just to throw people off the trail.

Lettie suddenly looked even more confused. "You know, lamb," she said in a papery voice, "I'll be seventy-eight next month. Everyone looks young to me."

18

❧

"*Thank goodness you're* back," exclaimed Drayton. "I have to make my bombe and I'm sure Mrs. Dimple will go crazy if she has to wait tables all by herself."

"You're talking about a pastry bombe?" asked Theodosia. Sometimes, when she stepped into the Indigo Tea Shop, she never knew what she was stepping into.

"Sort of," hedged Drayton. "It's a dessert for tonight, anyway. The Filmmaker Happy Hour Party at Solstice."

"I think Parker has a pastry chef," said Theodosia. She knew he did. A young man by the name of Jonas Whittaker who made a wicked crème brûlée and a to-die-for flourless chocolate torte.

"Maybe so," said Drayton. "But I offered to bring my famous coconut bourbon bombe and Parker accepted. Therefore I am duty bound to produce said bombe."

"At my expense." Haley laughed. "I had to bake the macaroons for Drayton's crust."

"And a fine crust it's going to be," said Drayton as he hunched over the work space.

While Haley assembled luncheon plates of marinated grilled shrimp, cucumber sandwiches, and chilled grapes lightly coated with sour cream and brown sugar, Drayton crumbled freshly baked coconut macaroons into a bowl.

"You want him out of here?" asked Theodosia. The kitchen was awfully crowded.

Drayton flashed a helpless look, and Haley, taking pity, shook her head.

"No," said Haley. "Drayton's a huge distraction, I'll grant you that. But I'll just work around him. Nothing I haven't done before."

"Once again," said Drayton, in a rather testy tone of voice, "might I point out that I am clearly *present*. That you are talking about me as though I were a rather large lump of pie-crust dough."

"We really do love you, Drayton." Haley chuckled. "Oh, and here's that cream cheese you wanted. Room temperature and ready to go."

"Thank you," came Drayton's soft murmur. "You know I really appreciate all your help."

"And my coconut macaroons," said Haley.

"Especially those," replied Drayton. He uncapped a bottle of bourbon, measured out a quarter cup.

"Hey!" Haley called out to a retreating Theodosia. "That pushy police detective called."

Theodosia ducked her head around the doorway. "Tidwell? What did he want?"

"Said to tell you he's coming over," said Haley. She poked her hair behind her ears. "Like we're supposed to think *that's* some sort of big whoop."

Out in the tea room proper, Miss Dimple was sprinting from table to table as fast as her short little legs could carry her. Upon seeing Theodosia, her eyes lit up, her elflike face relaxed.

"You're here."

"My apologies," said Theodosia. "Sorry to leave you in such a lurch." The tea shop was about half full, but give it another thirty minutes and the place would no doubt be jammed.

"Usually Drayton's out here barking orders at me, but today he's been hiding in the kitchen," said Miss Dimple.

"Making a special dessert," said Theodosia. "Sorry if everything fell on your shoulders, capable as they may be."

Miss Dimple beamed. "Thank you, honey. I'll admit I've been scrambling, but it was also kind of nice not to have Drayton breathing down my neck every single second." She paused and gazed up at Theodosia. "You know what I mean?"

"Yes, I do," said Theodosia. "He can be awfully particular at times." She raised a hand and gave a wave to Brooke Carter Crockett, who was seated by herself across the room. Brooke, a spry white-haired woman with a pixie cut, was the owner of Heart's Desire, an elegant jewelry shop just a few blocks away. Brooke specialized in estate jewelry and was a jewelry designer herself. Brooke had created sterling silver turtle pendants to help raise money for the preservation of the local loggerheads. And she made the most exquisite Charleston charm bracelets. This year's incarnation included a tiny sweetgrass basket, palmetto tree, crayfish, church steeple, wrought-iron bench, bag of rice, and model of Fort Sumter as charms.

"Brooke," said Theodosia, sliding into the chair across from her. "You're just the person I wanted to see."

"Then we're both in luck," said Brooke, "because I wanted to talk to you, too. I had a surprise visitor in my shop earlier today. Someone asking about rings."

"Tidwell," said Theodosia, the name popping out immediately from between her lips. Of course, Tidwell would be talking to local jewelers about the ring she saw—or thought she saw. Tidwell was famous for covering his bases.

"Yes," said Brooke. She leaned forward now and continued in an excited tone. "He mentioned that a particular type of ring might be connected to a recent murder."

"And you knew what he was talking about?" asked Theodosia.

"Pretty much," admitted Brooke. "But I didn't really put two and two together until I came in and talked to Drayton a half hour or so ago. He mentioned that you were right there, in the back of the Belvedere Theatre Sunday night! And that you might have spotted some sort of blue or greenish ring on the killer's hand!" She paused, breathless. "Now I know why Tidwell was so persistent."

So he is taking my witness statement to heart, thought Theodosia. *Isn't that interesting.*

"Tidwell wanted to know about sales of green or bluish-green rings?" asked Theodosia.

Brooke looked shaken. "At first he requested sales records for pretty much all ring sales."

"Did you give them to him?"

Brooke shook her head. "No. But that's how he kicked off his conversation and I must say it shook me a bit. I mean, *all* ring sales? Come on. I have customers who rely on my discretion. Then, once he saw that he'd been able to rattle me, Tidwell asked about specific rings. Blue rings, green rings, large rings."

"You can't sell that many pieces that fall into those categories," said Theodosia. "At least I don't imagine you do."

"Not so many," agreed Brooke. "I looked through my receipts and found maybe two dozen over the last year or two. After that, the records are in storage down in the basement. I told Tidwell he was welcome to tromp down there and paw around."

"Did he?" asked Theodosia.

"No. In fact, he looked rather offended at the suggestion."

"Good that you were able to offend him," said Theodosia. "Kudos to you."

The look of worry suddenly increased on Brooke's face. "The thing of it is Timothy Neville bought a rather large lapis ring for his granddaughter last Christmas."

"For Isabelle?" squeaked Theodosia. "Seriously? And you told Tidwell about this?"

Brooke nodded miserably. "Yes, I pretty much had to. But like I said, I didn't put any of this together, until I talked to Drayton a short while ago. He was going on about how Timothy Neville's granddaughter had fallen under some cloud of suspicion. And then Drayton told me you were looking into things for Timothy. Privately, I mean. So anyway . . . I stuck around so I could talk to you."

It was yet another twist, Theodosia decided. Tidwell had pretty much cleared Isabelle and now this ring thing had come up.

Brooke looked hopeful now. "I wanted to, you know, get you in the loop on this Tidwell thing. You are helping Timothy out, aren't you?"

"I sort of am," mumbled Theodosia.

Brooke reached across the table and clasped her hand over Theodosia's hand. "Good for you, honey. You go on and do your sleuthing. After all, we know you're doggone *good* at it."

When Burt Tidwell came through the front door some forty minutes later, Theodosia was ready for him.

"I think you're barking up the wrong tree," she told him.

Tidwell gazed at her as though she were an escaped mental patient.

"I've discovered a few things you don't know about," Theodosia told him. Then she led him to an out-of-the-way table. "You're less likely to disturb my guests over here."

"I have no intention of disturbing your guests," said Tidwell. He peered at her. "But your nervousness may set them on edge."

"Don't try to change the subject," Theodosia snapped.

"Pray tell, what *is* the subject?"

Theodosia glanced around quickly and saw that Drayton and Miss Dimple had begun ferrying luncheon plates to their guests. Which meant the coast was clear and she could fire away at Tidwell.

"There's more than one suspect walking around out there," said Theodosia. "You continue to focus on Isabelle while there are at least three other suspects that bear looking into."

Tidwell settled back in his chair. "Ah, the ring. Your little friend from the jewelry shop told you about the ring."

"Yes, she did."

"That bears looking into," he replied. "As for Nina van Diedrich, I've had several conversations with her. The woman is scatterbrained and uncooperative to the nth degree. But a murderer? Hmmm . . . doesn't really fit the profile."

"Don't be so sure of that," said Theodosia. And she proceeded to tell him about how she and Earl Grey were followed last night and how someone pitched rocks at them.

"You think it was Nina?" asked Tidwell. Now he looked a trifle more serious.

"I don't know," said Theodosia slowly. "Nina's wacky, I'll give you that. And she had some sort of fling with Jordan Cole. But did she murder him?" Theodosia shrugged. "Don't know. It *does* seem weird that his death doesn't bother her more. After all, they had a relationship."

Tidwell's beady eyes bore into her. "Is that what they had? A relationship?"

Theodosia just shook her head. She didn't really know.

"Tell me more," Tidwell intoned, in a voice that held a

mix of taunt and curiosity. "You said there are *three* suspects. Pray tell, who are the others you're trying to snare in your amateur web?"

So Theodosia told Tidwell about Homer Hunt, the owner of Crash and Burn. Told him how Homer had spoken out so vehemently against Jordan Cole. And was, it turned out, an accomplished scuba diver.

"Interesting," said Tidwell, leaning back in his chair.

"That's all you've got to say?" said Theodosia. "You said you subpoenaed customer lists from dive shops. Maybe you should check to see if Homer's name is on one of them."

He stared at her. "Yes, I do need to make a call."

While Tidwell was fiddling with the buttons on his cell phone, Theodosia raced into the kitchen and grabbed two luncheon plates.

"Say now," said Drayton, looking askance. "Those luncheons are spoken for. Table by the bay window."

"Let Theo take them," said Haley. "We've got lots more food. I can whip up two more plates in about thirty seconds."

"How come you're so agreeable to Theodosia and so finicky with me?" asked Drayton. His words were brusque but a smile played at his lips.

"Because you, my dear Drayton," said Haley, "are an all-fired delight to tease."

"*So* is *Homer* Hunt's name on any of the customer lists from local dive shops?" Theodosia asked.

Tidwell grasped his tea sandwich in his large hands, almost completely enveloping it. "Yes, absolutely," he told her. "But Hunt's name on a list proves nothing. It proves he's a diver, but that is information we already had."

"Huh?" said Theodosia. "I thought you just called your office to check the lists."

"No," said Tidwell, "I called on another matter entirely."

Theodosia was nonplussed. Here she'd thought she was three steps ahead of Tidwell. Turns out she might only be pacing him. And then not by much.

Tidwell rolled his eyes as he bit into his sandwich. "Hunt's photos are plastered all over the walls at his business. He has a spear gun hanging in his office." A dab of cream cheese squirted onto his plate and Tidwell poked at it with a pudgy finger.

"You've already been to Homer's office," said Theodosia. Her voice was small.

"What we *don't* know," said Tidwell, "is if Homer Hunt was present last night. If he was, he could have seen you and got it in his head to pursue you."

"Because . . . why?" said Theodosia.

"Because you don't mind your own business?" offered Tidwell, mildly. "Because you flashed that *Tinseltown Weekly* article to everyone and his brother? Because you might have made him slightly jittery for some reason?"

Theodosia thought for a moment. "We could check easily enough," she said. "To see if Homer was there last night. I'm sure Drayton still has the guest list."

But Drayton didn't need to consult his list.

"Yes, Homer was there," Drayton confirmed. "I chatted with him for a short while." Drayton poured out a steady stream of green tea into Tidwell's cup. "Now you're going to get a treat. That's a Huang Mountain green tea. A 2007 spring pick. Good body, slightly earthy."

"Can you tap Homer Hunt's phone?" Theodosia asked, once Drayton had moved on to another table.

Tidwell gave her a mild stare. "Only if he's a suspected terrorist."

"I'm serious," said Theodosia.

Tidwell shifted his bulk in the creaking chair. "So am I." He picked up his teacup, took an appraising sip of tea. "Yes,

I do taste that earthiness Drayton mentioned. Rather intriguing."

"Linus Gillette," said Theodosia.

Tidwell set his teacup down. "What about Linus Gillette?" He gave nothing away, barely looked interested.

"Cole was an intern for Linus Gillette several years ago. And Linus Gillette served on the Belvedere's restoration committee."

Tidwell's beady eyes seemed to narrow a millimeter. "A tertiary connection, yes," admitted Tidwell. "But what was Mr. Gillette's motive?"

"No idea," murmured Theodosia. But she wasn't about to let a little thing like that stop her.

19

❧

"That detective drives me crazy," Haley told Theodosia after Tidwell had left. "Snooping around here, always trying to pick your brain."

"Not today he wasn't," said Theodosia, feeling somewhat dismayed. She thought she'd developed some original ideas on the murder case; now she just felt deflated.

"And he's always eating our food," said Drayton, reacting to Haley's critical words. "Does the man ever pay? Does he ever spend a *cent*?"

"He left a very nice tip," said Miss Dimple as she pushed by them with a tray full of dirty dishes.

"He did, seriously?" asked Drayton. He brushed at the front of his apron as though he was pondering something. "He never left *me* a tip."

Haley couldn't resist. "Here's a tip," she said, grinning wickedly. "Try to chill out."

"You people." Miss Dimple laughed. She was already making a return trip. "So much camaraderie."

"That's right," quipped Drayton. "We're knee-deep in it."

"It's no wonder I love working here," continued Miss Dimple.

"It's us or the cats, isn't it," said Haley.

"The cats are my fur babies," admitted Miss Dimple. "But for sheer fun and madness, I'd have to pick you folks."

"Green Tea Lotion," murmured Theodosia. She was sitting in her office, trying to put together an order for the cosmetics manufacturer that whipped up her T-Bath products. So far, her line of tea-based cosmeceuticals, as she called them, had been selling very well. Retailed in her shop and on her website, Theodosia's T-Bath line was now being requested by some local gift shops. And wasn't that a retail coup!

"And I need to e-mail a JPEG of the new labels," she reminded herself. She had recently created a facial moisturizer of white tea, ginger, and chamomile that she'd named Chamomile Comfort Lotion. And a white tea and lemon verbena bath oil she called Lemon Aid. And, of course, she still needed a name for her hibiscus, tea, and rose hips nighttime moisturizer.

But Theodosia was finding it difficult to concentrate at the moment. Normally, she dove into projects like this, marketing projects, really, because that's where her expertise was. She'd spent a number of years honchoing product roll-outs, budgets, and creative strategies at one of Charleston's top marketing firms. But today it just wasn't coming together for her.

Like an overworked popcorn popper, her brain was bouncing around ideas concerning Sunday night's murder and tossing out strange possibilities. C. W. Dredd, angry at Jordan Cole because of professional rivalry. Isabelle, who'd been fired from his crew. Nina, who'd had a fling with Cole.

Homer Hunt, who despised the man. And Linus Gillette, who'd fired Cole once before.

A soft knock sounded at Theodosia's office door.

"May I come in?" It was Drayton's muffled voice.

"Yes, and hopefully you're bringing me a cup of tea," responded Theodosia. Honestly, that was exactly what she needed right now.

"You're in luck, dear lady," said Drayton, as he pushed his way in. "Because I did think you might benefit from a cuppa."

"Marvelous," said Theodosia as Drayton placed a small silver tray on top of her desk. It was meticulously arranged, of course. Small Lenox china teapot, matching cup and saucer, miniature sand clock for timing, tiny plate with a lemon wedge and two sugar lumps on it. Shining silver spoon.

"It's Keemun Mao Feng," said Drayton. "So you might want to let it steep another moment or two."

"Goodness," said Theodosia. "I forgot we even had this."

Drayton nodded. "Yes, and that's the problem." He glanced at her eagerly, then took a seat across from her desk on the oversized, overstuffed chair they'd dubbed the tuffet.

"What's the problem?" asked Theodosia. The rich aroma was intoxicating to her. An aromatherapy treatment that invigorated even as it relaxed.

"We have such a marvelous arsenal of teas," began Drayton. "Grown on almost every continent . . ."

"Except Antarctica," said Theodosia, taking a sip.

"Yes," said Drayton. "So I was thinking we should offer a tea menu." He held up a hand. "And not just a handful of teas, like we usually do, but a real list."

"Like a wine list," said Theodosia, catching on to his idea.

"Exactly," said Drayton. "Much like your friend Parker has."

"With everything on it?" asked Theodosia. They had to have at least three hundred different teas sitting in tins on those floor-to-ceiling shelves. Everything from small tea bricks of Puerh and tins of rooibos, to large bins of Darjeeling.

"We don't want to overwhelm our customers with too many choices," responded Drayton. "So maybe select twenty, possibly twenty-five teas, then rotate our lists every week or so. That way our customers will have a better idea of what we have to offer."

Theodosia thought for a few moments. "It's a good idea. No, it's actually a grand idea," she told Drayton. "After all, how long has it been since someone ordered the Pi Lo Chun?" Pi Lo Chun was a delicate green tea from China's Suzhou Province. The growers there planted peach, plum, and apricot trees between the rows of tea bushes so the tea leaves would absorb the fruit fragrances.

"It's been too long," said Drayton. "And what about our Taiwanese Pouchong? I'd love to educate tea drinkers about its slightly fermented flavor."

"Agreed," said Theodosia.

Now Drayton was rolling full speed ahead. "And it's been *months* since I brewed a pot of Hojicha green tea."

"We need to do a little one-line description for each tea," said Theodosia. "You know, like for the Pi Lo Chun, say something like, Picked in early spring, aromatic fruit flavors and buttery finish."

"That's perfect!" declared Drayton. "Just like that. I wouldn't change a word."

"But you're the real tea expert," said Theodosia. "So you have to compose the descriptions."

"With pleasure," said Drayton. And a grin began to form on his lined face. "Of course, I might have to refresh my . . . uh . . . memory from time to time."

Haley stuck her head in the door. "You've got a call from Nina van."

"Me?" asked Drayton.

"No," said Haley. "The boss lady." But Theodosia was already reaching for the phone. She knew exactly what this was about.

"Theodosia!" shrilled Nina. "Just a reminder. Five o'clock sharp."

"I haven't forgotten," said Theodosia, thinking the woman sounded positively manic. What was the clinical term? Manic depressive? Even though Tidwell seemed to have dismissed Nina from his list of suspects, Theodosia got the feeling there might be something bubbling just below the surface.

"Guess what," she told Drayton and Haley when she hung up the phone. "We're going to a séance. Courtesy of Nina van Diedrich."

"You're not serious," said Drayton, looking slightly put out.

"Sure she is," enthused Haley. Then she peered cautiously at Theodosia. "Aren't you?"

Theodosia gave a definitive nod.

"I for one am too old for parlor games," grumbled Drayton.

But Haley was loving the idea. "Very cool. I always wanted to commune with the spirit world."

"And this is to be staged at the Belvedere Theatre?" asked Drayton.

Theodosia nodded. "That's the plan. Nina's actually hired a medium."

"So you're *indulging* this woman?" asked Drayton.

"Delaine's going to be there, too," said Theodosia.

Drayton rolled his eyes. "Oh, that makes it so much more credible. And, more to the point, why the Belvedere Theatre?"

"Because of the murder," said Theodosia. "And the history, of course." Theodosia thought for a moment. "And I want to participate because every time I show up there, something strange happens."

"If you ask me," snorted Drayton. "I think it's more likely you'll end up communing with dust motes and spiders."

"Once again," said Haley, crossing her arms and giving Drayton her best look of reproach. "You're taking the fun out of everything."

"Then how about this," proposed Drayton. "What if the spirits don't want to commune with you? What if they're restless spirits . . . maybe even dangerous spirits . . . desperately searching for a pathway back to their own world?"

Haley grinned from ear to ear. "Now you're talking!"

20

Precisely at five o'clock, Theodosia knocked on the back door of the theater. Three sharp knocks, just as Nina had instructed.

"What's that supposed to be?" was Drayton's snide comment. "The secret knock that admits us to the Hardy Boys' clubhouse?"

The heavy metal door snicked open an inch.

"It's us," said Theodosia, and the door creaked open the rest of the way.

They stepped into darkness. And when their eyes finally adjusted, Nina was standing there in a long black dress, holding a flickering candle.

"Looks like she's in the road company of *Phantom of the Opera*," muttered Drayton, and Haley shot an elbow at him.

Ouch, pantomimed Drayton.

"Come in," beckoned Nina. "Welcome." She was obviously relishing her role as séance hostess.

"We don't have a lot of time," Drayton told her.

"Drayton," said Haley, in a cautionary tone. "These things can't be rushed."

"Not to worry," said Nina. "Everything's set. Delaine's already here along with Madame Zelda."

"Where do you intend to hold this séance?" asked Theodosia. Now that she was here, now that she was playing along with Nina, she was beginning to feel slightly foolish. Tarot cards, astrology, fortune-tellers—it all really did smack of parlor games, just like Drayton had pointed out. Did anyone ever *really* communicate with the spirit world? She didn't think so. Theodosia's parents were both dead and she truly believed that if there was some way to reach her, to assure her they were okay and send their abiding love, they would have done so. Thus far, however, she had received no spiritual telegram, e-mail, or text message from the other side.

Nina led them through a warren of rooms, then out onto the stage to a circular table where Delaine and Madame Zelda were already seated.

"I think this suits our needs perfectly," said Nina. "Close to where the most recent death in this theater took place."

"We're going to sit on the stage?" said Haley. "Wow."

"But there's no audience," Drayton pointed out.

"Not yet," said Madame Zelda, in an ominous tone. She sat at the table, a tiny woman with waves of red hair and a handful of rings.

"I take it that's the medium?" Drayton's voice was a low whisper in Theodosia's ear.

She nodded. "Mm-hm."

"Looks more like a small to me." He kept his eyes focused straight ahead, but mirth tinged his voice.

"Be serious," Haley hissed at him. "Or you're out of here."

Drayton rolled his eyes. "If only."

Delaine, who'd been sitting with Madame Zelda, immediately took charge of the introductions. Upon seeing this,

Nina stepped in and tried to overtalk her. There was a loud burst of chatter, as though a TV set had been cranked up, and then Delaine pumped up her volume.

"I'm hoping we might try to contact the ghost of Perdita," Delaine announced loudly.

"Who's Perdita?" asked Haley. Although she didn't really believe in spirits, she seemed to be having a rollicking good time.

"Ya'll know who Perdita is," Delaine announced to everyone. "She's that European actress who lived on Church Street almost a hundred and fifty years ago." Delaine suddenly put a hand to her forehead, as if she'd just remembered something. "Good heavens, she probably performed in this very theater!"

Drayton gave a low snort.

"Come and join our circle," invited Madame Zelda. "Take your places at the table and we'll commune together—harness the telepathic powers we each possess but are afraid to unleash."

They all sat down as instructed.

Madame Zelda reached into the pocket of her red silk jacket and pulled out a small blue-glass orb. It winked and twinkled in the dim light. "We shall use this orb to help focus our thoughts."

Okeydoke, thought Theodosia. *This really is wacky.*

"Now everyone join hands," instructed Madame Zelda, "and try your best to relax. Breathe in deeply, a cleansing breath, then push it out slowly."

Everyone breathed and cleansed and pushed out.

"That's right," Madame Zelda told them. "Keep breathing deeply until we are all in perfect harmony and our spiritual pathways are clear."

They sat there for three more minutes, breathing in, breathing out. And Theodosia had to admit she did feel more calm, more alert. Of course, she felt the same way when she jogged in the park with Earl Grey. Oxygen was like that. Good for the body and the brain.

Theodosia cast her eyes toward Madame Zelda. The woman was starting to sway gently now. And, strangely enough, there did seem to be a certain filmy aura surrounding her. Or maybe it was just an optical illusion caused by the candlelight.

"We come here," began Madame Zelda, "as knowledge seekers who have opened our hearts and minds."

Well, some of us have, thought Theodosia.

"Eager to be a conduit for greater enlightenment," murmured Madame Zelda.

Theodosia could have sworn a breeze suddenly fluttered across the stage. The candle licked sideways for a few moments and then flickered straight up. Of course, someone could have opened a door somewhere, too. Caused a minute shift in currents or air temperature. That had to be it, right?

Theodosia looked across the table at Delaine, who was suddenly sitting bolt upright in her chair.

She felt it, too. Crazy.

"We ask," intoned Madame Zelda, in a slightly wavering voice, "that you commune with us and move among us."

A low creak sounded off to their left.

Delaine's eyes were suddenly round as saucers. Even Drayton seemed to have tilted his head, listening for something.

"We ask," continued Madame Zelda, her voice rising and falling with great emotion, "that you give us a sign."

They all sat for a few moments, hardly daring to breathe.

And suddenly there *was* a sign.

A low, whooshing sound that seemed to grow louder with each passing second.

Theodosia stared across the dancing flame at Delaine, who suddenly jerked her eyes upward into the rafters. Then a look of supreme horror dawned on her friend's face.

Now what's freaking her out? wondered Theodosia. She tilted her head up to scan the vast depths of the darkened auditorium.

And couldn't quite believe what she saw!

A woman in a shimmering white dress was descending upon them!

Now everyone else, alerted by Theodosia and Delaine's reaction, was suddenly focused on this bizarre apparition, as well.

"What did you *do*?" Nina gibbered to Madame Zelda. "What on earth did you *conjure*?"

"Oh my lord!" screamed Delaine. "It's not of this earth!" She half rose in her chair and threw a hand up in front of her face as if to ward off impending danger. "It *is* a ghost! It's the ghost of Perdita!"

"Yeeeow!" Nina's teeth were actually chattering in her head now. "And it's . . . it's . . . coming to get us!"

"By George!" exclaimed Drayton, looking grim. "We've gone and disturbed something!"

Delaine was on her feet now, screaming at the top of her lungs. "Stay away! Stay awaaaay!"

Even Madame Zelda trembled as the ghostly apparition continued to descend. "What is it you want!" she squawked in a wobbly voice, her throat obviously constricted from fear.

"I can't believe this!" choked Haley. "This is some whacked-out stuff!"

And still the ghost kept coming at them, almost as though it was moving in slow motion, its white silk dress flowing out like a banshee in a horror film.

"This isn't happening," muttered Theodosia. "This isn't happening." She leapt from her chair, stared intently at the bizarre apparition that was hurtling toward them. Blinking, hoping she could summon enough nerve, Theodosia stood her ground as the ghost continued its downward path. At the last minute, she held out a hand and the ghost swooped by, its skirts just grazing the top of the table.

Theodosia felt the ripple of fabric, the swoosh of wind. And not much else. No cold ectoplasm, no ghostly presence, no spectral essence.

Theodosia gazed upward. The ghost had retreated into the rafters above the stage where it hesitated for a long moment. Then, like a bad, recurring nightmare, the ghost made a descent back toward them.

"Take care not to interfere with the spectral vision!" intoned Madame Zelda. For someone who had initially been scared out of her wits, she seemed to have regrouped fairly well.

But something about this descent looked fishy to Theodosia. Maybe it was the fact that the ghost seemed to be following the same trajectory.

"That's no ghost," said Theodosia, in a clear voice that seemed to resonate in the emptiness of the theater. And even though she sounded calm, inwardly Theodosia felt shaky. The way she sometimes felt when she ingested too much sugar.

"What?" screeched Delaine, peeping out from behind clasped fingers that shielded her eyes from the bizarre specter.

Theodosia made her bold move. She stepped into the path of the oncoming ghost, cognizant of the crack and ripple of fabric, the quick rush of air. Throwing up her hands, she was suddenly engulfed in layers of fabric.

"What are you doing?" screamed Nina, as Theodosia appeared to tussle with the creature. "Leave it alone!"

"Good heavens!" exclaimed Drayton. "She's gone and wrangled the darned thing!"

Theodosia struggled with the loose fabric, pulling hard, wrestling with it, trying to gather everything up into a giant ball. "Here's your ghost," she shouted, tugging roughly at the wire that supported it. "This is from the costume shop backstage!"

They stood and stared mutely at the strangely subdued ghost that was now puddled in Theodosia's arms.

"A ghost on a wire," Drayton finally murmured. He followed his comment up with a nervous laugh.

"Someone rigged this to scare us!" said Haley.

"A charade," declared Delaine. She sat down hard on one of the chairs, waved a hand rapidly in front of her face as if to fan herself. "A horrible charade that certainly did scare us." She seemed vastly relieved not to have been claimed by the ghost, yet a little glum she hadn't enjoyed an up close and personal visit with the spirit world.

"The thing is," said Haley, meeting Theodosia's angry, determined stare, "who would do such a rotten thing?"

Theodosia continued to rip at multiple layers of fabric. "That's what I intend to find out!"

By nine o'clock that night, Theodosia was happily ensconced at the Filmmaker Happy Hour Party at Solstice. Though she hadn't attended that evening's screenings, she enjoyed rubbing shoulders with the directors, cinematographers, screenwriters, judges, and fans, most of them familiar faces by now.

Parker Scully stood behind the bar, tossing ice cubes into a silver martini shaker. Theodosia, who was seated at the bar, watched him intently.

With great flourish, Parker set a martini glass in front of her and poured his freshly made concoction into it.

"Here you go," he told her. "A special martini just for you."

Theodosia stared at the stemmed glass. A floating, fluttering white object was suspended in the viscous liquor. "What's that supposed to be?" she asked. It didn't look like any martini she'd ever seen.

A grin split Parker's face. "Séance martini. Vodka, splash of vermouth, and a white anchovy."

Theodosia chuckled in spite of herself. "Drayton told you."

"Yeah, he did."

"It was a pretty bizarre séance," admitted Theodosia.

"Any idea who cooked up the ghost?" asked Parker.

"I'm still working on that," said Theodosia. "Obviously, it's someone who has access to the theater."

"And a grudge against you?" said Parker.

"Maybe." Theodosia eyed her martini again. "This looks awfully exotic. Like something 007 would drink just before he hops into his customized Bentley."

"Taste it," urged Parker. "And it *is* a real drink. Not just something I cooked up in the spirit of the moment. No pun intended."

Theodosia took a sip. It wasn't bad. Then again, it wasn't all that good, either. There was something about that floating anchovy and the oil slick it was leaving.

"I think I'd rather opt for a glass of wine instead," she told Parker.

"Easily done," said Parker. "How's about a Chardonnay?" He was already peering in the cooler and rattling bottles.

"Love it," said Theodosia. Thanks to Parker Scully she was rapidly expanding her wine repertoire. She'd always been a merlot-shiraz-Syrah kind of girl. Now, she was dabbling all across the board. Pinot, Bordeaux, Chardonnay, chenin blanc, frascati, even prosecco and champagne.

"An Aubert," said Parker popping the cork. "Soft with concentrates of lemon and orange peel." He poured two fingers of wine into her glass. "One of Sonoma's finest."

Theodosia picked up the glass by the stem and swirled it gently, releasing some of the bouquet. "Nice."

"Wait till you taste it. Kapow."

She already was. Little bursts of citrus exploded on her

tongue, followed by nuances of soft blossoms. "This is lovely. Is it terribly expensive?"

Parker grimaced, thinking. "Eey . . . maybe seventy bucks a bottle retail?"

"A little pricey then, but worth it," said Theodosia. She took another sip, set down her glass, and sighed.

"Tough day?"

"Strange day," Theodosia told him.

"You're too wound up in this crazy investigation," said Parker.

"I sort of promised Timothy . . ." Her voice trailed off.

"Yeah," said Parker, nodding, "I know. But you can only do so much. You've had to host all those events, serve as film judge, and run your tea shop at the same time." He paused. "Maybe you should throw in the towel. On the investigation, I mean."

"Maybe," she responded.

"But you're not going to, are you?" asked Parker.

"Let me think about it," she told him. "And I promise you, you'll be the first to know."

"Sure," said Parker, topping off her glass. "I bet."

Theodosia took another sip of wine, enjoying the smoothness and the richness of the Chardonnay. She could feel the first gradual effects of the alcohol as it slowly worked its way into her system. She felt relaxed. Like she'd been toting a twenty-pound load on her back and was finally able to put it down.

Parker popped the cork back in the wine. "Unfortunately, you do seem to have a feel for this stuff."

"I've been trying," allowed Theodosia.

"Hey," said Parker. "What say we mosey over to the buffet table and get something to eat. I know for a fact there's some pretty spectacular stuff laid out."

As they pushed their way through the crowd, they ran into Delaine and C. W. Dredd. Delaine looked ecstatic;

C. W. looked like he'd been hog-tied, branded, and dragged along for the ride.

"Theo!" exclaimed Delaine, delivering air kisses. "Parker!" More air kisses. "We were just *marveling* over the delightful spread your chefs put together." She gazed up at C.W. "Weren't we?"

"If you say so," said C.W. His eyes flicked from Theodosia to Parker, then back to Theodosia.

"We just screened the Historical Film category," said Delaine.

"Fun," said Theodosia.

"And C.W. served as one of the judges for the Experimental Film category."

Theodosia grinned at C.W. She rather enjoyed the fact that Delaine had laid claim to him and that he seemed unable to extricate himself.

"Was that ever some crazy stuff," continued Delaine. "So many films by students from local colleges and a few from the Savannah College of Art and Design. They have a video and film program there you know."

"Hard to pick a winner?" asked Parker.

"Lots of whimsy?" asked Theodosia.

"Hard to make money on whimsy," said C.W. "Especially in Hollywood."

Delaine let loose a high, tinkling laugh, as though C.W. had just uttered the most clever bon mot in the history of the world.

"Maybe that's why they call it experimental film," said Theodosia. "Maybe it's also a socioeconomic experiment."

"Socio what?" asked C.W. He threw Theodosia a quizzical look, but Parker was already tugging her arm, guiding her away from him and over to the buffet table.

"Why is it I can't *stand* that guy?" muttered Parker.

"Maybe because he likes me?"

"That's a big part of it," admitted Parker. "But I don't

trust C. W. Dredd, either. There's something slithery about him."

"Maybe he's just used to playing Hollywood politics," said Theodosia. Truth be known, she didn't trust C.W., either. Didn't trust him as far as she could throw him.

"If I was drawing up a suspect list for the murder of that Cole guy," said Parker, "old C.W. would be right there at the top. I hope your buddy Tidwell is keeping an eye on him."

"I'm guessing he is," replied Theodosia.

Parker grabbed a pair of silver tongs, delicately selected three perfect little oysters, and placed them on a small bone china plate for Theodosia to enjoy. "This is one of our new specialties," he told her excitedly. "Hama Hama oysters from Hood Canal, Washington, topped with a mango, lime, and soy salsa."

"Is there a right way to eat these?" asked Theodosia as she picked one up gingerly between her fingers.

Parker nodded. "There sure is. Just let it slide."

Theodosia tilted her head back and did as instructed. The briny little mollusk was tart in her mouth, the salsa a sweet counterpoint. "Good," she told him, thinking about the principles of food chemistry. Salty with sweet, sweet with sour, and so on.

"Ah, oysters," said Drayton, coming up behind them. "Truly one of the ocean's more challenging but rewarding tidbits."

"You're an oyster lover?" Parker asked.

"Point me toward a good South Carolina oyster roast," declared Drayton, "and I am in heaven. Of course, Rappahannocks from Virginia are quite a delicacy, as are Wellfleets from Massachusetts."

"You are an oyster connoisseur," said Parker.

"Are there any more of those pecan turtle bars?" Delaine asked loudly, pushing her way in between Drayton and Parker. "C.W. is positively in *love* with them."

"I think Jonas will be replenishing the dessert section any minute now," said Parker.

As the words slipped from Parker's mouth, the door from the kitchen flew open and the red-faced pastry chef appeared. Someone called to him from the kitchen and Jonas hesitated, balancing two large trays as he answered back, "Chocolate soufflé and a bombe!"

"What?" exclaimed Delaine. "A bomb?"

"No," said Drayton with a laugh, "you don't understand. He's . . ."

"There's a bomb?" shrilled Delaine. "In the kitchen!"

"With coconut . . ." Drayton was trying to explain.

But the buzz of conversation around them had suddenly escalated to a cacophony of shrieks. *Bomb? A bomb in here? Everyone outside!*

Like the old children's game of telephone, the "bomb message" spread from person to person, group to group, like wildfire run amuck.

Guests piled up against each other, shoving their way to the front door.

"Good grief," muttered Theodosia. She watched in vexation as the pandemonium spread across the room, from the buffet table to the bar to the entryway. "What next?"

21

❧

Entering Cotton Duck was like opening Pandora's box. Of course, Delaine's shop didn't look particularly exotic when you were outside on the sidewalk. There, horse-drawn jitneys clip-clopped down cobblestone streets lined with tall, stately brick buildings. But enter Delaine's domain and it was like entering another world. Racks of soft sea-island cotton dresses were jammed next to racks of diaphanous beach cover-ups. A circular rack held long ball gowns and filmy silk wraps to match. Antique highboys and secretaries spilled out offerings of belts with jeweled buckles, strappy sandals, hand-painted silk scarves, bangle bracelets, and beaded handbags.

"Theodosia!" Delaine Dish gazed up from where she was sprawled on the lush Aubusson carpet. She was in the middle of unpacking a giant cardboard box that had obviously just been delivered. Colorful silk skirts and matching shawls spilled out all around her. A commercial steamer billowed puffs of steam, guaranteed to remove the most stubborn wrinkles. "What are you doing here?" Delaine asked.

How to tell her? wondered Theodosia. *That the blue dress she gave me is now sadly in need of repair.*

"Wait!" Delaine scrambled to her feet and teetered toward Theodosia on four-inch stilettos. "You need key accessories, right? A woman always needs key accessories. Do you know, some of the most prestigious fashion columnists, people who are bona fide regulars at Fashion Week in Paris, Milan, and New York, are now saying you can tell a woman's income strata by her shoes and her bag?" Delaine's sharp eyes flitted from Theodosia's shoes—sensible, to her shoulder bag—practical. "Well, it's a *theory* anyway," she said, a slightly sour note creeping into her voice. Then she pulled her act together and put a big smile on her face. "So accessories, Theodosia? Of course, I'm assuming you'll want to wear the blue dress again. For tomorrow night's red carpet event. After all, not that many people got a chance to see it. It's not like you wore it on stage or anything."

No, thought Theodosia. *I just wore it while being terrorized by a maniac.*

"Uh . . . I'm afraid the blue dress needs dry cleaning."

"Something happened?" Delaine eyed her suspiciously. "An *accident*?"

"Just a spot."

"That dog of yours, hmm?" Delaine shook her head. She liked animals, but not when it came to rips or tears or what she euphemistically referred to as *pet stains.* Heaven forbid there be a *pet stain.*

"Something like that," said Theodosia. "Anyway, the point of my stopping in here was to find something new to wear." There, she thought that might appease Delaine. And hopefully take some of the heat off Earl Grey, who probably wouldn't appreciate being made a scapegoat. Or, in this case, scapedog.

"When you put it that way," murmured Delaine. "Yes, we do have a rather marvelous selection of dressy clothes right now. With the Lamplighter Tour just around the corner and the Charleston Symphony kicking off a new Masterworks Series . . . well, women just need beautiful new dresses and shoes and jewelry. It's as simple as that."

"The weather's still awfully warm," murmured Theodosia, eyeing a rack of featherlight dresses.

"So maybe a strapless dress," suggested Delaine. She darted toward the jam-packed rack of clothes and pulled out a sequined number. "Like this?"

"Perhaps a little too Vegas?" said Theodosia.

"Nonsense," said Delaine. "It's just shiny designy. And you can always tone it down with a plain clutch purse."

"Don't you have something a tad more conservative?" asked Theodosia.

"Honey," said Delaine, putting a hand on her hip and assuming a hectoring pose. "You're gonna walk the red carpet. You don't want to look like those poor sad publicity shlubs you always see accompanying stars at the Academy Awards. The ones in the black poly pantsuits who always look so frazzled."

"I don't want frazzle or dazzle, Delaine. I just want to look like me."

Delaine cocked her head, silently appraising Theodosia. "Yes," she finally muttered, "but what *are* you? What's your image?"

"Looking comfortable in my own skin as well as a new dress," said Theodosia.

Understanding began to dawn in Delaine's eyes. "Yes, I do hear what you're saying. Glam with a touch of the contemporary woman."

To Theodosia, Delaine's words sounded like the spin fashion designers tossed out when they were cornered by reporters. *It's minimalist but moody,* they'd say. Or, *My inspiration was derived from Tokyo's Harajuku.* Or, *It's modern but with a dash of retro.*

"Over here," said Delaine, beckoning for Theodosia to follow her to another rack. Delaine pawed feverishly through the clothes, hangers jangling like mad as she assessed, then discarded, piece after piece. Finally Delaine pulled out a sleek blue dress. "What do you think?" she asked, holding it up for Theodosia to see.

Theodosia relaxed. Delaine had selected a navy blue sheath dress with just a touch of white piping. It was classy. And comfortable looking, too.

"You like?" asked Delaine.

"I do like it," responded Theodosia.

"It's similar to pieces in Ralph Lauren's spring collection two seasons ago," Delaine told her. "But it's a timeless look, so I don't see a problem."

"That's a relief," said Theodosia, humoring her.

"And your white Dolce and Gabbana slides should pair beautifully with it," added Delaine. She turned toward a whitewashed wooden cabinet and pulled down a basket of jewelry. "I also have the perfect earrings." She held up a pair of rhinestone earrings. "See? Perfectamundo! The pinky gold of the stones will go beautifully with your coloring. And of course they're *vintage*."

"Vintage is big now, huh?" said Theodosia.

"Enormously popular," cooed Delaine. "I'm actually thinking about opening a special vintage section here in the store. Glance through any fashion magazine and what do you see? Pictures of celebrities wearing vintage clothing! Halston, eighties Dior, even a little Kenzo and Norman Norrell sprinkled in."

Theodosia eyed the earrings. They did have tons of sparkle and pizzazz. Might be fun. "Okay, I'm sold," she told Delaine.

"You'll look divine," promised Delaine. "Frankly, I can't

wait for tomorrow night. Just imagine—the glitterati of Charleston walking down our own red carpet! What a thrill." Delaine gave a little shiver and lowered her voice to a purr. "And if I continue to play my cards right, I'll be escorted by a certain Hollywood director."

"C. W. Dredd," said Theodosia. Of course.

Delaine eyed her nervously. "You're sure you don't mind, honey? Of course, you've got Parker." She playfully shook an index finger at Theodosia. "You can't collect *all* the good-looking, eligible men on your charm bracelet."

"I wish," said Theodosia, "that you'd be a little careful . . ."

Her words were interrupted by the front door flying open and banging into the wall.

"Gracious," said Delaine, a hand to her throat. Then she gave a little start. "Oh . . . it's Nina!"

"Good morning, Delaine. Why, hello there, Theo. Nice to see you again." Nina van Diedrich came steamrolling in, looking upbeat and slightly manic in a bright orange suit. "Although, I must confess, after last night, I feel like my world is getting stranger and stranger."

"That really was a shame," agreed Delaine. "I had high hopes for our séance. It would have been exciting to . . ."

"No, no, no," shrilled Nina. "I'm not talking about the séance. That was *obviously* a disaster."

"Surely you're not referring to the little misunderstanding about the bombe," said Delaine in an icy tone of voice. "Drayton should have known better than to bring along a dessert with such a *ridiculous* name."

"Something else has happened, Nina?" asked Theodosia, seeing the look of unhappiness on Nina's face.

"I'm talking about how my phone kept ringing all night long!" said Nina, really sounding cranky now. "First I had these strange dreams that I think were brought on by one of the films I watched, and then when I'd pick up the phone there was only breathing at the other end." She churned her arms in the air, as though searching for an explanation.

"Crank calls," said Delaine. She wrinkled her nose. "Awful."

"The thing of it is," said Nina, looking more than a little worried, "I had the strangest feeling it was really quite deliberate. That there was a real presence on the other end of the line, waiting to see how I'd react."

"Who do you think it was?" asked Theodosia.

Nina shook her head. "No idea. But I'm positive somebody's trying to scare me. I mean, add it up. The strange note I received with the encore message, yesterday's séance, and the phone calls last night . . ." She gave a slight shiver. "Somebody's working hard to scare me. And I have to admit they're succeeding rather well."

"Oh, honey," said Delaine, waving a hand. "You're upset over nothing. What you really need to do is focus on something positive—like tomorrow night." Her eyelashes fluttered as if she was entering a dreamlike trance. "I can hardly wait—the red carpet, live press coverage, the presentation of the Golden Palmetto Award, and then a fancy party afterward." She gripped a hand at the front of her neck in a theatrical gesture. "I do believe tomorrow night is going to be one of the most spectacular events Charleston has ever played host to!"

"It all sounds very grand," said Nina. "But don't you think I should be worried? Even a little?"

"Not in the least," said Delaine. She studied her nails, as if wondering if she had time to fit in a manicure.

Nina cast an inquiring glance at Theodosia. "Theo? You've got a good head on your shoulders. What do you think?"

Theodosia hesitated. What to tell Nina? Tell her to watch out, to be careful? Or give her the reassuring words she probably craved? After all, who really knew what was going on? She surely didn't. She hadn't been able to crack anything open yet. In fact, the only thing Theodosia was fairly sure of was that Detective Tidwell was right. Nina should probably be discounted as the murderer.

"I think we should all keep our eyes and ears open," Theodosia told Nina, finally. She knew it wasn't a great answer, but it was as truthful an answer as she could muster.

"See?" chirped Delaine. "No problem." She turned toward one of the racks and pawed through it hastily, pulling out a shimmery blue dress. "Did you have an outfit planned for tomorrow night?" Delaine asked coyly. "Or are you interested in this little number?" She held up a blue dress to show Nina.

"Oh, that's absolutely gorgeous!" cried Nina. "And the color! Is it the same periwinkle blue as Theodosia's dress?"

"It is," said Delaine in a silky smooth voice. "Because it's from the very same designer."

"So beautiful," murmured Nina, reaching for the dress, thoroughly enchanted. "Maybe I should go slip it on?"

Delaine spun on her heels. "Janine!" she yelled out at the top of her lungs. "Nina needs a dressing room! Pronto!"

Janine, Delaine's assistant, appeared out of nowhere. Red-faced, always looking a little harried, Janine led Nina off to one of Cotton Duck's oversized dressing rooms.

"I don't know why I keep that girl on," said Delaine, looking after them.

"You mean Janine?" said Theodosia. "I thought she was your right-hand person."

"She's loyal, I'll give her that," said Delaine in a grudging tone. "But she's not very dynamic when it comes to sales. You have to push people, you know."

"You mean twist their arms?" asked Theodosia, amused.

Delaine made a face. "It's more like encouraging customers in their decision making. Which is exactly what I'm going to do with Nina right now."

As Theodosia watched Delaine charge off, her phone twittered from inside her bag. She dug it out, pushed the on button, fully expecting her caller to be Drayton.

It wasn't.

"Hey, tea lady," came the booming voice of C. W. Dredd. "I barely got a chance to talk to you last night."

"You seemed to be somewhat occupied," responded Theodosia.

"Do I detect a slight snigger?" asked C.W.

"Not me," Theodosia told him. Then she lowered her voice, suddenly concerned that Delaine might still be in range. "Why are you calling me, anyway? And how exactly did you get this number?" How indeed. Probably from Haley, who was still glassy-eyed and starstruck over him.

"I'm calling to ask if I can be your escort tonight. To the animation screening and the Film and Food party afterward."

"You're not serious," said Theodosia.

"You bet your sweet Southern smile I am," said Dredd lightly. "I wouldn't kid about a thing like that."

"Well . . . I already have a date."

"That guy from the restaurant?" asked C.W. "The local yokel?" Hearty laughter echoed in Theodosia's ear, followed by the words, "Dump him."

"What did you say?" asked Theodosia. Did she really hear him right?

"You heard me. I said dump the guy."

"That's not going to happen!" Theodosia said emphatically. Glancing at herself in the three-way mirror, she saw she was frowning and shaking her head in a most unflattering way. She had to pull it together, she told herself as she watched Delaine emerge from the fitting rooms and slip behind her sales counter. Get rid of Dredd. Pronto.

"What's the big problem?" asked Dredd. "You been seeing this guy for a long time?"

"You could say that," said Theodosia.

"Has he asked you to marry him yet?"

"That's none of your business!" snapped Theodosia. Then almost bit her tongue as Delaine threw her a questioning glance.

"Aha!" crowed a triumphant Dredd. "When a woman gives that kind of answer it means the subject hasn't come up. The relationship is in limbo."

Is that where Parker and I are? wondered Theodosia. *Limbo? No, I don't think so.*

"So, are you gonna be my date or what?" asked Dredd.

Theodosia glanced over at Delaine again, who seemed to be focusing her somewhat snoopy, high-powered gaze directly at her. "Or what," she told Dredd. She didn't want to blow him off completely. He could, after all, be the murderer. And she wanted to keep her eye on him. And even if he wasn't directly involved in any crime, he might still hold some sort of key to solving the crime.

Theodosia's "or what" answer caught Dredd off guard. "Huh?" was all he said.

"But I'll for sure see you tonight," she told him. Then Theodosia thumbed the button on her phone before he could say anything and depressed the off button so her little phone wouldn't ring again and dropped it into the depths of her purse.

"Problem at the tea shop?" Delaine called in a syrupy voice. The voice she used when she was fishing around.

"Nope," said Theodosia, putting a quick smile on her face. She swore Delaine was either psychic or at least possessed of supersonic hearing. "Everything's just dandy."

Which, of course, it wasn't.

22

❧

"*Tell me again* why you're doing this," said Drayton. He was standing in the cramped Indigo Tea Shop kitchen, watching Haley prepare tea sandwiches and inhaling the intoxicating aroma of biscuits baking in the oven. Yet his face carried a puzzled look.

"Because it's fun," responded Haley. She took her daisy-shaped cookie cutter, placed it in the center of a slice of pumpkin bread, and pushed gently.

"And we don't have a special group coming in?" Drayton countered

Haley shook her head. "Not really."

"Nothing to do with the film festival?"

"Drayton!" said Haley, finally looking up at him. "Can you never just go with the flow?"

"What flow is that?" asked Theodosia, stepping into the kitchen. She'd slipped through the back door a few minutes ago. And, while hanging up her newly purchased dress and perusing a towering stack of morning mail, she had become aware of the exchange going on between Drayton and Haley. The heat had definitely been building.

Drayton spun to face Theodosia. "Haley's doing a daisy tea." Looking like he was in a quandary, he cast an inquiring glance at Theodosia as if trying to elicit her help.

"Sounds lovely," replied Theodosia.

"For no reason at all," added Drayton. For some reason he was having trouble processing this. "No special request, no groups coming in." He threw up his hands in a gesture of supreme bewilderment. "It's simply not on the agenda."

"You mean Haley's doing it just for the fun of it," said Theodosia, starting to get a kick out of Drayton's dilemma. "Out of pure spontaneity."

Drayton pursed his mouth as if he were about to say something, then changed his mind. "Yes," he said. "I suppose that's it."

"See," said Haley, tipping a glass plate stacked with daisy-shaped sandwiches for Theodosia to view. "Daisy sandwiches. And I thought we'd use the Staffordshire daisy pattern teacups and saucers, too."

"Set on cheery yellow place mats, I'd guess," said Theodosia.

"Sure," said Haley. She threw a triumphant glance at Drayton.

Drayton's shoulders slumped. "I'm not always the brightest bulb in the chandelier, but I can see when I'm being outmaneuvered. Is there anything *I* can contribute to this so-called daisy tea?"

Haley's eyes twinkled mischievously. "You could run down to Floradora and pick up a few bunches of daisies from Hattie. They'd look adorable bobbling from glass vases on our tables."

Now one of Drayton's furry eyebrows lifted. "And this is in our budget?"

"They're daisies, Drayton," said Haley. "Not rare blooms from the slopes of the Himalayas. I'm sure it won't be a problem."

Drayton held up both hands in a sign of capitulation. "Okay, okay, I'm just asking."

When all the tables were served, when four new pots of tea stood steeping on the wooden counter, when Theodosia herself finally paused to nibble a daisy sandwich herself, Timothy Neville came striding into the tea room. Isabelle followed in his wake.

Drayton scurried over to greet his old friend.

"Timothy, let me get you a table." Drayton's eyes read the floor in a millisecond. "Here, this one is clear." Drayton backpedaled across the tea room, hustling them to the table nearest the kitchen. "Just be seated and I'll return in a jiffy with linens and silverware." He spun on his heels, then caught himself. "Oh, and I just now finished brewing some of that Indian Munnar tea you like, Timothy. Awfully good with a splash of milk."

"We need to talk," said Timothy, a grim look on his lined face.

"Well, yes . . . of course," said Drayton. "I'll just, uh . . ."

"Can Theodosia join us?" asked Timothy.

Theodosia was at Timothy's table in a matter of seconds. "What's up?" she asked. She noted that Timothy looked awfully upset. And Isabelle seemed uncharacteristically subdued. What was going on? Was it something to do with her so-called investigation? Or something entirely new?

"Can I get a quick five minutes with the both of you?" asked Timothy.

"Not a problem," said Theodosia. She ducked between the velvet curtains and said, "Haley, can you cover the floor?"

When Haley emerged a few seconds later, wiping her hands on her white chef's apron, Theodosia sat down at the table with Timothy, Isabelle, and Drayton.

"First things first," said Timothy. "You're both well aware that my granddaughter Isabelle was initially viewed as a suspect, then cleared."

"Thankfully cleared," said Drayton.

Timothy held up a gnarled index finger. "Unfortunately, that situation has reversed itself. It now seems that because I purchased a certain lapis ring for Isabelle, she's once again fallen under a cloud of suspicion." He stared morosely across the table at Theodosia.

"I . . . I'm sorry to hear that," she told him. "I saw that silly glint of ring or cuff link and *had* to mention it. I certainly didn't intend for Isabelle's credibility to be impugned down the road . . ."

Timothy held up a hand to quell her words. "No, no, you misunderstand. I didn't come here to reprimand you, dear lady. Not at all."

"Okay," said Theodosia, slowly. Then what was going on?

Timothy reached over and clasped Isabelle's hand. She tilted her chin up and gazed at him. "The murder of Jordan Cole and the subsequent investigation," said Timothy, "has been nerve-wracking for all of us."

"It certainly has," agreed Drayton.

Timothy continued. "And while Isabelle and I certainly appreciate Theodosia's exemplary efforts at working behind the scenes, we are now asking that she basically cease and desist from any further, uh, shall we say, private investigating."

"Because . . . why?" asked Theodosia. Now that she'd been nosing around for a good five days, she wasn't sure she wanted to cease and desist, as Timothy had phrased it. And even though she'd actually considered throwing in the towel on more than one occasion, Timothy's words seemed to rekindle a spark deep within her.

"I think Isabelle has endured enough embarrassment," said Timothy.

He gazed at Theodosia with an impassive stare and she wasn't sure if he was referring to the fact that Isabelle's affair with Jordan Cole had been revealed, or if he was upset at Tidwell's probing questions in general. Theodosia decided that, for all she knew, maybe Timothy wasn't completely aware of Isabelle's little extracurricular activities with the deceased director.

"You really want me to stop," said Theodosia, rolling the idea around inside her head like a ball of clay, sort of prodding it and testing the notion.

"But of course she'll stop," said Drayton. He tucked his chin down and gazed speculatively at Theodosia. "You will, won't you?"

Theodosia drew in a deep breath, then let it out slowly. "Now I'm not so sure."

"What!" said a startled Drayton.

"Oh dear," muttered Isabelle, the first words she'd actually spoken.

"Why on earth not?" demanded Timothy Neville.

How to explain? Theodosia knew she had to choose her words carefully. "Because, Timothy, there appears to be more at stake now."

"What are you talking about?" asked a slightly wary Timothy.

"Several suspects have emerged and people have been threatened," said Theodosia. "I hate to say this, but *I've* been threatened."

"You're not serious!" said Drayton. "You've been threatened?"

Theodosia gave a quick account of how she'd been chased through Gateway Walk. As well as the strange note that had lured her to the Belvedere Theatre, an incident she'd pretty much whitewashed earlier.

"Gracious!" exclaimed Drayton.

"Then, of course," said Theodosia, "there was the séance yesterday. Somebody went to considerable trouble rigging up that amazing flying banshee trick." She gazed at Isabelle, saw not a flicker of reaction on the girl's face.

"I hadn't heard about that," said Timothy.

"The thing of it is," said Theodosia. "Now I feel committed. If that makes any sense at all."

Drayton shook his head. "Sounds like now is when you should *stop* investigating."

But Timothy was giving her a slow, almost grudging nod. "Yes, when you explain all that's gone on, I see your point."

Tears suddenly shimmered in Isabelle's eyes. "Timothy said you were a top-rate investigator and it looks as though you really are."

Theodosia gazed back at Isabelle, wondering if the girl's tears were real or if Isabelle was just a dang fine actress. "Well, thank you, Isabelle," she finally said. "I'll remember that." And to herself, Theodosia thought, *In for a penny, in for a pound. If I had any doubts, I don't anymore. I'm going to follow this thing to the end and see where it takes me.*

"*Yipes,*" said Haley. She was on her hands and knees, digging around under the front counter. A scatter of cardboard boxes surrounded her, and more were being unearthed with each passing second.

"Whatever are you *doing*?" asked Drayton. It was late afternoon and only two tables of customers remained in the tea shop. But Drayton was fretting as though they had a full complement of guests. "And kindly lower your voice," he instructed. "We still have customers."

"I'm trying to find those scented tea candles," said Haley. "Don't you remember? We agreed to contribute goodies for the swag bags tonight."

"Swag bags," said Drayton. "I really detest the sound of that."

Haley hunted through a few more boxes, sighing mightily when she still didn't find her candles. When Theodosia emerged from the back carrying a tin of Darjeeling, she looked slightly hopeful. "Hey, Theo?"

"Yes, Haley?" Theodosia gazed down at Haley. "And I'm not going to ask why you're down there scrabbling around on your hands and knees."

"She's hunting up goodies for tonight's swag bags," said Drayton in a disinterested tone. "Someone made a commitment, I guess."

Theodosia stood in the middle of the floor and touched the back of her hand to her forehead. "The swag bags," she breathed. "I completely forgot."

"They slipped my mind, too," said Haley. "But Kassie Byrd called a little while ago and said she's on her way to pick up our stuff. Except we don't really have any stuff!"

"How many swag bags does she need?" asked Theodosia.

Haley cast her eyes upward, thinking. "I think she said . . . ten."

"No problem," said Theodosia. "We've got lots of things that will work."

"Like what?" asked Haley.

"I suppose it depends on how generous we want to be," interjected Drayton.

"The first thing that comes to mind," said Theodosia, "are teapots. We've got a full case of them stashed in my office."

"Not my Brown Bettys," said Drayton in a proprietary tone. He crossed his arms over his chest to add impetus to his protest.

"You're not going to miss ten teapots," Theodosia told

him. "Plus we can throw in small tins of teas and jars of Du-Bose Bees Honey."

"And we can spare ten of everything?" asked Haley.

"I don't see why not," said Theodosia, nudging a stray box with her foot. Haley really had spread everything all over the place.

"Then what if we make up some of our own mini swag bags," suggested Haley. "Put the teapots, tea, and honey in our indigo blue take-out bags."

"I think that's a great idea," said Theodosia. "Then all Kassie has to do is pop our bags into her larger bags."

"No problem," said Haley. "I mean for her."

"Yes, yes," said Drayton, "we get it. Now can we *please* put away these boxes?"

"These are adorable," exclaimed Kassie. She was grinning over the bags Haley had assembled. "Each one's like a mini tea party in a bag."

"That's what we were going for," said Haley. She glanced over at Theodosia. "Weren't we?"

"If you say so," said Theodosia.

"Your contribution is also very generous," said Kassie. "After what happened . . . I mean this past Sunday night . . . a few businesses backed out and left us in the lurch. So some of our swag bags have been a little—how shall I phrase it? Meager?"

"We're glad to help," said Theodosia. "And if you need more contributions for tomorrow night, just let us know."

"Thanks," said Kassie, brightening. "But this'll be the last night of actual judging, so I think we're set." She stood at the counter, packing Haley's bags into a cardboard box. "You guys are coming tonight, aren't you?"

"For the animation films?" said Haley. "We wouldn't miss it."

"And afterward is the big Food and Film party," said Kassie. "The police already closed off Church Street so the giant tents can go up."

"I take it quite a few restaurants will be serving goodies tonight?" said Theodosia.

"Oh yeah," Kassie nodded. "It's going to be a veritable taste of Charleston. The Chowder Hound is serving their famous crab chowder, Blue Willow is doing fried green tomatoes, and Moby's will be serving Charleston red rice and poke sausage. And there's supposed to be an enormous seafood buffet in the VIP tent."

"Oh," said Haley, excited now. "Delaine promised us tickets for that so we can go inside and hobnob. I sure hope she comes through."

"You never know if she'll come through or not," said Drayton ominously, from across the room.

"Oh, you're in all right," Kassie assured them. "I saw your names on the list."

"You hear that, Drayton?" called Haley. "We're in!"

"Well, aren't we the lucky ducks," said Drayton.

23

✦

Theodosia giggled along with the rest of the audience as she sat in the darkened Belvedere Theatre, watching the presentation of animated short films. Right now, two delightful tabby cats named Beauregard and Beatrice were taking a road trip through Florida in a crazy animated romp appropriately titled *Pardon My Faux Paw.* And the film just before it had started off as live action, then quickly morphed into animation that reminded Theodosia of the early, loosely rendered cartoons of the 1930s.

To her left, Drayton was digging into his bag of kettle corn, chortling away. Haley, on her right, was squealing with laughter.

It was hard for Theodosia to imagine that, just five days earlier, a brutal, bloody murder had taken place here. One that had brought the audience to its feet in shocked dismay. Now, the murder of Jordan Cole seemed like a dim memory. Pushed aside, like the debris of popcorn and paper cups that lay at their feet.

When the house lights came up and applause rang through the plush theater, Drayton was still chortling.

"Delightful, absolutely delightful," he murmured.

"And you were so sure you wouldn't enjoy the animation," said Theodosia. Indeed, Drayton had been very dubious of it.

"My abject apologies," replied Drayton. "I had no idea how wildly creative these short pieces could be."

"My favorite was the cats," said Haley. "I loved how they got crazy on catnip before hitting the theme parks."

"What now?" asked Drayton as they eased their way to the side aisle and shuffled along with the crowd. "Off to the food tents?"

"What we need to do is find Delaine," said Theodosia. She looked around for her friend, but saw only a sea of moving faces. Many familiar, some not.

"There she is!" cried Haley. "Just working her way up the center aisle now. You see her?" Haley waved her arms, called out, "Hey, Delaine!"

Delaine looked around, spotted Theodosia, Drayton, and Haley, and gave an affirmative nod. She mouthed something that looked like *I have your passes*, then gestured toward the exit.

"I guess she wants us to meet her at the exit," said Haley.

"Why is Delaine suddenly so wrapped up with the film festival?" asked Drayton as the crowd continued to creep slowly toward the exits.

"Probably because she wants to be wrapped up with C. W. Dredd," quipped Haley. "You've seen how she looks at him."

"My heavens, Delaine can be a predatory woman," muttered Drayton under his breath.

And Theodosia, wondering to herself exactly who the predator du jour really was, said, "I think those sharply honed instincts of hers might come in handy."

"Darlings!" exclaimed Delaine, when they finally met up near the lobby. She was dolled up in a silver dress that featured a perky bow on one shoulder and a peekaboo neckline. Sterling silver hoops dangled from her ears. "I've got your VIP passes, although they're actually green wristbands that you snap on. So very Academy Awards, don't you think?"

"I don't know," said Drayton, gingerly accepting one of the wristbands. "Is this what they wear at the Academy Awards?"

"But of course," said Delaine, as if she had firsthand experience. "At the big, splashy after-parties. You're given a green wristband to get in, then a yellow one if you're invited into the swankier VIP section, then a red one for admittance into the upper echelon A-list star section. Of course, we only have one level of VIP tonight, so our wristbands are green." She shrugged, as if lamenting the fact that they didn't have a super-VIP level.

"This is really great," said Haley, snapping her wristband around her wrist and watching it slide down over her silver charm bracelet. "Let's go party."

"I'm not sure I completely approve of this exclusionary policy," said Drayton.

"Why, Drayton," said Haley. "I thought you practiced an exclusionary policy all your life."

Drayton reared back. "I have not."

"What if someone doesn't like history or lectures or exhibits at the Heritage Society?" pressed Haley.

"Then I would say it's their loss," said Drayton.

"And if someone doesn't like classical music?" pressed Haley. "Say they're more into jazz or rock or heavy metal?"

"I don't exactly pass *judgment* . . ." said Drayton, stumbling slightly with his words.

"I think he's getting the point," said Theodosia.

"Yes," said Drayton, "There's no need to clobber me over the head."

They crossed the lobby and came out onto Church Street. What had been a pretty vista of stately redbrick buildings set off with white columns and highlighted by rows of graceful palmetto trees was now obscured by two giant white tents.

"Amazing, isn't it?" said Delaine, waving her arms. "Tents." She pointed an index finger at the larger of the two tents. "That one on the left is for all ticket holders—that's the appetizer tent with a cash bar. The one on the right's the VIP tent. I understand there's a champagne bar and rather amazing seafood buffet."

Theodosia gazed at the crowd of people milling about. Most were dressed to the nines and chattering about the animated short films they'd just seen. "The crowd is really into this," she remarked. "The film festival, I mean."

"Oh, I think this is a truly spectacular event for Charleston," cooed Delaine. "Of course, tomorrow night will be the pièce de résistance—when the winner of the Golden Palmetto Award is announced!"

"So, the three feature films that are in contention have been playing all day?" asked Theodosia.

Delaine nodded. "Since ten this morning. They've been rotating and repeating them. They'll start again early tomorrow and run till about five. Hopefully that will give everybody an opportunity to see them."

"I'm off for the appetizer tent," announced Drayton. "Haley, care to join me?"

"Sure," said Haley. "I want to see if my friend Carrie Boone is working at the Chowder Hound counter."

"And I want to find C.W.," said Delaine, looking coy. "Theo, you care to wander around with me? I must say, you're looking suntanned and utterly adorable tonight in that white dress."

Theodosia had thought long and hard about wearing a long dress, but in the end had stuck with something short. And when she'd looked in the antique mirror in her dining room and tossed a plum-colored wrap around her shoulders, a shimmering, slightly glamorous image had gazed back at her.

"I'm supposed to meet up with Parker at the champagne bar," Theodosia told Delaine. But when she checked her watch, she saw it was only a few minutes past eight thirty, maybe a little too early for Parker to slip away from the restaurant.

Theodosia wandered over to the VIP tent anyway, flashing her coveted green bracelet to a volunteer, who unfastened the velvet rope and waved her in.

The crowd inside the tent was still fairly thin, so Theodosia wandered over to the ten-foot-long seafood bar. It was a heroic presentation of crushed ice topped with cracked crab, lobster tails, and shrimp the size of telephone receivers. Oysters on the half shell rested on a large silver tray that had been stuck into a sort of ice cave. Next to the oysters was a platter of Carolina blue crab and a bowl of shiny black caviar. On the very tippy-top of the pile of seafood-littered ice was an ice sculpture depicting one of the Golden Palmetto Award statues.

Theodosia's mouth watered at the thought of briny blue crab pulled from local waters, but she decided to do the polite thing and wait for Parker. And, hopefully, he'd be arriving soon!

At the champagne bar, Theodosia ran into Bill Glass. He'd just downed a flute of the golden liquid.

"Hit me again, will you, babe?" Glass said to the female bartender. Then he turned toward Theodosia and fixed her with a wide grin. "I can't seem to get enough of this French grape juice."

"You're referring to the champagne?" Theodosia allowed one of her eyebrows to arc upward. Bill Glass was never one to drip with Southern charm and manners, but tonight he seemed more uncouth than ever. And a little drunk, too.

"Yeah," said Glass. He stared at her and his eyes seemed to cross for a split second. "Hey, how come you're not hanging out with your hotshot director friend? I thought you two were an item."

"You thought wrong," said Theodosia as the bartender carefully refilled his champagne flute, then poured one for her, too.

Glass held his up in a toast. "Ah well, at least it's been a great week . . . filled with killer parties."

"Did you cover the screenings, too?" asked Theodosia. She took a little sip of champagne, mentally strategizing how she could get away from him.

Glass shook his head vehemently. "Nope." He gestured with his glass again, this time toward the crowd that was beginning to swell within the VIP tent. "All the action's right here. When people attend these fancy events, they drink, cut loose a little too much, and maybe say the wrong thing or get caught cozying up to the wrong people." Glass smiled crookedly at Theodosia. "That's where I come in. Ready for anything that presents itself."

"In other words," said Theodosia, "you're only in this for the dirt."

"And the swag bags," said Glass. He cackled wildly then kicked a large silver bag that rested at his feet. "For some reason they keep giving me these lousy swag bags."

Theodosia frowned. She was pretty sure the teapot, tea, and honey she'd donated was resting in the swag bag that sat on the ground. Oh well . . .

Bill Glass edged closer to Theodosia. "Can I . . . uh, buy you a drink?"

"I already have one," said Theodosia. She looked over at the bartender, a pretty blond with short-cropped hair. The girl threw her a what-can-you-do look and rolled her eyes.

"I don't generally care for fizzy drinks," said Glass, smacking his lips together, "but this stuff is doggone good."

"Then let's alert the media, shall we?" came Parker Scully's disapproving voice from behind them.

Glass spun around, albeit a little shaky. "Hey, I *am* the media."

"You are a gossip tabloid," remarked Parker. "Not to be confused with legitimate media."

"Hold on now . . ." began a sputtering Bill Glass.

"And another thing," said Parker cutting in, "that fizzy drink you're guzzling happens to be a Beaufort Grand Cru from Montagne de Reims in the heart of Champagne, France. Probably aged in oak vats for at least fifteen years. So kindly give it the proper respect it deserves, will you?" He turned toward Theodosia. "Theodosia?" Parker extended a hand. "Care to visit the buffet table?"

"You couldn't have come sooner," said Theodosia, enjoying the fact that she was actually able to flounce away from Glass into the arms of a very attractive man. It was a maneuver rife with theatrics. Like something Bette Davis might have done.

Theodosia and Parker surveyed the display of chilled seafood.

"All I can say," said Parker, "is I'm glad we didn't have to put *that* together."

"Catering can be a challenge," agreed Theodosia, "but there's a limit to what you can do."

"For sure," said Parker, chuckling. "Man, that is the Mount Rushmore of seafood."

Theodosia giggled at Parker's analogy.

"Shall we try a technical ascent?" invited Parker. He picked up a frosted glass plate from a nearby stack and handed it to her.

"Let's," said Theodosia. "Because I'm absolutely starved."

They wandered down the length of the seafood bar, still

marveling at the towering mound, delighted by the quality of the shellfish. Theodosia selected a small lobster tail and two jumbo shrimp. She dipped a silver spoon into the cut-glass dish filled with caviar and dabbed a tiny shimmering mound onto a cracker. Reaching for a crab claw from the mountain of crushed ice, she decided there was nothing like blue crab, fresh and sweet and a teensy bit briny. But as she tugged at the claw embedded in the crushed ice, it didn't seem to want to pull free.

What's the problem?

Theodosia gave a slightly harder tug.

"Having trouble?" Parker asked. He was busy stacking tiny Kumamoto oysters around the perimeter of his plate.

"This crab claw," said Theodosia, finally pulling it out and unintentionally bringing a rather large chunk of ice along with it. That little movement set off a miniature landslide, causing shrimp, crab claws, and lobster tails to slither down the mound of crushed ice.

"Oh dear," lamented Theodosia as another hunk of ice tumbled off the table and landed with a thunk on the floor. "I think I . . ." Theodosia stopped midsentence and suddenly gasped at what her efforts had revealed.

A human hand projected from the mound of ice! Ghastly blue in color and clenched in rigor mortis!

"Parker!" Theodosia clapped a hand over her mouth, trying to quell her own scream.

"Oh no!" came Parker's hoarse murmur. His face had blanched white; he looked shocked, like he was ready to pass out.

"We've got to . . ." Theodosia choked out.

An hysterical shriek pierced the air. The woman directly behind Theodosia gazed at the frozen hand, screamed again, and dropped her flute of champagne. It exploded on impact, sounding like a rifle crack and sending glass shards hurtling through the air. Which, of course, set off even more shrieks.

Then it seemed like dozens of people were screeching and moaning, sending up a harsh cacophony that made Theodosia's nerves jangle. Jostling and shoving immediately followed and Theodosia suddenly felt like she was trapped at the vortex of a soccer scrum gone bad as the more morbid of the guests pressed in close, vying for a better look.

"Call the police!" rasped one woman.

"Call an ambulance," cried a man in a high, reedy voice.

And then Parker was bent over the table, scooping mounds of crushed ice with his hands, trying to see just what . . . or who . . . was really imbedded in that ice.

"Be careful," warned Theodosia, working alongside him, her bare hands tingling from the freezing cold. "The police will want to treat this as a crime scene."

And then, like a long-lost climber being unearthed from the unforgiving, death-zone slopes of Everest, a frozen face came partially into view.

"Quick," demanded Theodosia, "give me your hanky."

Parker pulled a clean white hanky from his pocket and handed it to Theodosia. Gently now, she cleared away more ice, hoping against hope that whoever lay under this layer of ice was still . . . what? Alive?

Caught in a viselike grip of revulsion as well as perverse curiosity, Theodosia frantically brushed away the final shards. And when she finally saw who it was, she was rocked to the core with horror.

Nina van Diedrich lay with her eyes closed on the pallet of crushed ice. A streak of red seafood sauce had splattered and frozen across her pale cheek. Not a single breath escaped her blue-tinged lips.

More screams then, and Theodosia was vaguely aware of someone trying to shove her roughly out of the way. It was Bill Glass, thrashing with his elbows even as he aimed his camera lens directly at Nina's frozen face.

"Don't!" cried Theodosia, her throat constricting. She

was horrified that Glass would take advantage of such a disastrous situation.

"Call me crazy," muttered Glass. "But I think I just found my page-one photo."

Theodosia stared at Bill Glass as he raised his camera. Then the flash exploded, bouncing off the ice, and making Nina's pale face appear even more corpselike. Taking a step back, Theodosia decided that Glass reminded her of a jackal who'd arrived late at a fresh kill. Snarling and snapping at the outer perimeter, fearful of the larger predators, yet biding his time to steal in and snatch a bite.

24

Timothy Neville lived like a prince. Or maybe an archduke. Ensconced in his palatial mansion on Archdale Street, he spent considerable sums of money doing little nip-tucks on the plasterwork, brick chimneys, wrought iron, and graceful pillars, finials, and balustrades that graced his historic home. Inherited money was always the best, of course, and Timothy had spared no expense on the elegant Hepplewhite furnishings, Chinese rugs, and gleaming oil paintings that hung inside his hallowed halls.

"I brought scones," Theodosia said, almost apologetically. "And strawberry jam and Devonshire cream for anyone who wants it." She gazed at the glum faces that looked up at her from Timothy Neville's baronial dining-room table. Like her, they'd been summoned to this emergency meeting to put their collective heads together and help decide if tonight's finale should even take place.

Probably, Theodosia decided, most everyone would rather have slept in this Saturday morning. The murder of poor

Nina van Diedrich last night had made for a long, stressful evening. Along with the arrival of four police cruisers, an ambulance, and a cadre of investigators, the tents had been cordoned off and almost a hundred people questioned. What was supposed to have been a festive, fun affair had quickly spiraled downward into a grinding, grim police investigation.

Drayton came out of the butler's pantry carrying two steaming teapots. "You're here, Theodosia," he said. "Good. We're just about to have a little wakeup tea. Lord knows, we can all use it."

"Let me take these into the pantry and arrange them," she said, lifting the bag of scones.

Drayton nodded.

But when Theodosia came out with her plate of scones, more faces had appeared, as if by magic, at the table.

Timothy and Drayton were there, of course. Along with Linus Gillette from Trident Media and Gavin Dorfman from the Charleston Arts Committee.

But the two new surprise faces were Delaine and C. W. Dredd.

Theodosia set her plate down with a thud. She wasn't pleased that Delaine had dragged Dredd along. Not at all.

"You've seen this?" Timothy asked Theodosia as he held up the morning edition of the Charleston *Post and Courier.*

Theodosia nodded. Of course she had. It had landed on her doorstep early this morning and she'd rushed down in her nightgown to fetch it. The front-page banner screamed "Festival on Ice?" in thirty-six-point type.

She slipped into a chair next to Drayton where she could keep an eye on C. W. Dredd at the other end of the table. "What do you think?" she asked of no one in particular. "*Is* the event on ice?"

Timothy picked up his teacup and took a sip. "Bracing," he murmured. Then he looked around the table. "That question is precisely what this group must determine rather quickly. Shall we stay the course and blunder on to a conclusion? Or simply scrap tonight's award program?" He paused, his gnomelike head glistening from the morning sun that streamed through lead-pane glass. "Any ideas, people?"

Throats were cleared, feet were shuffled, fingers twitched, but nobody seemed willing to step up to the plate and declare themselves.

"Well?" said Timothy, looking nonplussed. Most times you could hardly muzzle these people. Now nobody uttered a peep.

"I'd like to speak first," said Theodosia. She'd learned from her years in marketing that the person who spoke first in a meeting, the one who engendered their own idea right at the outset, often carried the day. Unless, of course, you were dealing with a really cantankerous group. Then all bets were off.

"What say you?" asked Timothy, in his formal, chairman-of-the-board-*Robert's-Rules-of-Order* voice.

"I think tonight's award show should proceed as planned," said Theodosia. "We have dozens of directors, filmmakers, cinematographers, and screenwriters who traveled here to Charleston to participate. I don't think it's fair to penalize them for something they had nothing to do with."

Linus Gillette fixed her with an angry glare. "Are you sure about that?" he snapped.

C. W. Dredd gave a low snort.

"As far as we know—as far as the police are concerned—no one has yet been deemed a suspect in last night's murder," said Theodosia. She wasn't sure she was 100 percent correct, but it helped to make her case.

"She's right," agreed Drayton. "And, not to be completely mercenary, but we did sell nearly two thousand tickets over the past week for the various screenings. That tells you how high interest has been. So it would be a huge disappointment if we cancelled."

Timothy didn't look convinced. "I'm not so sure we shouldn't just award the prizes in absentia," he said, tapping his square fingers against the mahogany table.

Theodosia decided to take another tack. "Look at it this way," she said. "If the Charleston Film Festival is not a fait accompli, we may come under pressure to return some of that ticket money."

"Return the money?" asked Timothy in a steely tone. This was something he obviously hadn't thought of.

Theodosia nodded. Now she had his full attention. In these tight times of garnering donations and gifts for the Heritage Society as well as the Charleston Arts Board, Timothy was more than mindful of each and every penny.

"That wouldn't be good *at all*," said Timothy. His face sagged, the back of his neck glowed pink.

"I don't see the problem with continuing," spoke up Delaine. "I mean, it's just one more night, isn't it? The judges have cast their ballots, the program is pretty much set, the award statues are sitting on a table backstage." She cocked her head coquettishly and let her eyes travel the length of the table, occasionally lingering on one man or another.

Now Gavin Dorfman from the Charleston Arts Committee spoke up. "It seems to me someone is bound and determined to bring this entire film festival to its knees. Which certainly bodes ill for all of us."

"Are you talking about a conspiracy?" asked Drayton. "Or just one person."

"I don't know," said Dorfman, in a testy tone of voice. "If the police don't know, how am I supposed to know?"

"We can't just *not* have it," said Delaine in a petulant tone. "It wouldn't be fair."

She wants to wear her dress, thought Theodosia. *And walk the red carpet with Dredd.*

Linus Gillette nodded suddenly, as though he'd just made a momentous decision. "I think Delaine is right." He glanced over at Theodosia. "And you, too, Theodosia. We should proceed as planned. Certainly, if we have enough police protection . . ."

"We're going to need a lot of police protection," snapped Timothy. "In the audience as well as backstage."

"Especially backstage," said Dredd. He gazed toward Theodosia and gave her a wink. She stiffened, but pointedly ignored him.

"Do you think we can get that kind of security?" Timothy asked, shifting his gaze to Theodosia.

Why was he focusing on her? wondered Theodosia. "I suppose we'll have to run that by the police," she said to him. "See what they're willing to offer."

"You think we can get Tidwell over here?" Timothy asked her.

Drayton jumped up from his chair. "I'll go call him."

"If we're still on for tonight," said Linus Gillette, "I'll alert the media."

"We have a consensus then?" asked Timothy. "Everyone is in agreement to proceed with tonight's festivities? Conditional, of course, on obtaining extra police protection."

There were nods and murmurs all around the table.

"All right," said Timothy, still looking unhappy. "Meeting adjourned."

"Theodosia," said Timothy, as she was wrapping a piece of plastic wrap over the scones. "You can stay?"

She nodded. "Sure. But . . . why? What's up?"

"Burt Tidwell's on his way," Timothy told her. "And

since you two seem to have formed some sort of bond, it might be helpful."

"We don't have a bond," said Theodosia. "Most of the time we're completely at odds."

"Still," said Timothy, unwilling to take no for an answer, "you may be of help."

But Theodosia didn't feel a bit helpful when, twenty minutes later, Detective Burt Tidwell showed up, flanked by two other homicide detectives.

Not bothering with introductions, Tidwell swaggered into the dining room and plopped himself down at the table, along with Theodosia, Drayton, and Timothy. Oblivious to all, he thumbed through a small black spiral notebook that looked dwarfed in his big hands. The other two detectives, obviously used to this type of treatment, sat down, too.

"Drayton spoke to you about an increased police presence?" asked Timothy. Sitting at the head of his handcrafted table that held an easy eighteen dinner guests, the decision made to proceed with the award show, he now looked calm and in control.

Tidwell inclined his large head and gazed at Timothy with bright, beady eyes. "The department can spare twenty uniformed officers for tonight."

"What about you?" Theodosia asked Tidwell. "Will you be there as well?" She indicated the men sitting next to him. "Along with your cohorts?"

Tidwell's eyes shifted and a look of exasperation crossed his ample face. "I'll be wherever I'm needed. No need to worry about me, Miss Browning."

"I never do, Detective."

"Excuse me," said Drayton, looking nervous at this somewhat hostile exchange. "Would anyone like a cup of tea?"

No one answered.

Drayton cleared his throat. He was going to remain friendly and a touch formal if it killed him. "Scones then?"

Now the two detectives looked slightly interested.

"Scones," Drayton repeated for their benefit. "Sort of like . . . muffins?"

"Sure," said one.

"Great," said the other.

Relieved, Drayton made a fast escape to the butler's pantry.

"I was just wondering," said Theodosia, addressing Tidwell again, "if you've ascertained the exact cause of Nina's death?"

Tidwell nodded. "Penetrating trauma," he told her in a friendly tone. "Probably an ice pick to the back of the neck."

Theodosia had to work hard to stifle her revulsion. It sounded like a terrible way to die. "And do you have any suspects?" she asked in a halting tone. Although Theodosia hadn't been the best of friends with Nina van Diedrich, she was finding it difficult to inquire about the woman's death. The revelation about the ice pick truly sickened her . . . and the image of Nina's pale, frozen face was still freshly etched in her mind.

"We do have what you might call a short list," said Tidwell. "Although it is far too early for speculation. Especially on *your* part."

"What I'm also curious about," said Theodosia, plowing ahead, "was who set up the seafood buffet?"

Drayton arrived back with the scones. "I wondered about that, too," he said as he passed around small plates that each held a scone, dabs of jam and Devonshire cream, along with a small silver knife.

Tidwell glanced at his notebook with its notations in small, cryptic handwriting. "Harper's Seafood Purveyors," he told her. "Owned by a Mr. Dell Harper."

Theodosia had met Dell Harper once. Had even gone to

an oyster roast at his home over on Edisto Island. Harper was one of Parker's suppliers at Solstice and the oyster roast had been their first date. Certainly Dell Harper had nothing to do with this. So the question still remained . . . who had stabbed Nina van Diedrich with an ice pick, then hidden her body under the ice?

Tidwell put his hands flat on the table. "I'd like to talk to . . . Isabelle," he announced. "Is she here?"

Timothy gave a sharp intake of breath. "Why are you asking about my granddaughter?"

Why was Tidwell asking? wondered Theodosia.

Tidwell settled back in his chair and wiggled his shoulders. He crossed his pudgy arms over his stomach. "She was seen talking with Nina van Diedrich late yesterday," said Tidwell.

"Isabelle is part of the film festival!" thundered Timothy. "Of course they were talking!"

"Is Isabelle a suspect?" asked Theodosia. "Do you intend to bring charges against her?"

Tidwell's lips formed into a pout. "I only wish to *speak* to her. There's no need to jump to conclusions. There'll be no interrogations, intimidation, or threats."

Hah, thought Theodosia.

"She is here," said Timothy. "Upstairs. But I'm not sure I want you questioning her without a lawyer present."

"Again," said Tidwell in a kinder, almost wheedling tone, "I only want to speak with the girl. Ask a few simple questions."

Timothy sat immobile in his chair, seemingly unable to make up his mind. Finally, Theodosia interceded.

"Why don't I go up and get Isabelle?" she said.

"Good idea," replied Drayton. He glanced nervously at Timothy. "All right, Timothy?"

"Yes," Timothy responded in a papery voice.

Theodosia was out of her chair and charging down

Timothy's center hallway in a flash. Bounding up his circular staircase, she took the steps two at a time. She paused at the top, noting that Timothy had added several more amazing oil paintings to the long hallway that stretched off in either direction and served as his private art gallery.

And where would Isabelle's room be? Theodosia wondered. *Front of the house? Back of the house?* The place was so vast it was hard to decide.

Figuring Timothy was probably ensconced at the front of the mansion, where the view toward Charleston Harbor was quite spectacular, Theodosia stepped lightly down the Aubusson carpet toward the rear of the house. All the doors were closed and, for a brief moment, Theodosia wondered just what went on behind them.

She knocked on one of the doors. There was no answer, no sound, save the ticking of a clock on the landing.

Theodosia tiptoed to the next door. Again, nothing.

The third door she knocked on, her efforts were rewarded.

"Yes?" came a soft voice.

"Isabelle," said Theodosia. "It's Theodosia, may I come in?"

There was no answer and Theodosia thought Isabelle might be simply ignoring her. But then the brass handle jiggled and the door creaked inward a few inches.

"Is your meeting over?" asked Isabelle. She wasn't particularly friendly but she wasn't totally hostile, either.

"It is," Theodosia told her.

"The film festival is proceeding?" asked Isabelle.

Theodosia nodded. "Yes." She peeked through the crack at Isabelle's face. "May I come in?"

Isabelle gave a shrug, then pulled the door open all the way. "Suit yourself," she said.

Following Isabelle in, Theodosia quickly surveyed the room. It was as gorgeous as the rest of Timothy's house.

Done in pinks and grays, it held a hand-carved four-poster bed, a wooden dresser, an upholstered love seat, and a French decoupage screen with Chinese figures.

"I take it you wanted something?" asked Isabelle. Now there was a guarded crispness to her voice.

Theodosia dove right in. "Your grandfather would like you to come downstairs and speak with Detective Tidwell and his men for a few minutes."

"My grandfather wants me to have a conversation with them or Tidwell himself suggested this?" asked Isabelle.

"Tidwell actually made the request," said Theodosia. "And your grandfather agreed."

Isabelle shuddered. "That man . . . Tidwell. Such a boor."

Theodosia couldn't argue with her there. Last night, after she'd gone over her story what seemed like two dozen times, she'd seen Tidwell wandering around with a plate of crab claws. She didn't know if the crab claws were crime-scene evidence or if Tidwell had been helping himself to a tasty little snack. After what had happened, Theodosia really hadn't cared to speculate.

"Isabelle," said Theodosia. "Is there something you're afraid to talk about?"

Isabelle just stared at her.

"You could tell me, you know," said Theodosia. "I promise I won't pass judgment. In fact, I'll try to help if I can."

"There's nothing to tell," said Isabelle. She turned toward a small chest of drawers that looked suspiciously like a Chippendale and had what appeared to be a real Tiffany dragonfly lamp sitting on top of it. Picking up a gold bangle bracelet, Isabelle slipped it onto her wrist.

"Have you been threatened, Isabelle?"

Isabelle almost jumped out of her skin. "No. Of course not." She pulled open the top drawer, rummaged around nervously, finally pulled out a ring. Her gaze was uneven as she slid it on her finger.

"That's the lapis ring Timothy gave you?" asked Theodosia.

Isabelle bobbed her head.

"Beautiful," said Theodosia.

Isabelle held out a trembling hand to admire it. "It really is, isn't it."

As the ring glinted and shone in the spill of light from the Tiffany lamp, Theodosia wondered if it was the same ring she'd seen glinting from the dumbwaiter. Could sweet little Isabelle have actually committed murder that night? Was she the one who'd jabbed Jordan Cole with a bang stick? And then, for whatever sick reason, attacked Nina last night?

"Would you do me a favor, Theodosia?" Isabelle was gazing at her now, a slightly inquisitive look on her face.

"Yes. Of course," replied Theodosia. *Is she going to spill something to me? Could it be her conscience is consumed by guilt?*

Isabelle reached into her top drawer again and pulled out a CD. "Take this over to the Belvedere Theatre for me? I have a feeling it's going to be a while before I extricate myself from Burt Tidwell's sticky clutches."

"Sure," said Theodosia, reaching to accept the CD in the shiny plastic jewel case.

"It's background music for tonight's award show," Isabelle explained. "Some of it's classical music, some of it's sort of Academy Award-sounding. A few of Timothy's friends from the Charleston Symphony recorded pieces, then Timothy had it mixed and timed out over at Crash and Burn. Nina had a copy, too, but . . ."

"Who knows where that is," finished Theodosia.

"Right," said Isabelle, sighing.

"Sure, I can drop it by. Where to?"

"Oh, just make sure it finds its way to the audio department," said Isabelle. "I'm sure someone will be there to receive it."

"And the audio department is . . . where?" asked Theodosia.

"Backstage," answered Isabelle. "Next to the costume department."

25

❧

Theodosia pulled her Jeep into the back parking lot of the Belvedere Theatre and listened as the engine ticked down. She stared at the massive brick building, thinking how inviting theaters always looked from the front sidewalk and how shabby and ominous they appeared from back alleys. She would have preferred to enter through the front, but one of the tents was still there and the area was cordoned off so a genuine red carpet could be rolled out for tonight's festivities.

Gathering up her purse, Theodosia grabbed the CD Isabelle had given her. And continued to sit in her car.

It wasn't that Theodosia was *afraid* to go inside. She was just . . . well . . . hesitant.

So many strange things had taken place in the Belvedere Theatre. Of course, this was the last day she'd probably have business backstage. Once the awards were handed out tonight, the film festival would be a distant albeit sad memory. Not a great film festival all in all, but participants and volunteers had soldiered through and pulled it off. She rapped bunched knuckles against her dashboard. *Hopefully* pulled it off.

Theodosia crossed the back lot, mindful of gravel crunching underfoot. Then knocked on the back door, a massive rust-colored metal contraption that looked like it might have been installed a century earlier.

Nothing.

She tried the handle. It clicked loudly, then the door swung open on creaking hinges.

Creaking hinges, thought Theodosia. *Why are there always creaking hinges?*

She poked her head into darkness.

"Hello? Anybody here?"

No answer. Pulling the door all the way open, Theodosia hoped it would remain open so she could at least see where she was going.

And, probably, there were lots of people scurrying around backstage. Tonight was the big night, after all. Sets had to be readied, podiums rolled in place, lighting and microphones had to be tested. And the music . . .

Well, she had the music.

Theodosia decided she'd saunter in and hand the CD to the first person she met. If she could find her way, that is. She'd only come this way once before and that was with Nina (poor Nina!) who'd led the twisty-turny path with a flickering candle, while she, Drayton, and Haley had stumbled and giggled behind her.

Ten steps in, the door slammed shut and Theodosia was plunged into total darkness.

Startled, she dropped the CD, heard it clatter loudly on the floor.

Oh great.

Theodosia bent down, felt around with her hands, and found the plastic jewel case right away. Straightening up, she decided she was definitely going to locate the audio department, toss 'em the CD, and get the heck out of Dodge.

Taking a few more tentative steps, Theodosia pushed on. And even though navigation wasn't her strong suit, she knew if she proceeded straight ahead, she'd hit the stage sooner or later. And probably a whole cadre of volunteers.

Directly ahead, looking like a giant spiderweb in the dim light, was a network of ropes and pulleys. Most of them led to a complex overhead system that controlled all the various curtains and sets.

And flying banshees.

Yes, Theodosia told herself. *Let's not forget the amazing flying banshee trick.* Probably, whoever rigged that little charade was familiar with live theater workings.

But who would that be? she suddenly asked herself.

Because, aside from volunteers, all of the people involved in the Charleston Film Festival were screenwriters and cinematographers and directors and production people. People who'd been involved in TV and film, not live theater.

So did that point to a volunteer? Had the murders of Jordan Cole and Nina van Diedrich been committed by someone local? And by the same person? Someone intimately familiar with the backstage workings of live theater? Could Isabelle somehow be connected to this? Had she beat Theodosia to the theater and was now lying in wait? All good questions. Terrifying questions.

More anxious than ever to drop off the CD and get to her tea shop, Theodosia pushed her way through the darkness, wound her way past two giant sets—a garden gate and some kind of castle scene—and emerged in a dim hallway.

Probably, she decided, this hallway led to the costume shop and the dressing rooms.

She put her left hand against the wall, letting her fingers guide her. It was slightly lighter here, which made her heart feel lighter, too. Maybe once she rounded the corner just ahead she'd be home free.

"Hey there!" A voice rang out, a dark figure loomed menacingly in front of her.

Startled, Theodosia stopped dead in her tracks and threw up an arm for protection.

And then the figure seemed to bend toward her and a familiar voice said, "Theodosia?"

Huh?

"What are you doing back here?" asked the voice.

It was C. W. Dredd.

"What are you, *crazy*!" shrilled Theodosia. "What are you trying to do? Scare me to death?"

"Not at all," came Dredd's smooth voice. "I was looking for the stage manager."

"Well, I doubt he's back here," said Theodosia, sounding scared and very cross.

"Here," said Dredd, "take my hand."

"I'm *mad* at you," said Theodosia. Her heart was pounding inside her chest like a timpani drum.

"My sincere apology," said Dredd. "Really. Hey, I've got something to show you. Delaine tells me you're supposed to be a crack investigator, you tell me what you think it means."

"Now what are you talking about?" asked Theodosia.

"Just come with me, you'll see," promised Dredd.

"I'll *follow* you," said Theodosia. She was keenly aware that C. W. Dredd could just as easily be the murderer as anyone else. That being the case, he probably wasn't the ideal candidate to follow around in the dark.

"Okay, suit yourself," said Dredd, striding off. "It's right over here."

Walking cautiously behind him, Theodosia dogged his footsteps as they turned left, then right, then left again. Finally Dredd stopped outside one of the dressing rooms. "In here," he said.

"You want me to go in there," said Theodosia. Warning bells sounded in her head. Was he trying to lure her in?

"I just noticed this maybe fifteen minutes ago," said Dredd. "When I was hunting for the stage manager. I think it's pretty weird."

"You go in first," said Theodosia. "I'll follow."

He ducked in first. "You really don't trust me, do you?" said Dredd. He seemed to find her discomfort amusing.

"What?" asked Theodosia in a sharp tone. "What did you want to show me?"

Dredd brushed past a rack of costumes and moved into the far corner of the little room. "This," he said gesturing downward.

Theodosia peered in. In the dim light all she could see was a tangle of rags. Or maybe it was limp blankets.

"I think someone's been sleeping back here," said Dredd. His voice held a mixture of curiosity and dismay. "Or hiding out. See the way this stuff's folded?"

Theodosia took in the pile of old coats and dirty quilts that had been folded and twisted into a kind of sleeping pallet. And wondered who on earth would hide out in an old theater? Especially at night. And did they, could they, have anything to do with the terrible things that had gone on here?

"It's like some kind of nest," said C.W., kicking at the pile with his foot.

"A rat nest," said Theodosia. "Maybe even inhabited by a human rat."

"You guys," said Haley, stepping inside the tea shop, shuffling through the envelopes and flyers that had just arrived in the morning mail.

"What?" asked Theodosia and Drayton at the same time. Drayton was polishing a silver teapot; Theodosia had just returned from dropping the CD with the audio department. To say nothing of her little side trip with Dredd.

"Looks like we got a complimentary copy of *Shooting Star*, Bill Glass's nasty little tabloid."

"Oh dear," said Drayton, a look of dismay on his face. "You know this won't be good."

Theodosia put an index finger to her lips to shush him. They only had a handful of customers at the moment, but the last thing she wanted was to upset anyone.

So the three of them clustered together at the counter as Haley ripped off the brown paper sleeve.

"Hurry up," urged Drayton.

"Hold your horses," said Haley as the final bit of paper peeled off. "Oh man . . . !" She blinked rapidly, then tilted the glossy tabloid to get a better look. "It's her all right." There on the front page was a grainy, slightly out-of-focus photo of Nina's ghostly face.

"Awfully poor taste," grimaced Drayton. Peering over his half-glasses, he looked more than a little owlish.

"I can't believe Glass really used that photo," said Theodosia. "And with such a nasty headline."

"'Diva on the Half Shell,'" read Haley. "Hmph. Nina wasn't *that* much of a diva."

"Yes, she was," responded Drayton.

"Either way," said Theodosia, feeling outrage bubble up upside her. "To be brutally murdered last night and mocked today . . . *nobody* deserves that!"

"Particularly the murder part," said Haley. "I still can't believe you were right there. And that we missed all the excitement."

"Trust me," said Theodosia, still shaken from her experience. "It wasn't exciting. Finding Nina was horrific at best."

"And I suppose Tidwell questioned everyone for hours," said Drayton.

"He's thorough," said Theodosia with a sigh. "I'll say that for him."

"It's funny that Tidwell never advised Timothy or the arts people to cancel tonight's award show," mused Haley.

"The subject never came up," said Drayton.

"You don't suppose . . ." began Haley. Then stopped suddenly.

"What?" asked Drayton.

"Nothing," said Haley.

"Something," prompted Theodosia.

Haley shook back her hair and stared at them with questioning eyes. "You don't think Tidwell *wanted* tonight's show to go on, do you?"

"What are you talking about?" asked Drayton.

But Theodosia immediately caught Haley's drift. "You think he's trying to draw out the murderer?" she asked.

Haley gave a succession of rapid nods.

It was, Theodosia decided, exactly how Tidwell's mind worked. Devious, clever, almost delicious in its brilliance.

"What a terrifying idea," said Drayton, glancing nervously at Theodosia. "Tidwell wouldn't expose everyone to a risk like that, would he?"

She thought for a moment. "Of course he would."

26

❧❧

The navy dress was a stunner, making Theodosia appear taller and thinner than she really was. And when she experimented in front of the mirror, gathering up her mass of auburn hair, brushing it back, then twisting it into a loose chignon, she knew she'd found her perfect red-carpet style.

The sparkling earrings were the perfect glam touch—Delaine had been right about that. And her white Dolce & Gabbana slides gave her another three and a half inches. Put her up there with the tall gals. Sort of.

"Whoa," said Parker, as he climbed the back stairs to Theodosia's apartment. "You look terrific." He pulled her close, gave her a long, lingering kiss.

When they finally broke apart, Theodosia noticed he was wearing a tux.

"You look great, too," she told him. "I love that tux. Very *GQ*."

"Ah." He waved a hand, pleased. "It's just my headwaiter's outfit."

"Still . . ." she said, smiling.

"Hey," he said. "I'm glad we're still going to this shindig tonight. Even after what happened with Nina. I'm glad the organizers decided not to cancel."

"Timothy and Gavin Dorfman came awfully close," Theodosia told him. "But they didn't want to disappoint all the directors and cinematographers and screenwriters who traveled here to participate." What she left unspoken was what Haley had proposed earlier. That Tidwell might actually *want* the award show to go forward tonight in hopes of drawing out the murderer.

Parker held up a split of champagne he'd brought along. "How 'bout we have a glass of bubbly first? It's a vintage Laurent Perrier my wine dealer brought by yesterday. If enough people like it, I'll probably add it to our wine cellar."

Theodosia went into her dining room and grabbed two Baccarat champagne flutes from the china cabinet. When she was positive Parker was focused on gently easing out the cork, she blew quickly into the flutes to dislodge any little particles of dust. Though she was fastidious about her tea room, dusting all the stemware and English Staffordshire dog figurines in her apartment wasn't exactly her strong suit. After all, life was short, right?

"Watch for a soft, silky mousse and a fine perlage," Parker instructed. "The perlage basically being tiny bubbles. Then you should get a bright taste of apples and pears."

Theodosia sniffed, sipped, and drank. It tasted like champagne. Fizzy. A little sweet, a little dry. Nice.

"Did you pick up a hint of pears?" Parker asked expectantly.

"I think so," said Theodosia.

Parker beamed. "All that tea drinking's given you an educated palate and a supersensitive nose."

But do I have a nose for sniffing out a killer? she wondered.

Giant searchlights lit the night sky above Church Street. As the bright white beams shot upward, they bounced off thin wisps of clouds creating a warm, hazy glow. A perlage in the sky, Theodosia decided.

A press paddock had been set up right on the street. There, photographers and news crews milled about, clicking strobes, changing lenses, elbowing each other out of the way. They were kept at bay only by a set of velvet ropes and a few uniformed officers. As guests were disgorged from limousines and town cars and began their walk down the red carpet, the frenzy picked up as cameramen vied for shots. Of course, not all guests got their pictures taken.

"Theodosia!" called out one photographer. "This way. Look this way!"

Hanging on Parker's arm, Theodosia stopped, turned obligingly, and posed.

Then another photographer called out to her as well.

"How come you're so well known?" asked Parker. "Are you a high-society gal and I don't even know it?"

"Please," said Theodosia, steadying herself on his arm. "That guy was from the *Goose Creek Tribune.* They did a little piece on tea once and I helped out."

Entering the lobby, there was a press of people, a buzz of excitement. If opening night had been thrilling, then this was an over-the-top gala. Long gowns, cocktail dresses, and tuxedos were the norm. It would appear that the social elite of Charleston hadn't been intimidated in the least by last night's tragic event.

Theodosia, who had an almost contact high by now,

surreptitiously peeked at rings and cuff links, studying the hand of every gentleman she saw.

"You think you're going to catch a glimpse of that green stone ring again?" asked Parker. He was both bemused and a little taken aback by Theodosia's doggedness.

"Maybe," said Theodosia. "You never know." There was, she figured, a slight possibility that the killer could get careless. Might wear the same ring or cuff links, or whatever it was, again. In fact, that was how a surprising number of criminals were apprehended. They made silly, careless little errors, such as having an expired license tag or a burned-out taillight, that caught the attention of police officers.

"You're not really thinking your suspect is going to show his face again, are you?" asked Parker. "Or his ring finger?"

"I'm not sure what to expect," responded Theodosia. She wasn't psychic, but she did feel a sort of energy vibe rippling through the crowd. So she was trying to keep herself open to whatever might happen.

As they pushed their way through the crowded lobby, a woman's face, smug and defiant, bobbed in front of Theodosia.

"Hello, Theodosia," snapped Abby Davis. This was the one person Theodosia had truly wanted to avoid tonight.

"Hello, Abby," responded Theodosia. She managed a half smile only out of sheer politeness. Because she'd been raised in Charleston and had her manners drilled into her like a cadet at the Citadel. The sad fact was that ever since her breakup with Jory, Abby Davis had been hostile and rude to her.

"Hello," said Parker. He gave Abby a friendly smile, assuming she was a friend of Theodosia's. He waited a few moments, then threw a questioning glance at Theodosia. Still she made no attempt to introduce them.

"You know," said Abby, sidling closer to Theodosia and seeming to delight in the tension she was causing. "I'm one of the nominees for the Women in Film and Television Award tonight." Her words came across as a taunt. "I'm doing hard news now. Investigative reporting. It won't be long before I'm in the anchor slot at Trident."

"Good luck then," said Theodosia, trying to edge past her, struggling to keep her cool. There was no way Abby was going to goad her into a catfight. Not here, not now.

But Abby seemed to be reveling in their little exchange.

"Oh, and some interesting family news, too." She tossed her head like a show pony. "Jory will probably be moving back from New York." Abby paused a beat, then added, "I also hear he just got engaged."

"How lovely," said Theodosia. Her voice was brittle and her grip on Parker's arm tightened considerably. As expected, he received her signal loud and clear and they moved on.

When they were out of earshot, Parker said, "Why was that woman so darned snotty to you? And who's this Jory guy?"

"Ancient history," said Theodosia, as they stepped into the dimly lit theater. But from the look on Parker's face, she knew she owed him a better explanation. Just not right now.

They had excellent seats tonight. Right on the aisle, tenth row from the front. Drayton was already seated, but Haley was missing.

"Where *is* that girl?" fussed Drayton as the house lights dimmed, the curtain began to rise, and the music swelled. "She's going to miss everything!"

The first award was for the Short Films category. Theodosia had screened and judged these films and pretty much fallen in love with all of them. But she was thrilled beyond words when *Gingerbread and Rainbows* won. It was the film she'd voted for. About the gorgeous and fanciful architecture of Charleston.

Timothy Neville was the presenter for the next two awards, the Documentary category and the Video Art category. The first award went to *The Pelicans of Cat Island*, which somewhat disappointed Theodosia. She'd been hoping the service dog film would win.

Haley slid into the seat next to Theodosia just as everyone was applauding. "Sorry I'm late," she whispered.

"Where have you been?" asked Drayton. "You're missing everything."

"I ran into Delaine in the lobby," said Haley, "and I couldn't get away." Haley leaned over and touched Theodosia's arm. "Delaine is completely freaking out. The presenter for the Women in Film and Television Award backed out at the last minute and she's been asked to go on."

"So what's the problem?" muttered Drayton, as the audience burst into applause once more. "She should be delighted. Delaine usually *basks* at being in the limelight."

Haley shook her head. "It's not that. She just had *words* with C. W. Dredd."

"What kind of words?" whispered Theodosia. The audience was on their feet, clapping and whooping now, so they could conduct this little exchange without being disruptive.

"Upsetting words," Haley whispered back. "Apparently Dredd told her to take a hike."

"Oh great," said Theodosia. "Where's Delaine now?"

"Backstage," said Haley. "But she's really in a bad way. Sniffling, crying, you know."

"I'm going to go see what I can do," said Theodosia. "Maybe she just needs a few words of encouragement."

"She is awfully upset," said Haley.

"Aw, don't go," said Parker. "They're just getting to the good awards."

Theodosia patted his hand. "I won't be long. Promise." Theodosia edged past Drayton. "If I'm not back here in five minutes," she said under her breath, "you come backstage, okay? You make the presentation for Delaine?"

Drayton nodded. "Of course." He always enjoyed being needed.

Back in the wings of the theater, Theodosia hunted for Delaine. Found her huddling against the back wall, her shoulders shaking as she dabbed at her eyes with a hanky.

She put a hand on Delaine's shoulder. "Are you okay, honey?"

Delaine gazed at her with tear-streaked eyes. "Theo? What are you doing back here?"

"I came to see how you are."

Delaine buried her head in her hands. "Ooh, don't ask. I'm so embarrassed," she said in a muffled voice.

"You have nothing to be embarrassed about," said Theodosia.

Delaine shook her head. "Yes, I do." She lifted her head and stared at Theodosia with sorrowful, red-rimmed eyes. "I feel like such a fool!" As her voice rose, the two dozen or so people waiting in the wings exchanged embarrassed glances.

Theodosia plucked at Delaine's sleeve and pulled her to her feet. Then she guided her across the back of the theater, over to the far side of the stage where it was pretty much deserted.

"This isn't about you," Theodosia told her gently. "It's about male ego and one-upsmanship and drama." She peeked into one of the darkened dressing rooms, pulled Delaine in, eased her into a chair.

Delaine was still sniffling loudly, making little choking sounds. "It sure feels like it's about me." She balled her fists and wiped at her eyes, leaving twin smears of mascara on what had been artfully rouged cheeks.

"Delaine," said Theodosia, "maybe we should get someone to take your place as presenter."

"Do I look that bad?" Delaine asked, then leaned forward and peered into one of the mirrors. Upon seeing her image, Delaine's sobs seemed to intensify. "I look horrible," she moaned. "Twenty minutes ago I looked pretty and now I'm a fright. And all because he . . . he was a cad. A horrible, rotten cad."

"Well, we knew that," said Theodosia in a soothing tone. She was listening with half an ear to what was going on at the podium. And knew Delaine's turn was fast approaching. Theodosia pulled a lace hanky from her evening bag and passed it to Delaine. The girl definitely needed a backup. "Should we have Drayton go on for you?"

Delaine nodded, pathetically grateful now. "Do you think he'd do that?"

"I know he will," said Theodosia. In fact, she figured Drayton was probably headed back here right about now. "You just sit here and relax, okay, honey?" She patted Delaine's hand. "Have a good cry. This is all going to look different tomorrow."

"Oh, Theo," blubbered Delaine, "you're such a good friend. I know you've been jilted yourself, so you really do understand."

"Uh . . . right," said Theodosia. It that what Jory had done? Jilted her? And all along she'd thought she was the one who'd caused the breakup. Wasn't that an interesting and perhaps topsy-turvy perspective?

"You stay right here," Theodosia told Delaine. "I'm just going to check on . . ." She darted out the door and peered around the corner, half expecting to see Drayton heading toward them.

Instead she saw Burt Tidwell talking to Kassie Byrd. They seemed locked in conversation until Kassie gazed her way and waggled her fingers in a friendly manner. Tidwell just stared directly at Kassie, intense as always.

Theodosia darted across the back of the theater, hoping to locate Drayton. She'd buttonhole him and tell him to go on, do the presentation as best he could.

Halfway across, a note of warning pinged in Theodosia's brain. Something about the exchange she'd just witnessed didn't feel right. There'd been tension between Tidwell and Kassie. And even though Theodosia had caught just a quick glimpse of them, the body language had seemed all wrong. It was as if . . . what?

As if Kassie had some kind of strange hold over Tidwell?

And something else, too.

Theodosia fought to ignore the music and applause that suddenly sounded so loud. *But what?*

27

❧

The answer came to Theodosia not like a bolt from the blue, but more like a feeling of cold dread stealing across her heart. Kassie had been wearing turquoise jewelry. A squash blossom necklace and matching ring. But not the beryl-blue turquoise that was so popular, the coloration was more . . . green?

Tiny hairs prickled on the back of Theodosia's neck.

It couldn't be, could it?

Theodosia knew she had to go back there and get a closer look at Kassie's ring. And see what Tidwell had been so formal about. Had he made some sort of connection, too? Was he right now interrogating or maybe even arresting Kassie?

Theodosia hurried back to where she'd seen them. But when she got there, there was no one in sight.

"Kassie?" she called in a tentative voice. "Detective Tidwell?" Her voice a little stronger this time.

What just happened here?

"Theo?" called Delaine. "Everything okay?"

"Stay there!" commanded Theodosia. "Stay in the dressing room."

Suddenly, there was a burst of bright light followed by a strange electrical zapping sound. Theodosia darted around a corner just in time to see Burt Tidwell stagger back on his heels, reel to and fro in a sort of suspended animation, then fold forward and drop to his knees. When his knees hit the wooden floor boards, it sounded like twin gunshots.

"Detective, are you . . . ?" began Theodosia, just as Kassie turned toward her with a nasty snarl on her face.

"What did you do to him?" Theodosia hissed. She clenched her fists, ready to do battle.

"Shut up!" snapped Kassie. Extending an arm, Kassie pointed a gun directly at Theodosia's chest. Snub-nosed and boxy, with a dull gray finish, it looked menacing and dangerous in the dim backstage light.

Theodosia tried to choke back her fear. "What did you *do* to him?" she demanded again. Tidwell was on the floor in a heap, groaning pitifully.

"Taser," said Kassie through gritted teeth. "Lovely little weapon, don't you think? A five-thousand-volt charge that can drop a bull elephant at twenty feet." She looked disdainfully down at the floor. "Or a fat detective."

"Hello!" called a melodious male voice. "Does someone need a pinch-hit presenter?"

Drayton! Oh no!

Drayton came around the corner. "There you are, Theo! I just spoke with Delaine and she said . . ." He stopped, frowned, suddenly noticed Tidwell on the floor and the gun in Kassie Byrd's hand. "Oh my!" was his stunned response.

"You're not going to get away with this!" yelled Theodosia. Her voice rose sharply. She hoped everyone in the wings, at the podium, and in the audience could hear her.

"Shut up!" hissed Kassie. She swung her arm around and pointed the gun directly at Drayton. "You!"

"Me?" squeaked Drayton. He touched a hand tentatively to his chest.

"Yes, you," said Kassie. "Get over here!"

"Don't even think it," said Theodosia, taking a step forward. She had a single moment of madness where she wondered if she could wrest Tidwell's gun out of his shoulder holster and try to get the drop on Kassie. Then she decided it was a bad plan. Stupid. Way too risky.

Drayton was wavering between them now.

"Get over here!" Kassie commanded. Reluctantly, Drayton edged toward her.

"You don't want him," said Theodosia. She was so angry she was almost shaking. "Let him go. If you're so intent on having a hostage, take me instead."

"Shut up," said Kassie. She tapped Drayton in the middle of the chest with the stun gun. "You, old man. You're coming with me." She waved the gun toward the back of the theater. "That way. Get moving."

Helpless, Theodosia watched as Drayton and Kassie disappeared into the darkness, until she could only hear their footfalls as they shuffled through the backstage maze.

Dropping to her knees, Theodosia tried to rouse Tidwell. "Tidwell! Tidwell!" she called, her fingers grappling at his sport coat, tugging, pulling, trying to get his attention. "You've got to get up!"

Tidwell's eyes flew open and fluttered slightly, like he was trying to recall just what had happened. And he was breathing hard. Wheezing and sputtering like a tea kettle. Sounding way too overexerted for a man his size. Theodosia thought of his overtaxed heart and fear flooded her chest. She pulled at his arm, trying to get him moving. It was like trying to move a mountain.

Still, Tidwell was recovering enough so he could talk.

"Wha-happen?" he asked, his beady eyes rolling like a wonked-out pinball machine.

"Kassie Byrd shot you with a stun gun!" yelled Theodosia, trying to get through to him. "Then she took Dayton hostage! Come on, we've got to go after them!"

Tidwell lifted a big paw and rubbed his head cautiously. "We've no idea where she's gone." He seemed cognizant and was starting to make sense again.

"Yes, we do," said Theodosia. "I'm pretty sure I know where she's headed!" She tugged at him again. "Where's your car?"

"In back," murmured Tidwell, making a halfhearted gesture.

Pulling and pushing, she got Tidwell to his feet. "Now c'mon!" she yelped. Together they lurched through the warren of rooms until they were at the theater's back door. They pushed it open and burst out into the warm, dark night.

It all felt so wrong, Theodosia decided. This lovely, warm, moonlit evening was supposed to have been an exciting time for everyone. Now it was turning into a night of terror.

Theodosia spotted Tidwell's burgundy Crown Victoria immediately. "Give me your keys," she told him, driving him forward like a beast of burden. "You're in no condition to drive."

She shoved Tidwell into the front passenger seat, snatched the keys from his hand. When she climbed into the driver's seat, he stared at her belligerently, as if he'd just woken up from a bad dream and found himself in very strange circumstances.

"You can't drive this car," he thundered. "It's . . . uh . . . police property."

"Paid for with good old taxpayer money," replied Theodosia as she turned the key over in the ignition. "So in a way it's partly mine." The engine roared to life and she tromped down hard on the accelerator.

Tires churning wildly, they kicked up a hail of tiny

stones. Then they lurched forward and rocketed down the alley.

Man, does this baby have pickup!

"You are in so much trouble!" Tidwell bellowed.

"Let's deal with that later," said Theodosia, fighting to keep Tidwell's boat of a car from fishtailing all over the road. "Right now, please get on the horn and put out an APB or police alert or whatever it is you people do."

Her nattering at him worked, because within seconds Tidwell was muttering into his radio, sounding rather official though a tiny bit out of it. Static crackled back at him as they barreled across the Cooper River Bridge, water gleaming darkly below. Burt Tidwell turned his great head toward her, one eye seeming not to focus. "Where are we headed?" he asked.

Theodosia had but one single image burned in her brain. The demonic bird with the long wagging tongue she'd seen flash on the screen that day she'd been lured to the Belvedere Theatre. She hadn't put it together until just now, but she was fairly sure that image was part of the ruins of the Old Chester Church out in Four Hole Swamp. A carved relief that depicted Adam and Eve being expelled from the Garden of Eden.

The Old Chester Church had been burned by Sherman in his March to the Sea in 1865, but parts of the walls still stood like a carcass of bleached bones. She'd seen some of the carved wall images years ago and they'd haunted her. Strangely enough, Kassie had chosen one of those images with which to taunt her. Probably, that old church had served as the focus of Kassie's film, *Low-country Ghosts*. Too bad she hadn't been a judge on that one. Maybe she would have figured everything out a lot sooner!

Theodosia swerved around a slow-moving produce truck bristling with green and a horn blared behind her.

"Careful, careful," cautioned Tidwell.

Theodosia pushed her speed up to eighty, felt the car start to shimmy. Tidwell had radioed for help, but who knew what that would bring?

"You're sure you know where you're going?" Tidwell asked her for about the twenty-seventh time.

With crystal clarity, Theodosia knew Four Hole Swamp was exactly where Kassie was running to. Kassie had mentioned she was from Bowman, and Bowman was within the swamp's perimeter. Theodosia figured that's exactly where Kassie would go to ground, so to speak. An unstable, murdering girl who held Drayton as her hostage.

The big question now was, would they get there in time?

28

❧

Jouncing down a lonely dirt road, Theodosia entered Four Hole Swamp via the southwest corner. She knew a few people lived out here within its boundaries, but nothing was marked—least of all a route to the Old Chester Church.

Still, her sense of direction told her this was the part of the swamp where the church's ruins might be located. But as the road seemed to simply peter out, her anxiety grew. Was this right? Was the church nearby? Was she taking a terrible risk?

Jumping from the car, Theodosia was struck by the dark, foreboding feeling of the forested swamp. A canopy of trees blocked faint moonlight. Strangler fig vines hung down in large tendrils. The hoot of an owl contributed to the overall feeling of isolation.

Theodosia didn't know if they were in the right place, but something deep inside was driving her, was telling her the Old Chester Church was somewhere in this vicinity.

Grunting, Tidwell hefted himself out of the passenger

seat and came around the back of the car. "We should wait for backup," he cautioned. "If we can even communicate appropriate directions."

"Drayton's out there," said Theodosia, her jaw set firmly. "And Kassie's killed two people already. You're nuts if you think I'm going to just sit here and wait for backup."

"It's the smart thing to do," said Tidwell with a grimace. "It's *procedure*."

"Do you not hear me?" hissed Theodosia. "*Drayton's* out there." She pointed toward a stand of colossal trees that looked like they were right out of *Jurassic Park.*

"We need a plan," pressed Tidwell.

"Here's the plan," said Theodosia. "The dirt road ends here. There's a path. We're going to follow it. We're going to try to find those ruins." She knew it was time for action, not just words.

"Madness," muttered Tidwell.

Theodosia struck off anyway. Creeping down the dark path as though she were stalking an animal. Quiet, all senses on full alert.

Fifty yards in, the path ended and two narrow trails split off.

"Not good," whispered Tidwell behind her.

Theodosia stood in the dark, contemplating what to do next. She gazed up at the heavy forest canopy, looked down at her feet. And was suddenly stunned when she noticed the back end of a car sticking out of the bushes.

"Is this her car?" she asked.

Tidwell hesitated. "Not sure. I . . ."

"Has to be," said Theodosia. "So you take one fork and I'll take the other. Okay?" Tidwell remained silent. "You going to do this with me or not?" she asked.

His dark eyes burned back at her. "Yes."

"Do you have a gun?"

Tidwell lifted an arm halfway and gestured at the

underarm holster he wore. "Yes, of course," he whispered back. "I'm a detective first grade, remember?"

"Let's hope *you* remember how to use it," she muttered to herself. Back at the theater, Kassie had obviously surprised him and gotten the drop on him. How long had it been since Tidwell had really been out in the field? How long since he'd had to defend a life?

Fifteen minutes after they split up, the trail Theodosia was following dwindled to a narrow, twisting rut. What had been sandy and slightly spongy now turned damp and squishy. Theodosia decided her sandals were more of a hindrance than a help. She bent down, slipped them off. Now it was easier going. Quieter, too.

Though they were barely forty miles from downtown Charleston, Four Hole Swamp was serious swampland. Bald cypress trees rose like giant pillars, black water encircled her. This was the provenance of poison ivy, alligators, and cottonmouth snakes. Theodosia had been here once before as a child, when her dad had brought her fishing for crayfish. But that was a long time ago and this whole area felt like unfamiliar territory.

In fact, now that she thought about it, the Old Chester Church might be down the *other* trail, the trail Tidwell had taken. If so, she could walk for hours and never find a thing. Not even come close to rescuing Drayton.

Theodosia was on the verge of turning back when she saw some sort of obstruction ahead of her. She tiptoed closer, mud squishing between her toes. It was a wooden sign, splintered and silver with age. The tips of her fingers traced the words. Sand Boil Springs.

That name struck a familiar chord with her. She'd heard of this place.

Sand Boil Springs is . . . what?

She racked her brain. Finally came up with a bit of South Carolina lore she thought she'd long forgotten. Sand Boil Springs was a natural, bubbling spring where groundwater, really ancient groundwater, moved up through a crack in the bedrock. Every few minutes or so, the water would erupt in a gush and gigantic bubbles, some three feet across and at least that high, would appear on the surface of the pond. The water, in effect, appeared to be boiling.

Parting some low-hanging branches, Theodosia tiptoed closer to the pond. Off in the distance an alligator barked his hoarse cough. She shivered. Terrifying.

As her feet sank into mud up to her ankles, a sulphurous smell assaulted her nose. Theodosia stared across the surface of Sand Boil Springs as bubbles continued to rise slowly, looking for all the world like bubbles in a teakettle just before the water broke into a rolling boil. The bubbles puffed and swelled, growing enormous on the surface. They quivered like giant primordial blobs for a few seconds, then burst with a slow-sounding *pffft*.

But nothing here, Theodosia decided. No Old Chester Church and no Drayton.

She started to turn away, caught a glint of something out of the corner of her eye.

What?

She stared again, saw nothing. Decided it must have been a bubble reflecting a patch of moonlight.

But, no, wait. There it was again.

Parting a dangling sheet of leafy kudzu, Theodosia stared intently across the expanse of bubbling pond. And saw . . . a yellow flicker? There for an instant, then gone again.

Firefly? No, too late in the season.

Someone stomping about with a flashlight? Maybe.

Or . . . a lantern?

Theodosia crept back to the narrow rut, wondering what kind of people lived in this part of the swamp. Trappers?

Poachers? She wondered who might be moving about in the darkness just ahead.

Twenty feet more and Theodosia began to make out the shadowy outline of something. A building of some sort? A lean-to?

No, it was a swamp shack. Set on stilts out over the water.

What is this place? Theodosia wondered.

She stopped beside a large tupelo, put a hand on the damp bark. Prayed there was nothing slithery in its overhead branches waiting to drop down upon her.

Crickets chirped, a few cicadas whirred, wind stirred the leaves of verdant undergrowth. The swamp was talking.

And so was someone inside that shack.

The words drifted across to her in low, barely audible tones. Theodosia crept closer, mud sucking at her feet until she reached a sort of boardwalk. She followed the trail of boards with her eyes.

It led to a wooden catwalk that seemed to extend around the shack.

Theodosia moved closer, then crept up onto the catwalk. The weather-beaten hide of a nutria was tacked to the shack's outside wall. Alligator jaws, bleached white, hung there, too.

And the words coming from inside the shack were more distinct.

She heard . . . angry voices.

Closing her eyes, Theodosia tried to make out what was being said.

Did you really think . . . won't stand for this . . . someone . . . pay dearly.

Moving in as close as she dared, Theodosia peered through a dirt-crusted window.

She saw a kerosene lantern flickering on a small wooden table and Kassie Byrd pacing back and forth, ranting like a lunatic and waving her stun gun. Drayton sat on a primitive wooden chair facing her. He was trying to get a few words in, but wasn't having much luck. Kassie Byrd, on a righteous, murderous tear, looked stark raving mad!

What to do? wondered Theodosia. Run back down the trail and try to find Tidwell? Try to signal him? Attempt to locate the backup he'd radioed for?

Or . . . should she try to make some sort of stand here and now? All by herself?

In Kassie's sarcastic rant back at the theater, she'd said something about the stun gun working up to twenty feet. Theodosia figured that was a dangerously long distance. If she just walked in and tried to talk to her, Kassie could easily Taser them both.

She had no idea how to do it, but Theodosia knew she'd have to somehow disarm Kassie.

Searching the area for some sort of weapon, Theodosia didn't see much to choose from. An old broom, a rake, some fishing poles jumbled together against a railing. Not much help. She finally noticed a gaff leaning up against the shack. A six-foot pole with a sharp, barbed hook on one end. If she could burst in on Kassie and jab her hard, throw her off balance . . . Well, maybe she could even knock that lantern over.

No time to worry what might happen, she told herself. Just have to act! Have to be decisive!

Pressing her shoulder up against the rough wooden door, Theodosia heard Kassie's low cackle.

On three, she told herself. *One . . . two . . .*

Theodosia lunged hard at the door, putting all her strength into it. The door held for an agonizing moment, then the old wood shuddered and burst inward with a loud crack. In a piece of luck, the door landed partially on top of Kassie, hitting her on the head and momentarily stunning her. In the melee, the kerosene lantern went spinning to the floor. Shocked by Theodosia's surprise entrance, Drayton leapt from his chair just as flames spread across the floor.

"Drayton!" cried Theodosia. She clambered across the fallen door to get at him, knowing the little shack was probably tinderbox dry. Drayton reached out toward Theodosia as a wall of dancing flames flared up around them. Kassie, still on the floor, let out a loud groan.

Then Kassie was struggling to get up even as she batted at flames and searched frantically for her stun gun.

"This way!" said Theodosia. She tugged at Drayton and stepped through a low window, pulling him after her as they retreated to the rickety deck that hung out over the pond. All around them now, flames were shooting skyward.

One side of the deck was already cut off by a swirl of fire, so Theodosia and Drayton circled around the other way. Kassie Byrd met them halfway, a murderous grin on her face and the stun gun clutched tightly in her hand.

Theodosia knew if Kassie hit either of them with that fifty thousand volt charge, they'd die right here in the fire. Only one option left.

Grasping Drayton's arm, Theodosia flung herself against him, pushing him against the rickety railing. Just as she figured, it snapped like a matchstick and they tumbled down into the pond in a tangle.

The water was warm, covered in duckweed and water fern. Beneath the tips of their toes, bottomless mud.

Like a madwoman, Kassie ran back and forth on the deck as flames swirled high into overhanging trees. Finally, driven by the sheer heat and force of the fire, Kassie uttered a shrill scream and plunged in to join them.

Not a strong swimmer, Drayton floundered pitifully, kicking his legs wildly, slapping at the water with open palms.

"Get to the opposite bank," Theodosia told him, spitting water, trying to grapple him and propel them both away from Kassie.

"I see you!" Kassie shrieked triumphantly. She waved her stun gun wildly above her head.

Theodosia and Drayton were making no progress at all. If anything, they'd floated back toward the burning shack. Now hot embers rained down upon their heads.

"Duck under!" she told him. "Grab a breath and go under!"

Drayton did as instructed, but fifteen seconds later popped up again. "Can't," he croaked.

That gave Kassie a chance to get a bead on them. "There you are!" she chortled. "Right where I want you!"

"Grab on to the pilings and try to make your way to shore," Theodosia told Drayton as she struck out away from him. "Don't try to swim, just pull yourself along." If she could put distance between herself and Drayton, Kassie would have to make two perfect shots. Not so easy in the water and the darkness.

As Drayton clung to the pilings, easing himself around to the side of the shack, the moon came out from behind a bank of clouds, casting its silver shadow on the brackish water and revealing another peril! Two ominous eyes and a gnarled, bumpy back slid through the green algae toward Drayton.

An alligator!

This was the fabled *Alligator mississippiensis* found in brackish waters as well as freshwater ponds throughout South Carolina's low country. Growing as long as twelve feet, an alligator could outrun a horse for a short distance. In the water it had no equal.

Tasting real panic now, Theodosia beat at the water, trying to draw the giant reptile toward her. The alligator was not deterred in the least.

Frantic now, Theodosia's hands flailed about, trying to find something, anything, to wield as a weapon. Her fingertips grazed rotted pilings half hidden below the surface and happened upon a metal chain.

Huh?

Theodosia explored with her hands, struggling to pull the metal toward her. And came up with . . . a fish stringer. Dirty, rusted, with two skeletal, smelly fish heads still attached.

She grappled with it, then raised the stringer up and slapped it hard against the water. "Here," she cried to the alligator. "Try this instead."

The alligator held his course for a few long moments, then slowly his broad tail swished and altered his direction. Now Theodosia could see jaws, eyes, and a great humped back heading right for her.

"Are you crazy!" screeched Kassie, who was now only a few feet away. "What do you think you're doing!"

Jiggling the chain, taunting the giant reptile, Theodosia waggled the string at him as if it were a fishing lure.

"You're insane!" screamed a bedraggled Kassie. Now her main focus seemed to be getting away!

A splashing sound from the other side of the lagoon caught Theodosia's attention. Burt Tidwell had slogged his way to the edge of the water!

Theodosia gestured toward the alligator that was slowly gliding toward her. "Shoot him, shoot him!" she screamed.

Tidwell pulled his nonregulation Smith & Wesson 10mm from his shoulder holster and assumed a wide-legged combat shooting stance.

"Hurry up!" shrieked Theodosia as the alligator slid relentlessly toward her.

Tidwell, hunkered in muck up to his knees, looked like an overblown John Wayne. Still as a statue, using a two-handed grip, he sighted down the barrel, aiming for the alligator. Just as he eased the trigger back, Kassie rose up, a triumphant grin on her face and the stun gun clutched tight in her right hand. She was aiming directly for Theodosia's head.

A huge explosion filled Theodosia's ears just as the chain was tugged rudely from her hands and a leathery, ridged back slipped past her. Like a submarine, it disappeared silently beneath the murky water.

"What the . . . ?" she cried as a spew of pink froth bubbled up and a tiny chunk of something damp hit her cheek.

Five feet away, floundering in the water, Kassie's face, once purple with rage, had turned alabaster white. She grasped her shoulder and threw her head back, her mouth cracked wide in a rictus of pain. "I'm hit!" she howled. "Help me, I'm hit!" She beat one arm frantically against the water and a froth of blood bubbled up around her.

Theodosia, paddling tiredly in the dark water, turned to face Tidwell and screamed in sheer frustration at him. "I told you to shoot the *alligator*!"

Tidwell lowered his gun slowly. His face was ashen, his shoulders slumped, his entire being looked completely drained.

"Of the two," he choked out, sounding like he was on the verge of collapse, "the girl seemed far more dangerous."

29

❧

Even though it was a warm night and Drayton had a blanket wrapped around him, he was still shivering. Tidwell, taking pity on him, constructed a pyramid of kindling and logs in the little stone fireplace, lit a match, and began fanning madly.

Haley flew around the Indigo Tea Shop, grabbing cups and saucers and brewing tea.

Theodosia had already changed into dry clothes, but Drayton, insisting on stopping for a bracing cup of tea first, sat stolidly in his damp, ruined clothes.

Timothy, Delaine, and Parker, alerted by Tidwell, had just arrived in a wild, nervous flurry.

"Oh, honey!" Delaine exclaimed to Theodosia. "If you fell into a swamp, then your dress was probably ruined." Her voice carried a note of reproach. "*Another* dress gone."

"It didn't fare too well," admitted Theodosia.

"If you ask me," said Drayton, doing his best to put on a brave face, "Theodosia's going to have some major dry-cleaning bills." He coughed, sneezed, glanced hopefully toward the counter. "Is that tea ready yet, Haley?"

"In a sec," she called back.

"We missed the whole award show," said Theodosia. She sounded a little forlorn even though everyone was gathered around her.

"We thought you were all backstage," said Parker. He sat in a captain's chair next to her, his arm around her shoulders. "We had no idea you were out chasing around Four Hole Swamp!"

"Or that Detective Tidwell got Tasered," said Delaine. She reached out and patted his hand sympathetically. "Poor, dear detective. Feeling better now?"

"Hmph," said Tidwell. He was on his cell phone, mumbling and rumbling to his police minions.

"Here's that tea," said Haley. "I brewed some nice, strong Irish breakfast tea." She set a silver tray down on the table, passed around teacups and saucers.

Tidwell clicked his cell phone closed. "Well, it certainly checks out," he announced loudly.

"What checks out?" asked Theodosia, hoping to fill in some of the blanks.

"When I received personnel records from Jordan Cole's production company earlier today, Kassie Byrd's name was listed."

"As what?" asked Theodosia. This was a surprise!

"PA," said Tidwell.

"What's a PA?" inquired Drayton.

"Production assistant," said Theodosia. "So that's why you went to the Belvedere to talk to her?" she asked Tidwell.

Tidwell nodded. "Only she was ready for me. Or for whoever was next on her list."

"Are we to believe Kassie Byrd was dumped to make way for Isabelle?" asked Timothy Neville. He looked unhappy but relieved.

"Probably," said Tidwell. "And then Isabelle was fired . . ."

"Because she was inconveniently in the way when Jordan hooked up with Nina," said Theodosia. It was all coming together for her now.

"Which obviously left Kassie smoldering," said Tidwell.

Theodosia turned toward Timothy. "Do you think Isabelle was being threatened?" she asked.

Timothy gave a tired nod. "*Something* was wrong. So, yes, yes, I do."

"Sounds like Kassie had turned into the classic stalker," put in Parker. "Dangerous and deluded." He gazed worriedly at Theodosia. "Just think, if she'd set her sights on C. W. Dredd, you could have been next."

"Don't say that!" implored Drayton. "Please. Not after everything we've been through."

"And we weren't even close to catching her," murmured Theodosia.

"But in the end, you knew where to find her," replied Tidwell in a low voice. "That was good work."

"Thank you," murmured Theodosia.

"Uh, do we know who won the Golden Palmetto Award?" asked Drayton. He'd finally stopped shivering.

Delaine gave a derisive snort. "C. W. Dredd."

"Did Abby Davis win the Women in Film and Television Award?" Theodosia asked.

"No," said Haley, "somebody else got it."

"Good," said Theodosia.

Drayton let loose a wide yawn, then quickly covered his mouth. "Oh, *excuse* me!"

"Poor Drayton," said Haley. "You must be completely drained after your horrible ordeal. I mean . . . being kidnapped and spirited off to that swamp!"

Drayton bobbed his head. "It was absolutely terrifying. There we were, up to our eyeballs in horrible green slime with this hideous prehistoric beast bearing down upon us . . . and Theodosia actually mustered the courage to *taunt* it. That brave girl lured the alligator away from me!" He let loose another dry cough, wiped a finger in the corner of one eye. "She saved my life."

"Too bad you couldn't capture that alligator and have a nice pair of shoes made." Delaine laughed. "Two pairs, if he was as big as you say."

"Oh no," said Tidwell, taking a sip of tea and letting it burble noisily across his tongue. "Per South Carolina fish and game statutes, it's deemed illegal to feed or entice an alligator."

"Is that a fact," said Theodosia.

"Absolutely," replied Tidwell. His furry eyebrows rose as he focused squarely on her. "In the eyes of the law, your actions have incurred a fine of five thousand dollars."

Theodosia gazed at Tidwell across the top of her teacup. She saw the mirth in his dark eyes, the mischievous smile he was fighting to keep under wraps.

The corners of her mouth twitched. "So bill me."

FAVORITE RECIPES FROM
The Indigo Tea Shop

Key Lime Scones

2½ cups flour
2 Tbsp brown sugar
1 Tbsp baking powder
½ tsp salt
1 stick butter
1 cup milk
1 large egg
Grated zest from 3 or 4 small key limes

MIX flour, brown sugar, baking powder, and salt in a large mixing bowl. Cut in the butter using a fork until mixture is crumbly. In a separate bowl combine milk, egg, and lime zest. Now add this to the flour mixture and stir until well blended and dough is quite sticky. On floured board, form dough into a roll. Slice off circles and place on lightly greased cookie sheet. Brush circles lightly with milk and bake at 425 degrees for approximately 20 minutes. Serve with Devonshire cream and garnish with thin lime wedges.

Haley's Simple Devonshire Cream

    1 (3-oz) pkg cream cheese, softened
    1 Tbsp sugar
    ⅛ tsp salt
    1 cup heavy cream

CREAM together cream cheese, sugar, and salt. Then beat in cream until the mixture forms stiff peaks. Chill until serving. Yields about 2 cups.

Drayton's Slightly More Complex Devonshire Cream

    1 (8-oz) pkg cream cheese, softened
    1 (12-oz) carton sour cream
    1 lemon, juice only
    2 tsp vanilla
    2 cups powdered sugar

CREAM all ingredients together, making sure sugar is thoroughly dissolved. Chill until serving. Yields about 3 cups.

Cat Head Biscuits

2 cups self-rising flour
2 Tbsp butter or margarine
1 cup buttermilk

PLACE flour in mixing bowl and create a small depression. Add butter and small amount of buttermilk and begin mixing. When butter is blended, add in the rest of the milk and mix until just blended and dough forms a ball. Place dough on floured surface and pat out gently to a 1½-inch thickness. Cut out 6 biscuits and place on greased pan. Bake at 400 degrees for about 14 to 16 minutes, or until golden brown. Remove from oven and brush with melted butter.

Chilled Strawberry Soup

2 cups frozen strawberries
2 cups milk
¾ cup heavy cream
¾ cup sour cream
3 Tbsp sugar

COMBINE strawberries, milk, cream, sour cream, and sugar in food processor and pulse until smooth. Chill at lest 8 hours in refrigerator before serving in chilled bowls. Garnish each serving with a mint leaf, fresh strawberry, or dab of vanilla yoghurt. Yields about 8 appetizer-sized servings.

Down-Home Cinnamon Raisin Muffins

¼ cup oil
1 egg
1 cup milk
½ cup sugar
½ tsp salt
1½ tsp cinnamon
1 Tbsp baking powder
2 cups flour
½ cup raisins

COMBINE oil, egg, milk, sugar, salt, and cinnamon in a large bowl. Mix well with a wire whisk. Add in the baking powder, flour, and raisins. Mix again until batter is moist and everything is incorporated—but do not overmix. Spoon batter into paper muffin cups or well-greased muffin pan. Bake at 400 degrees for approximately 20 minutes.

Lemon Tea Bread

½ cup butter, softened
1¼ cups sugar
2 eggs
½ cup sour cream
½ cup lemon juice from 3 large lemons
2 cups flour
2 tsp baking soda
¼ tsp salt
¾ cup chopped walnuts or pecans

CREAM together butter, sugar, eggs, sour cream, and lemon juice. In separate bowl combine flour, baking soda, salt, and nuts. Now stir the dry ingredients into the creamed mixture, but do not overmix. Grease and flour 4 mini loaf pans, then pour equal amounts of batter into each. Bake at 325 degrees for 45 to 50 minutes, or until wooden pick comes out clean. Allow to cool in pans for 10 minutes, then finish cooling on a rack. Serve slices with jam or Devonshire cream or drizzle on your favorite topping.

Apple Spice Cake

2 cups sugar

2 medium eggs

2½ cups flour

1 cup oil

2 tsp baking soda

1 tsp salt

1 tsp vanilla

1 tsp ground cinnamon

4 cups apples, diced

1 cup walnuts, chopped

⅓ cup butterscotch chips

MIX sugar, eggs, flour, oil, baking soda, salt, vanilla, and cinnamon together. Fold in apples and walnuts. Pour into a greased 9-inch-by-13-inch pan and sprinkle the top with butterscotch chips. Bake at 350 degrees for approximately 50 minutes.

Lavender Scones

2 cups flour
1 Tbsp baking powder
6 Tbsp butter
3 Tbsp sugar
2 tsp dried culinary lavender, chopped
1 egg
½ cup buttermilk

SIFT flour and baking powder together. Cut the butter into flour mixture until it has the consistency of bread crumbs. Stir in sugar and lavender. In separate bowl, beat egg and buttermilk, then add to mixture, forming dough. Place dough onto well-floured surface and shape into a circle. Pat down dough until it is about 1 inch thick. Use a floured cutter to stamp out 12 scones. Place scones on parchment-lined cookie sheet and sprinkle with a little sugar. Bake at 425 degrees for 10 to 12 minutes or until golden brown. Serve warm with jam or preserves.

Apple and Cheese Bruschetta

½ cup goat cheese, softened
¾ tsp dried thyme
¼ tsp freshly ground black pepper
1 large apple, peeled, cored, and diced
10 slices French bread

PREHEAT broiler. Combine cheese, thyme, pepper, and apples. Place bread on baking sheet and put under broiler until just lightly toasted. Remove from broiler and spread cheese/apple mixture on each slice of bread. Broil until cheese softens and bubbles slightly. (Note: shredded cheddar cheese may be used in place of goat cheese.)

Haley's No-Fuss Sponge Cake

4 eggs, separated
1 cup sugar
4 Tbsp cold water
1 cup cake flour, sifted
1 tsp baking powder
Whipped cream or whipped topping
Sliced strawberries or peaches

BEAT together egg yolks and sugar. Add water. Sift together flour and baking soda, add to batter, and beat. In separate bowl, beat egg whites until stiff, then fold into batter. Pour batter into a well-greased small angel food cake pan. Bake at 350 degrees for approximately 30 minutes. Once baked, cool completely and invert onto cake platter. Slice cake in half, horizontally, and fill with whipped cream or your favorite whipped topping. Now top with remaining whipped cream and add sliced strawberries or peaches.

Strawberry Cobbler

4 cups strawberries, hulled and sliced
1 cup flour
½ tsp baking powder
1 cup sugar
1 egg, beaten
¼ cup butter

ARRANGE strawberry slices in a greased 9-inch baking dish. In a bowl, stir together flour, baking powder, and sugar. Add egg and mix with fork until all ingredients are incorporated and mixture is crumbly. Spread mixture over strawberries and dot with pieces of butter. Bake at 375 degrees for 45 to 50 minutes. Serve in fancy parfait glasses and top with whipped cream.

Drayton's Coconut Bourbon Bombe

4½ cups soft coconut macaroon cookie crumbs (about 24 cookies)
¼ cup bourbon
1 (8-oz) pkg cream cheese, softened
1 (14-oz) can sweetened condensed milk
1 (12-oz) container frozen whipped topping, thawed
1 cup pecans, crumbled and toasted
Your favorite chocolate or caramel topping

PUT cookie crumbs in large bowl and drizzle with bourbon. Toss well and let everything soak for 30 minutes. Coat the interior of a 9-cup mold or large round mixing bowl with cooking spray, then line with plastic wrap. Gently press bourbon-soaked crumbs into prepared mold, forming a shell. Set aside. Combine cream cheese and condensed milk in a bowl and beat at medium speed until smooth. Fold in whipped topping and pecans. Spoon mixture into cookie shell. Cover and freeze bombe until firm. When ready to serve, invert frozen bombe onto a chilled serving platter. Wrap a damp, warm towel around mold to help loosen. Slide off mold and peel off plastic wrap. To serve, slice bombe into wedges and serve with your favorite chocolate or caramel topping.

Turn the page for a preview of the
first book in the new Cackleberry Club
Mystery series by Laura Childs . . .

EGGS IN PURGATORY

Available in paperback from Berkley Prime Crime!

❦

"*We are officially* out of wild rice sausage," Toni announced. She stood behind the lunch counter, hands on skinny hips, wearing an AC/DC concert T-shirt and tight jeans, her reddish blond frizzled hair pulled on top of her head like a show pony. All around her forks clacked noisily against plates, coffee was slurped loudly, and the gaggle of men hunched at the counter watched her surreptitiously. For Kindred and the surrounding area, Toni was pretty hot stuff.

"I'll grab another package from the cooler," Suzanne told her, moving quickly, pushing her way into the kitchen.

It was nine in the morning, and the mercury had already hit eighty, the heat gathering momentum, building into a steamy midwestern August day. Toni, as waitress supreme, was handling the morning rush with aplomb, if you could call eight men perched at an eight-stool counter a morning rush. Petra was the short-order cook, rattling pots and pans, making magic at the grill, slipping in a few strips of turkey bacon here and there, doing her small part to help keep their patrons from suffering cardiac infarctions before they hit fifty.

Suzanne, as one part inventory manager, one part marketing guru, and one part majordomo, ran herd on the rest of the place.

The rest of the place, the Cackleberry Club *in* toto, was a homey, crazy-quilt warren of rooms that almost defied description.

There was the café, of course, the counter and a half dozen battered tables that turned into a tea shop in the afternoon. The whitewashed walls were decorated with antique plates, grapevine wreaths, old tin signs, and turn-of-the-century photos. Vintage hats hung from pegs, wooden shelves were jammed with ceramic chickens and forties-era salt and pepper shakers.

The small Book Nook across the hall carried CDs and boasted a fairly decent children's section. Toni led the book club on Tuesday nights. Their first few meetings had started out academic and scholarly, the women discussing writers such as Jane Austen and Charlotte Brontë. But after someone brought along a jug of wine and everyone had a glass or two of sweet, jammy Shiraz, the women pretty much admitted that bodice-busting romances were really top of mind.

Next door was the Knitting Nest, a cozy corner filled with overstuffed chairs and stocked with a veritable rainbow of yarns and fibers. Petra taught Hooked on Wool classes Thursday nights. This was a slightly more crunchy-granola crowd, distinguished by their nubby sweaters and Swedish clogs.

The adjoining bakeshop sold fresh-baked breads, potato rolls, corn muffins, and apple and strawberry pies. Locally grown produce was also carried in season, inventory being what folks trucked in that morning. Today the shelves held blueberries, plums, tomatoes, green beans, and honeydew melons, as well as rhubarb jams and native grape jellies made by Petra in the same double boiler her grandma had once used. The small, secondhand display cooler offered wheels of organic blue and cheddar cheese produced by Mike Mullen, their neighbor down the road who owned a herd of long-lashed, doe-eyed Guernseys. And there were fresh eggs, brown, white, and the speckled variety, from local poultry producers.

Eggs were the morning specialty at the café. Puffy golden omelets bursting with sautéed mushrooms and molten with pungent Gruyére cheese. Monte Cristo Eggs Benedict served with a sidecar of sour cream and strawberry jam. Slumbering Volcanoes, a concoction of baked eggs, pepper jack cheese, and roasted garlic atop grilled artichoke hearts. Toad in the Hole with pork sausages surrounded by a flaky golden crust of baked eggs. Plus Scotch Eggs, Eggs on a Cloud, and Huevos Rancheros. Hence the name, of course: the Cackle-berry Club.

Suzanne wasn't surprised when, at half past nine that morning, Bobby Waite came ambling in. Bobby was Kindred's most popular attorney, a nice enough fellow who always had his polo shirt tucked neatly into his khaki slacks and wore well-buffed Cordovan leather loafers.

As Suzanne's lawyer, Bobby had been a gentle guiding force through the myriad death certificates, probate red tape, and other documents that the banks, courts, and Social Security Administration had required.

"Got a few more papers for you to sign," Bobby told her. He slid onto a just-vacated stool and shoved the documents across the counter.

"More government stuff? They sure love to poke their nose in a person's business," said Suzanne, fumbling for the pen tucked into her jacket pocket, finding it wasn't there.

Then again, neither was the jacket. These days she was comfortable and unapologetic in faded blue jeans and a white shirt tied at the waist. Serious jewelry traded for silver earrings and a simple turquoise bracelet that somehow looked exotic against her suntanned skin.

Bobby reached into his briefcase, fished out a silver Bic. "Here. Use mine."

As Toni was wont to do, she sidled over. "Whatcha want for breakfast, honey?" she asked Bobby.

He shook his head. "No time. I'm on my way into the office, then I have to drive over—"

"You gotta have breakfast," cut in Toni, who wasn't about to let him off so easily. "It's the most important meal of the day. Fortifies the body and the spirit. Maybe you want to take somethin' with you?"

"Okay, sure," Bobby relented, a grin on his face. "Your Eggs in Purgatory then." Eggs in Purgatory was Petra's version of baked eggs swimming in lethal Tabasco and chipotle-laced tomato sauce. Besides being delicious, you were assured of getting your capsaicin fix.

"You got it," said Toni, with the enthusiasm of an insurance salesman who'd just landed a major account.

Suzanne scrawled her signature where Bobby had affixed little plastic tabs with red arrows. Idiot-proofed it, she told herself, for people like her who needed a professional to deal with the nits and nats of legal documents. So she could focus on more broad-concept topics. Like . . . eggs.

"Got another call last week," said Bobby. "About your land." Suzanne owned a two-hundred-acre portion of land nearby. Well, actually, it had been Walter's land, an investment of sorts when he'd signed on as doctor at the Westvale Clinic. Now the land was hers, and she continued to lease it to a farmer named Ducovny who produced corn and soybeans from the rich, black soil.

"A serious offer?" she asked. "Beaucoup bucks?"

Bobby shrugged. "More like a casual inquiry from an agent. You still not interested in selling?"

"I'll think about it," Suzanne told him. But she knew it wouldn't be top of mind. She was noodling lots of plans for the Cackleberry Club. And maybe even a sister restaurant that offered fine dining. Suzanne had a real passion for cooking and food concepts, especially when it involved fresh ingredients that were locally sourced. And Kindred, with its dairy farms, boutique cheese makers, and organic farms, was a rich source.

"Well, let me know," said Bobby. He stashed the papers back inside his well-worn briefcase and then fumbled for the white plastic container that Toni slid across the counter.

Suzanne thanked Bobby again, then grabbed an order book and threaded her way through the cluster of wooden tables where two more groups of customers had made themselves comfortable.

It was crazy, she decided. The Spur station had done a reasonable business, had been a good investment. But this place, the Cackleberry Club, was going gangbusters. Suzanne still wasn't sure what the magic charm was that drew folks in. It could be the home-cooked angle. Men loved Petra's breakfasts, and women adored their tea service in the afternoon. Or maybe it was the eclectic mix they'd stumbled upon: the food, the books, the yarns. Whatever it was, business was good. In fact, three months after launching, they weren't just eking out a living, they were edging toward making a profit, a difference that didn't sound like much, but was immense in the scheme of things.

"*Bobby Waite is* sitting out back," Teddy Harlingen told Suzanne some twenty minutes later. He slipped onto a stool and winked at her. Teddy Harlingen was a World War II vet who'd served with George Patton in the Battle of the Bulge, got bayoneted in the gut, and never let anyone forget it.

Unfortunately, Teddy's mind had slipped a few cogs since his glory days with the hard-charging general.

"What are you talking about?" asked Suzanne.

Teddy giggled as he tilted his head sideways and rolled his eyes. A three-day stubble covered his wrinkled cheeks, and his eyes were a transparent blue, as though he'd been gazing out to sea too long.

Suzanne knew that Teddy always showed up the day after his Social Security check arrived, ordered a humongous breakfast of scrambled eggs and sausage, then caromed off down the road on the balloon-tired Schwinn bicycle his son had outfitted with training wheels. Probably, Suzanne figured, that vehicular arrangement neatly offset Teddy's penchant for splurging on a pint of Mad Dog 20-20, then following it up with a night of beer and bull at Schmitt's bar.

"Did you do something to Bobby's car?" asked Suzanne. Teddy was known for his practical jokes. He'd once jammed firecrackers and fresh cow manure into the tailpipe of Joe Dumar's milk truck. That had caused a big stink in more ways than one.

"Didn't do nothin'," shrugged Teddy. "Just walked by, saw Bobby sittin' there."

"And what did Bobby say?" asked Suzanne. Her eyes slid over to meet Toni's, who was doing her darndest to ignore the old coot. Toni shrugged. An I-don't-know-what-the-heck-that-old-geezer's-talking-about shrug. But Suzanne was suddenly aware that Baxter, her aging Irish setter, was barking his fool head off out back. Baxter, who napped out there pretty much every day, was rarely disturbed by anything, save the occasional Harley-Davidson that rumbled into their parking lot or a lone jackrabbit that poked its furry nose out of the fringe of woods the property backed up to.

"I'm gonna go out back and check on Bobby," Suzanne told Toni. "Sounds like he might be having car trouble."

But Toni was suddenly busy, trying to explain the subtle but critical variances between Eggs Florentine and Eggs Neptune to a customer at the counter.

Suzanne pushed her way back into the kitchen, where she was once again enveloped in a rich cocoon of aromatherapy-like smells. Pepper jack cheese melted on sizzling eggs, mettwurst sausage and cinnamon French toast fried on the grill, blueberry scones and ginger muffins baked in the oven.

"Hey," said Petra, who was handling the grill like a jolly maestro, flipping cakes and prodding sausages, then spinning deftly to plate each breakfast. Already in her fifties, Petra was smart, intuitive, and a calming influence. With her bright brown eyes and kindly, square-jawed face, she was always quick with a smile. And though her body was full-figured, it was still curvy in all the right places.

Suzanne couldn't resist snatching a piece of turkey bacon from the grill, then pulling open the oven door for a quick peek. "Lookin' good," she declared. Petra was also baking one of her trademark carrot cakes.

"No you don't," warned Petra. "Remember what happened when you snuck a peek at my pineapple upside-down cake? Poor puppy went flat as a board."

"Not my fault," Suzanne grinned. "That was due to a barometric imbalance in the stratosphere that produced gobs of humidity."

"Oh you are so full of it," laughed Petra, as Suzanne eased the oven door closed then slipped out the back door.

Baxter's barking could mean the coyotes were back, Suzanne decided. She'd seen one last week when she was hauling out garbage. A small female, skinny and mangy. She'd felt so sorry for the miserable little thing that she'd tossed it a hunk of chicken. Now she wished she hadn't. She'd probably just encouraged the little pest to pay a repeat visit.

Off in the distance Suzanne could see a hawk circling lazily in the sky, probably zooming in on a nest of field mice. She winced inwardly, suddenly thinking of the shrieking intrusion that would come cannonballing out of the sky, the tiny lives lost. Since Walter died, she thought about death a lot. Yesterday, she'd set a little red spider outside rather than swat it.

Suzanne crossed the back lot, a patchwork of hardpan, grass, and struggling violets. A slight breeze had sprung up, and she felt it instantly dry the tiny beads of sweat on her forehead. Her silver dangle earrings fluttered gently, caressing her throat like butterfly wings.

"Hey, Baxter," Suzanne called. "What's going on, fella? What's got you so hot and bothered?"

Baxter, his brow furrowed, his muzzle starting to go white, pulled himself up to greet her and give an answering woof. Although Baxter didn't seem particularly upset now, something had gotten him riled up. And Bobby Waite's shiny black Ford pickup *was* parked over there by the old shed. If he was hunting around in there for tools, he was out of luck. There was nothing in there now except a sputtering Toro lawn mower and a few bags of fertilizer that were probably well past the statute of limitation on germination.

Car trouble? Suzanne wondered as she crossed the backyard. She figured maybe Bobby had phoned Lou Marcy at the Conoco station, then didn't want to wait around for the tow truck to show up. Maybe Bobby had caught a ride into Kindred with one of her customers. He was a busy lawyer, after all, with a meeting to go to.

Suzanne edged up to the truck. With the sun tasering down in a cloudless blue sky, it was hard to see in, lots of reflection off the glass. She had to press her nose up against the passenger side window.

And then wished she hadn't.

Bobby Waite was in there, all right. Along with his take-out order of Eggs in Purgatory. The whole shebang was splashed across the dashboard and up the front window. Gobs of sauce obscured the speedometer, dripped off radio dials, and soaked Bobby's shirt. In fact, it looked like a damn ten-gallon can of industrial-strength tomato sauce had exploded in there. Except, Suzanne realized, some of the red stuff was blood.

DON'T MISS THE NEXT
TEA SHOP MYSTERY!

Oolong Dead

As Theodosia's horse, Captain Harley, hurtles over the fourth jump in the Wildwood Hunt Club's Point-to-Point Race, he suddenly spooks and she is thrown from the saddle. Groggy and sore, Theodosia opens her eyes to discover a dead body. Upon close inspection, it looks like it just might be the sister of her old boyfriend Jory Davis!

WATCH FOR THE NEXT
SCRAPBOOKING MYSTERY
ALSO FROM LAURA CHILDS

Death Swatch

When a Mardi Gras party turns deadly, Carmela Bertrand, owner of Memory Mine scrapbook shop, is pulled into a bizarre investigation that takes her into the dark recesses of a Vampyr Club, hurricane-ravaged buildings, and a haunted bayou where the pirate Jean Lafitte's treasure may be buried.

A Special Invitation to Readers

PLEASE DON'T MISS THE
FIRST BOOK IN THE BRAND-NEW
CACKLEBERRY CLUB MYSTERY SERIES.

Eggs in Purgatory

In a rehabbed Spur station outside the small town of Kindred, three semi-desperate, forty-plus women have launched the Cackleberry Club. Eggs are the morning specialty—fluffy omelets, slumbering volcanoes (a lethal combination of Tabasco sauce, pepper cheese, and roasted garlic), toad in the hole, and eggs on a cloud. This cozy little café even offers a book nook and yarn shop—and business has been good. But two murders, a runaway girl, a vicious widow, and a messianic cult leader just might lead to the club's undoing.

I think you're going to like these women, they're spunky, funny, and very real. And it wouldn't be a Laura Childs mystery without plenty of recipes!

Blessings,
Laura Childs

FIND OUT MORE ABOUT THE AUTHOR
AND HER MYSTERIES AT
WWW.LAURACHILDS.COM.

AVAILABLE IN HARDCOVER

Cozy up with the new
Tea Shop Mystery from
Laura Childs

OOLONG DEAD

While riding her new horse in a race through the
South Carolina low country, Theodosia Browning
finds her arch nemesis, Abby Davis, dead. What's
more, the victim's brother is Theodosia's old flame.
Who would have guessed they would be reunited
through cold-blooded murder? Theodosia's investigation takes her from the low-country thicket to
the backstage maze of a darkened theater where
a maestro of murder waits for the next cue. All
proving that when it comes to high drama, Theodosia can give Verdi a run for his money.

"Murder suits Laura Childs to a Tea."
—*St. Paul Pioneer Press*

penguin.com

Introducing the
CACKLEBERRY CLUB MYSTERIES from
the author of the TEA SHOP
and SCRAPBOOKING series
Laura Childs

Eggs in Purgatory

Eggs to go. Murder on the side.

Suzanne, Toni, and Petra lost their husbands
but found independence—and, in each other,
a life raft of support, inspiration, fresh baked
goods, and their own business. But when the
Cackleberry Club café opened its doors in the
town of Kindred, who'd have guessed that the
cozy oasis would become the scene of a crime?

penguin.com

The Tea Shop Mysteries by
Laura Childs

DEATH BY DARJEELING
GUNPOWDER GREEN
SHADES OF EARL GREY
THE ENGLISH BREAKFAST MURDER
THE JASMINE MOON MURDER
CHAMOMILE MOURNING
BLOOD ORANGE BREWING
DRAGONWELL DEAD
THE SILVER NEEDLE MURDER
OOLONG DEAD

"A delightful series."
—*The Mystery Reader*

"Murder suits Laura Childs to a Tea."
—*St. Paul Pioneer Press*

penguin.com

M314AS0808

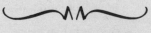